Once and for All

The Ego Is Always at the Wheel
In Dreams Begin Responsibilities
Last and Lost Poems
Screeno: Stories and Poems
Summer Knowledge: Selected Poems

ONCE AND FOR ALL
THE BEST OF
DELMORE SCHWARTZ

Introduction by John Ashbery

Edited by Craig Morgan Teicher

A NEW DIRECTIONS BOOK

Essays and letters in this volume originally appeared in the following publications:
The Selected Essays of Delmore Schwartz, ed. Donald A. Dike and David H. Zucker, Univer-
sity of Chicago Press, 1970; *Letters of Delmore Schwartz*, ed. Robert Phillips, Ontario Review
Press, 1984; and *Delmore Schwartz and James Laughlin: Selected Letters*, ed. Robert Phillips,
W. W. Norton, 1993. The verse plays were collected in *Shenandoah and Other Verse Plays*,
ed. Robert Phillips, BOA Editions, Ltd., 1992.

Manufactured in the United States of America
New Directions books are printed on acid-free paper
First published as a New Directions Paperbook in 2016

Library of Congress Cataloging-in-Publication Data
Schwartz, Delmore, 1913–1966.
[Works. Selections]
Once and for all : the best of Delmore Schwartz / edited, with a preface, by Craig Teicher ;
introduction by John Ashbery. — First American paperback edition.
pages cm
Includes bibliographical references.
I. Teicher, Craig Morgan, 1979– editor. II. Ashbery, John, 1927– writer of introduction.
III. Title. IV. Title: Best of Delmore Schwartz.
PS3537.C79A6 2016
818'.52—dc23   2015022095

10 9 8 7 6 5 4 3 2 1

New Directions Books are published for James Laughlin
by New Directions Publishing Corporation
80 Eighth Avenue, New York 10011

CONTENTS

UNPUBLISHED POEMS

VERSE DRAMA

CRITICISM

LETTERS

FOREWORD

Though Delmore Schwartz's reputation is sadly diminished from what it was at his beginnings in the late 1930s, it has been kept alive thanks to James Atlas's excellent if depressing biography, which appeared in 1977, eleven years after the poet's early death. Alas, the biography was a success not so much because people were at the time interested in Schwartz's poetry, but because of the cautionary nature of his life story. Readers indifferent to modern poetry could still take grim relish in the classic saga of a brilliant poet, first heralded as a genius, the greatest young poet of his day, who quickly burnt himself out due to mental illness and addictions to alcohol and narcotics, and died almost forgotten at the age of fifty-two in a seedy hotel room in New York's Times Square district. In a way, Atlas's biography is the contemporary counterpart of Samuel Johnson's great essay on the little-known eighteenth-century poet Richard Savage, which has become a classic study of the self-destructive, paranoid artist. Unfortunately, the story of Delmore Schwartz's life hasn't really sparked an ensuing revival of interest in his poetry. It has, however, kept his *Selected Poems* and several other collections of his writings in print at New Directions, which first published him in the thirties, and also resulted in the publication of a volume of his letters and a copious selection from his unpublished notebooks. The patient, that is to say his reputation, is still alive, if not exactly well. But the extent of Schwartz's fall from grace can be measured by the fact that, although his early work was admired by Eliot, Auden, and Wallace Stevens, and such influential critics as R. P. Blackmur and F. W. Dupee (who wrote, "Since Auden's early poems appeared, there has been no verse so alive with contemporary meaning"), he is not included in Helen Vendler's comprehensive *Harvard Book of American Poetry* and is represented by only two poems in Richard Ellman's canonical *New Oxford Book of American Verse*. Nor can one really fault the editors: Delmore Schwartz is but one, albeit perhaps the most distinguished, of a group of poets of his time whom a revolution in taste (in Schwartz's case speeded by a decline in the quality of his later poems) has swept from view; perhaps he will be swept back in by some future revolution when his time has come.

Now, however, with this spendid *Once and for All*, the reader can see Delmore Schwartz whole again and take in his entire career.

Delmore, as everyone called him, including those who didn't know him, was born in Brooklyn on December 8, 1913, to the unhappily married Harry Schwartz and Rose Nathanson, both immigrants from eastern Europe ("Atlantic Jews," as Delmore would characterize their class in his poetry). He both loved and hated the artificially English-sounding name Delmore, and offered various explanations of its origin. James Atlas tells us: "Sometimes he would insist he had been named after a delicatessen across the street from the house where he was born, sometimes that his mother had been fond of an actor who was named Frank Delmore. In still other versions, the name was taken from a Tammany Hall club, a Pullman railroad car, or a Riverside Drive apartment house." (His one sibling got off lightly with the given name Kenneth.) In his verse play *Shenandoah*, the protagonist's parents, Mr. and Mrs. Fish, set about choosing a "distinguished and new and American" name for their firstborn, who becomes Shenandoah Fish, an alter ego appearing in a number of

Schwartz's works. Other ponderously named Jewish characters in his writings include Hershey Green (the Anglo-Saxon name Harold transformed to the Jewish Herschel and then to the name of a brand of chocolate), Rudyard Bell, Faber Gottschalk, and Richmond Rose; and Delmore himself would become the character Von Humboldt Fletcher in his friend Saul Bellow's roman à clef *Humboldt's Gift*, published after Schwartz's death.

The circumstances of Delmore's childhood and later life would be continually recalled in his writing, which is in a sense one vast mythification of himself and his family. Harry Schwartz was handsome, a successful businessman and a philanderer. Rose's natural bitterness intensified as the marriage failed; in desperation, she secretly cashed a French war bond, the gift of a European uncle, to pay for an operation which would enable her to have children, thinking in this way to attach her husband. The operation was a success, but the marriage wasn't. One particularly traumatic event occurred when Delmore was seven, and his mother discovered his father's car parked outside a restaurant; going inside, they discovered Harry entertaining a "whore," in his mother's term; the ghastly scene that followed would later be enshrined in his poem "Prothalamion":

> ... the speech my mother made
> In a restaurant, trapping my father there
> At dinner with his whore. Her spoken rage
> Struck down the child of seven years
> With shame for all three, with pity for
> The helpless harried waiter, with anger for
> The diners gazing, avid, and contempt,
> And great disgust for every human being.

But all the small tragedies of childhood, situated and magnified against the backdrop of Europe (especially Russia, his father's homeland) and the war that raged there, would become grist for Schwartz's writing. In one of his best-known poems, "The Ballad of the Children of the Czar," he compares himself, eating a baked potato in Brooklyn in 1916, with the Czar's children playing ball "six thousand miles away"; he knocks the potato off his tray and loses it, just as the children's ball escapes through a gate, and the ramifications extend even further back into history and myth: "In history's pity and terror / The child is Aeneas again; / Troy is in the nursery, / The rocking horse is on fire. / Child labor! The child must carry / His fathers on his back." History, he observes, has no "ruth," no pity, for "the individual, / Who drinks tea, who catches cold," that is to say, everybody. And in his most famous short story, "In Dreams Begin Responsibilities," the poet himself moves backward in time, dreaming he is in a movie theater watching a silent film of his parents' courtship at Coney Island years before. At a crucial moment "I stood up in the theatre and shouted: 'Don't do it. It's not too late to change your minds, both of you. Nothing good will come of it, only remorse, hatred, scandal, and two children whose characters are monstrous.'"

Schwartz was an astoundingly prolific writer. He seems to have written almost continuously, not only in the various literary genres of poetry, fiction, and criticism at which he excelled— he was amazingly erudite—but also journals, letters, unfinished projects, and scraps and jottings of every kind. The bulk of his work is unpublished and probably unpublishable. The fragments from notebooks which his widow, Elizabeth Pollet, collected in a volume called *Portrait of Delmore*, run to 650 pages, and though there are treasures to be found in it, they are few and far between. For me and for most readers, his most rewarding phase is that of the early lyric poetry and the book of short stories, *The World Is a Wedding*, some of which are so good that one deplores the fact that there aren't more of them (other uncollected short stories do exist), or that he never wrote any of the novels for which numerous sketches abound.

Schwartz's most ambitious published work is the unfinished epic poem *Genesis*, published in 1943. The temptation to write the great American epic poem was particularly keen in the 1930s. Besides the obvious examples of Pound's *Cantos* and Eliot's

The Waste Land—which (unlike the longer *Four Quartets*) I think must be considered an epic despite its relative brevity—together with Stevens's "The Comedian as the Letter C"), there were other examples of would-be epic verse: Robinson Jeffers's "Tamar" and "Roan Stallion"; the volume of a thousand sonnets called *M* by Merrill Moore, a member of the southern Fugitive group; *Taal* by the female poet Jeremy Ingalls; while still to come were Auden's "The Sea and the Mirror" and, much later, James Merrill's *The Changing Light at Sandover* (both of these arguably influenced by Schwartz's epic), Berryman's "Homage to Mistress Bradstreet," Williams's *Paterson*, and Olson's *Maximus Poems*—all products of an inherent American urge to make it big as well as new.

Genesis is a disappointment, but it fails on a lavish scale. It was intended to be Delmore's twentieth-century Brooklyn version of Wordsworth's *The Prelude*, though a more immediate stylistic precedent was Hardy's *The Dynasts*, which Delmore studied. In *Genesis*, the forebears of the hero, Hershey Green, live out horrible adventures in Europe and manage to emigrate to America, where the real substance and sorrow of their lives begin. As in *The Dynasts*, a chorus of disembodied spirits comments ironically on the saga as it unrolls; lyric passages, many of them of great beauty, alternate with rather stiff expository stretches of "biblical" prose, printed as long run-on lines of poetry but nonetheless prosaic, though the ear gradually gets used to the contrast. Wrapped in this prose padding like precious objects stored away, the intermittent brilliant passages stand out all the more strikingly:

> "The act of darkness which begins the world
> Fosters what gross mistakes!" another said,
> "Because the lovers lie like scissors close,
> And face hides face, love's plaza absolute,
> Their eyes are shut, they cannot see, alas!
> And from the cache and spurt what lies are born!"

We see here how subtly Delmore could manipulate undertones of language. The "lovers lie like scissors close"—closed as well as close, one assumes, and yet the idea of the lovers as sharp blades capable of inflicting harm even on each other, as well as being two parts of a single entity, galvanizes the image. Similarly the phrases "love's plaza" and "the cache and spurt" are both bizarre yet somehow right. The "plaza" suggests the bullring where the antagonist lovers will meet, and also the Plaza Hotel where the upwardly-aspiring couple might, with luck, celebrate their marriage one day. And the dimly heard sexual innuendo of "cache and spurt" (an odd pairing of nouns, to say the least) alludes not only to the female and male sexual organs but also the "cash" which will play an important role in the union.

A little further on occur the lines, "Asking what every sore throat may have meant / And what the burnt match, what the cane, / The necktie and the boredom of the will—." Delmore was always adept at conjuring a specific world out of a sparse sprinkling of abstract and concrete words. The sore throat evokes "the individual / Who drinks tea, who catches cold" (cold symptoms abound in Delmore's work), who is situated in a precise environment by the words match, cane, necktie, boredom of the will. This singular but singularly appropriate list of particulars echoes Auden, whom Schwartz admired (and vice versa). James Laughlin, Delmore's publisher and a poet himself, called Schwartz "The American Auden"—no small compliment, though today one tends to forget that Auden was then considered the major poet of his generation. And Delmore's list suggests similar lists in Auden: "The croquet matches in summer, the handshake, the cough, the kiss, / There is always a wicked secret, a private reason for this."

"Boredom of the will." Indeed. Here, as so often in *Genesis*, as throughout his work (and his work is really all of a piece, the same retelling of birth, migration, new disappointment, damaged hopes, ordinary lives being turned into the stone of history), one is again at the core of the poem; the phrase, like so many of his others, is a rabbit hole down which one plummets to an exasperatingly real and unsatisfactory Wonderland. It always comes back to the recounting of sorrow in new and breathtakingly beautiful ways which lighten the sorrow. For a while. "It seems that few actions remain unobserved, and fewer yet remain unsuspected by human beings, of each other," observes the nameless narrator of *Genesis*. At the end of the short story "A Bitter Farce," a college professor named Mr. Fish "returns to his home to await the arrival of innumerable anxiety feelings which had their source in events which had occurred for the past five thousand years." In a 1959 prefatory note to his *Selected Poems*, Delmore surprisingly interjected: "Every point of view, every kind of knowledge and every kind of experience is limited and ignorant; nevertheless, so far as I know, this volume seems to be as representative as it could be." And at the end of "America! America!," the brilliant short story, Shenandoah Fish says: " 'I do not see myself. I do not know myself. I cannot look at myself truly.' He turned from the looking-glass and said to himself . . . 'No one truly exists in the real world because no one knows all that he is to other human beings, all that they say behind his back, and all the foolishness which the future will bring him.'" These works are later than the early lyrics collected in his first book *In Dreams Begin Responsibilities*, but for me they are the most valuable part of Delmore's oeuvre.

A brief sketch of his biography may cast some light on a few passages from his greatest poetry.

During the first decade of his life, the family was shunted back and forth between cramped apartments in Brooklyn and the upper-Manhattan neighborhood of Washington Heights. Harry Schwartz finally left his wife for good in 1923 and moved to Chicago, where his insurance business prospered, leaving Delmore with the illusion that he would someday inherit wealth. This was not to happen, though he did inherit a few thousand dollars long after his father died in the spring of 1930. Delmore studied for a year at the University of Wisconsin, then at New York University, and finally Harvard, which he left without taking a degree.

Despite his unwillingness to be considered a Marxist, he joined the staff of the leftist intellectual journal *Partisan Review*, which had switched its allegiance from Stalin to Trotsky. During the latter half of the thirties, he taught at Harvard, but often in menial positions: His continual attempts to get a tenured position there, at Cornell, at the University of California and elsewhere, were always foiled by circumstance, or, more often, by his erratic behavior. As a Jew at Harvard, he keenly resented the snobbery of the largely WASP faculty, but even more the success of the suave and cosmopolitan scholar and critic, Harry Levin, who, though Jewish, was somehow "accepted," or so it seemed to Delmore. I took Levin's celebrated course in Proust, Joyce, and Mann, though I never studied with Delmore, nor met him at Harvard, for reasons I can no longer remember, since I admired his poetry even before coming to the university; he was, in fact, one of the reasons I wished to study there. My friend Kenneth Koch did, however, take a course with him, from which he reported great things. (I did get to know Delmore slightly several years later in New York, and was delighted when he accepted my poem, "The Picture of Little J. A. in a Prospect of Flowers," for *Partisan Review*.) Our lack of contact at Harvard may have been a problem of scheduling; Schwartz on at least one occasion canceled his course abruptly and returned to New York to breathe the freer air of Greenwich Village. Still, the cultured ambience of Harvard attracted him, too, and he became friends with such rising, slightly younger poets as Robert Lowell and John Berryman, whose genius and chaotic temperament he shared. Berryman for his part memorialized Delmore in some dozen of his *Dream Songs*, one of which contains the passage: "He looked onto the world like the act of an aged whore. / Delmore, Delmore. / He flung to pieces and they hit the floor."

Meanwhile, Delmore's literary career had begun auspiciously, dazzlingly, with the publication of *In Dreams Begin Responsibilities*. James Atlas has attempted to explain the powerful effect of the book when it appeared in 1938. When I first discovered it some five years later, it still retained this aura, palpable even in the dog-eared copy I found in a public library: "It devolved upon Eliot to become Delmore's model; he was, after all, the quintessential modernist, and, what was perhaps more significant, he provided an example of the recognition conferred on those who managed to establish a new poetic idiom. Yet ... authoritarian, dignified, remote, Eliot had achieved a stature that infuriated Delmore even as it filled him with envy; restrained by the limitations of his own background from emulating Eliot's cultivated manner, Delmore could only follow an opposite course, and eventually found more congenial models in those exemplary figures of revolt Rimbaud and Baudelaire." Atlas sees "Baudelaire's emphatic style of declamation ... tempered by a note of ineffable sadness" in the poem "Tired and Unhappy You Think of Houses," though a more immediate antecedent may have been Thomas Mann's story "Tonio Kröger"; and the peripatetic domestic life of Rose Schwartz and her two boys, ever shuttling between meaner and cheaper lodgings after their relatively comfortable earlier life, no doubt also plays a role.

In "Tired and Unhappy You Think of Houses," as throughout his poetry, the transition is dangerous, unexpected; the peaceful, somnolent bourgeois interior is abruptly supplanted by the world underground, perhaps a further allusion to Gluck and Orpheus. "The weight of the lean buildings is seen," that is the pilings sunk deep into the earth; the rush is on; "well-dressed or mean, so many surround you." One thinks of Dante's (and Eliot's) "I had not thought death had undone so many"; and the final line with its exclamation point (a favorite device of Delmore's, often used with great skill, as here) echoes both the slamming of iron gates and the imperious ringing of a cash register totaling up the bill.

Atlas points out the power of Delmore's titles, which inveigle and buttonhole the reader in the manner of the Ancient Mariner. Others one could cite for their suasive force are "Out of the Watercolored Window, When You Look," "Someone Is Harshly Coughing as Before," "All of Us Always Turning Away for Solace," and "A Dog Named Ego, the Snowflakes as Kisses." Often in one of those seemingly tiny variants which Delmore is always inserting into his poetry and which can produce a seamless unexpectedness, he will use the title as the first line with a minor variation, as in the first lines of two of the poems just mentioned. "Out of the Watercolored Window, When You Look" becomes "When from the watercolored window idly you look" and "Someone Is Harshly Coughing as Before" becomes "Someone is harshly coughing on the next floor."

"The Heavy Bear Who Goes with Me," perhaps his most famous poem, is one of a group he calls "The Repetitive Heart: Poems in Imitation of the Fugue." I haven't seen an explanation of what he meant by "in imitation of the fugue," but these poems use the device of variants ringing changes on a theme in the manner of Bach, or, even more, of Mozart, where a subtle modulation can slip past the ear's attentiveness and suddenly alter the music's landscape and mood.

The clandestine linking of images has the football of the first stanza returning in the word "scrimmage" in the last line (Delmore was an avid sports fan and reader of sports journals). The perhaps likable if clumsy bear, who "climbs the building, kicks the football," turns terrifying at the end, participating in "the scrimmage of appetite everywhere," one of Delmore's most riveting phrases.

Another of Delmore's "fugal" poems, "Calmly We Walk through This April's Day," encapsulates a number of his constant themes: the life of the city, names of friends he knew ("Many great dears are taken away"), and above all an apprehension of the whirling universe (in the mundane décor of a municipal park).

Note how matter-of-factly he begins setting the stage: "In the park sit pauper and *rentier*" (another of his favorite words; how desperately he wished to be a *rentier*!). But then: "The screaming children, the motor-car / Fugitive about us, running away, / Between the worker and the millionaire." It's impossible to know who is running with whom: the screaming children, the car, the worker, the millionaire, all swarming, "fugitive about us"—though why the motorcar and the millionaire should be fugitive is unclear. The spelled-out dates: "Nineteen Thirty-Seven," "Nineteen Fourteen," as well as the names of people we don't know (Bert Spira and Rhoda, it turns out, were actual friends of Delmore from his college days) read as desperate attempts to pin down the fleeing scene, give it permanence, but all is swept away in flames. This time the fugal repetitions end in a painful thud of closure.

A somewhat lighter but still disturbing poem is "Far Rockaway." The name of this lower-middle-class sea-resort near Brooklyn is almost a joke for New Yorkers; there is nothing "far" or "away" about the place, and the joke is compounded by Delmore's use of an unidentified epigraph from Henry James: "the cure of souls" (could it be from *The Wings of the Dove* with its larger-than-life doctor character, Sir Luke Strett?). James would certainly have felt ill-at-ease in Far Rockaway, worlds away from Newport.

"The radiant soda," or a multicolored assortment of soft drinks in their bottles, fun fashions, foam, and freedom (not only on the beach but in the breaking waves as they catch the light). "The sea laves / The shaven sand"; "laves" and "shaven" offer a marvelous echoing of sounds, as well as a precise image of what the sea does to the sand, brutally sandpapering it. "And the light sways forward / On the self-destroying waves." Finally, an image of destruction undermines the airy gait of the scene; the light collapses inward; the waves self-destruct in coming to be. And at the end the "tangential" author seeking the cure of souls in what greets his gaze is doomed to failure. His nervous conscience amid the "concessions"—a brilliant play on words, concessions can mean commercial stalls such as would flourish along a boardwalk, selling soda, etc., and also the demeaning compromises the writer must accept in lieu of a cure—is the haunting (romantic) and haunted (macabre) moon.

One last example of these early poems is "I Am to My Own

Heart Merely a Serf." Here again are arrayed many of the motifs that occur throughout Schwartz's poetry: the sea, tall buildings, automobiles (Delmore loved to drive and even during his most penurious periods usually managed to hang on to some old wreck of a car), sleep, dreams and their responsibilities, his own past, and history. There are some fabulous configurations here: he "climbs the sides of buildings just to get / Merely a gob of gum, all that is left / Of its [that is, his heart's] infatuation of last year." The phrase, as awkward but hallucinatory as the act it describes, suggests a forgotten episode of a love affair: the speaker, it seems, was infatuated with a girl last summer and left a wad of chewing gum stuck to the side of a building by the sea, intending to retrieve it later. Now, that disgusting object is all that is left to the lover, menial as a serf to the commands of his heart. Now he is as sick of his heart's "cruel rule" "as one is sick of chewing gum all day," a wonderfully comic, cruel image. In sleep anger can spend itself, but when sleep too is crowded and full of chores, the tyranny of the past takes over. The poet must find the right door in a row of maddeningly identical ones, carry his father on his back, or rather, the poem implies, carry a carriage with his father in it on his back. Then the language starts to become increasingly garbled, as speech heard in a dream: "Last summer, 1910, and my own people, / The government of love's great polity, / The choice of taxes, the production / Of clocks, of lights and horses, the location / Of monuments, of hotels and of rhyme ..." Why, among other questions that spring to mind, the date 1910, three years before his birth? The lines become more nonsensical until finally anger causes the dreamer to start awake, with an exclamation mark. But the finality dies into "merely wake up once more," leaving the humiliated dreamer to contemplate yet again his condition of being a "servant of incredible assumption."

The pain of Delmore's poetry is only a pale reflection of the painful life from which it grew. I'll abridge the downward drift of his later years: two failed marriages, erratic employment as a teacher and a book and film reviewer, increasing poverty, alcohol and various other addictions. When his second wife, the novelist Elizabeth Pollet, left him in the summer of 1957, his life was really over, though it dragged on for another nine years, during which he became steadily more deranged, imagining that his wife was the mistress of Nelson Rockefeller and that President Kennedy and the Pope were plotting against him. Friends, including Bellow, took up a subscription to pay for psychiatric treatment, but he never stayed in the mental wards long, returning to his favorite Greenwich Village haunts and increasingly squalid living quarters. Lowell, who had published a poem about their drinking days in Cambridge back in the forties in *Life Studies*, wrote another about his last years which is probably chillingly accurate:

> Your dream had humor, then its genius thickened,
> you grew thick and helpless, your lines were variants
> alike and unlike, Delmore—your name, Schwartz,
> one vowel bedeviled by seven consonants ...
> one gabardine suit the color of sulphur,
> scanning wide-eyed the windowless room of wisdom,
> your notes on Joyce and porno magazines—
> the stoplights blinking code for you alone
> casing the bars with the eyes of a Mongol horseman.

Yet he continued to write poetry. In 1959, he published *Summer Knowledge*, a collection of poems from previous volumes along with many new ones. Critics have tended to dismiss these, and perhaps rightly, though some have lately come to their defense, notably David Lehman. The late poetry does seem to lack the electric compressions and simplifications that animate his early writing, tending toward bald assertiveness. James Atlas calls it "haphazard, euphonious, virtually incomprehensible effusions ... imitative of Hopkins, Yeats, Shelley." And he may be right. Yet there is something there, perhaps indeed the ruin of a great poet, but perhaps something more. It turns out that critics were premature in condemning the late work of Picasso and Stravinsky;

perhaps Delmore will one day get a similar reprieve. Read the title poem from that last collection; I leave it to you to decide, adding only that I think that the repetitions in his defining what he means by "summer knowledge," though they seem labored at first, end by achieving a new kind of telling, with an urgent bluntness of its own.

JOHN ASHBERY

EDITOR'S PREFACE

For readers of at least the last two decades, it has been extremely difficult to construct an accurate picture of the shape of Delmore Schwartz's career. Between Schwartz's death in 1966 and the early 1980s, a number of posthumous books were published. These included volumes that are now already out of print: James Atlas's excellent biography, *Delmore Schwartz: The Life of an American Poet*; *Portrait of Delmore*, containing excerpts from Schwartz's journals, edited by his second wife Elizabeth Pollet; *The Selected Essays of Delmore Schwartz*, edited by Donald Dike and David Zucker; two collections of letters; and *Shenandoah and Other Verse Plays*, edited by Robert Phillips. Schwartz's own original collections of poetry and prose—his 1938 debut *In Dreams Begin Responsibilities*; *Genesis: Book One*, the only published volume of his uncompleted epic; *The World Is a Wedding*, his first book of stories; *Vaudeville for a Princess*, his second book of poetry and prose; and *Successful Love*, his last story collection—have all been unavailable for decades. Some prose and poetry from these books is contained in various editions published by New Directions. But none of these selections give a truly accurate sense of the *development* of Schwartz's art and the unfolding of his literary career.

It is my goal to offer in this single volume the best and most representative of Schwartz's writing, much of it available for the first time in years, some of it published for the first time. I hope readers will be able to gain a broad, if not complete, understanding of Delmore Schwartz the literary artist. Selections from *Genesis* are reprinted here for the first time since the book's original publication in the 1940s; as a whole, the poem is unsuccessful, but, as John Ashbery says in his introduction, there are many stunning passages. I have tried to select a few that represent the whole work. I have also added two unpublished poems found in Schwartz's archives, held at Yale. The book includes, for the first time, selections from Schwartz's unpublished book on T. S. Eliot, commissioned by James Laughlin for his Masters of Modern Literature series. This series, containing critical books about single authors, was published early in New Directions' history.

As it is my goal to portray the unfolding of Schwartz's career, I have grouped the pieces according to the order of their original publication in Delmore's own books, though where pieces were reprinted in later books, I have used the later book as my textual source. In *Summer Knowledge,* Schwartz seemed to have found a more appealing order for the poems in his first book, so I have used that ordering. I am not a textual scholar; I have done my best with the material from the archives to interpret Schwartz's handwritten drafts and corrections. I only hope any mistakes I have made will be corrected by a future researcher.

I owe thanks to many people, foremost among them my wife Brenda Shaughnessy, who has had to suffer Schwartz's long residence in our household. I am also grateful to Robert Phillips, Schwartz's literary executor, for his support of this project. Barbara Epler, Jeffrey Yang, Declan Spring, and Laurie Callahan of New Directions carried forward James Laughlin's devotion to Delmore, an early author and advisor to the press, and I am eternally thankful to them for giving life to this project. Thank you to John Ashbery for the use of his lecture as the foreword to this book. I am also grateful to my research assistant Monica Sok, and to Don Share and Stephen Burt for much help and advice.

CRAIG MORGAN TEICHER

Fiction

IN DREAMS BEGIN
RESPONSIBILITIES

I

I think it is the year 1909. I feel as if I were in a motion picture theatre, the long arm of light crossing the darkness and spinning, my eyes fixed on the screen. This is a silent picture as if an old Biograph one, in which the actors are dressed in ridiculously old-fashioned clothes, and one flash succeeds another with sudden jumps. The actors too seem to jump about and walk too fast. The shots themselves are full of dots and rays, as if it were raining when the picture was photographed. The light is bad.

It is Sunday afternoon, June 12th, 1909, and my father is walking down the quiet streets of Brooklyn on his way to visit my mother. His clothes are newly pressed and his tie is too tight in his high collar. He jingles the coins in his pockets, thinking of the witty things he will say. I feel as if I had by now relaxed entirely in the soft darkness of the theatre; the organist peals out the obvious and approximate emotions on which the audience rocks unknowingly. I am anonymous, and I have forgotten myself. It is always so when one goes to the movies, it is, as they say, a drug.

My father walks from street to street of trees, lawns and houses, once in a while coming to an avenue on which a streetcar skates and gnaws, slowly progressing. The conductor, who has a handlebar mustache, helps a young lady wearing a hat like a bowl with feathers on to the car. She lifts her long skirts slightly as she mounts the steps. He leisurely makes change and rings his bell. It is obviously Sunday, for everyone is wearing Sunday clothes, and the street-car's noises emphasize the quiet of the holiday. Is not Brooklyn the City of Churches? The shops are closed and their shades drawn, but for an occasional stationery store or drugstore with great green balls in the window.

My father has chosen to take this long walk because he likes to walk and think. He thinks about himself in the future and so arrives at the place he is to visit in a state of mild exaltation. He pays no attention to the houses he is passing, in which the Sunday dinner is being eaten, nor to the many trees which patrol each street, now coming to their full leafage and the time when they will room the whole street in cool shadow. An occasional carriage passes, the horse's hooves falling like stones in the quiet afternoon, and once in a while an automobile, looking like an enormous upholstered sofa, puffs and passes.

My father thinks of my mother, of how nice it will be to introduce her to his family. But he is not yet sure that he wants to marry her, and once in a while he becomes panicky about the bond already established. He reassures himself by thinking of the big men he admires who are married: William Randolph Hearst, and William Howard Taft, who has just become President of the United States.

My father arrives at my mother's house. He has come too early and so is suddenly embarrassed. My aunt, my mother's sister, answers the loud bell with her napkin in her hand, for the family is still at dinner. As my father enters, my grandfather rises from the table and shakes hands with him. My mother has run upstairs to tidy herself. My grandmother asks my father if he has had dinner, and tells him that Rose will be downstairs soon. My grandfather opens the conversation by remarking on the mild June weather. My father sits uncomfortably near the table, holding his hat in his hand. My grandmother tells my aunt to take my father's hat. My uncle, twelve years old, runs into the house, his hair tousled. He shouts a greeting to my father, who has often given him a nickel, and then runs upstairs. It is evident that the respect in which my father is held in this household is tempered by a good deal of mirth. He is impressive, yet he is very awkward.

II

Finally my mother comes downstairs, all dressed up, and my father being engaged in conversation with my grandfather becomes uneasy, not knowing whether to greet my mother or continue the conversation. He gets up from the chair clumsily and says "hello" gruffly. My grandfather watches, examining their congruence, such as it is, with a critical eye, and meanwhile rubbing his bearded cheek roughly, as he always does when he reflects. He is worried; he is afraid that my father will not make a good husband for his oldest daughter. At this point something happens to the film, just as my father is saying something funny to my mother; I am awakened to myself and my unhappiness just as my interest was rising. The audience begins to clap impatiently. Then the trouble is cared for but the film has been returned to a portion just shown, and once more I see my grandfather rubbing his bearded cheek and pondering my father's character. It is difficult to get back into the picture once more and forget myself, but as my mother giggles at my father's words, the darkness drowns me.

My father and mother depart from the house, my father shaking hands with my mother once more, out of some unknown uneasiness. I stir uneasily also, slouched in the hard chair of the theatre. Where is the older uncle, my mother's older brother? He is studying in his bedroom upstairs, studying for his final examination at the College of the City of New York, having been dead of rapid pneumonia for the last twenty-one years. My mother and father walk down the same quiet streets once more. My mother is holding my father's arm and telling him of the novel which she has been reading; and my father utters judgments of the characters as the plot is made clear to him. This is a habit which he very much enjoys, for he feels the utmost superiority and confidence when he approves and condemns the behavior of other people. At times he feels moved to utter a brief "Ugh"—whenever the story becomes what he would call sugary. This tribute is paid to his manliness. My mother feels satisfied by the interest which she has awakened; she is showing my father how intelligent she is, and how interesting.

They reach the avenue, and the street-car leisurely arrives. They are going to Coney Island this afternoon, although my mother considers that such pleasures are inferior. She has made up her mind to indulge only in a walk on the boardwalk and a pleasant dinner, avoiding the riotous amusements as being beneath the dignity of so dignified a couple.

My father tells my mother how much money he has made in the past week, exaggerating an amount which need not have been exaggerated. But my father has always felt that actualities somehow fall short. Suddenly I begin to weep. The determined old lady who sits next to me in the theatre is annoyed and looks at me with an angry face, and being intimidated, I stop. I drag out my handkerchief and dry my face, licking the drop which has fallen near my lips. Meanwhile I have missed something, for here are my mother and father alighting at the last stop, Coney Island.

III

They walk toward the boardwalk, and my father commands my mother to inhale the pungent air from the sea. They both breathe in deeply, both of them laughing as they do so. They have in common a great interest in health, although my father is strong and husky, my mother frail. Their minds are full of theories of what is good to eat and not good to eat, and sometimes they engage in heated discussions of the subject, the whole matter ending in my father's announcement, made with a scornful bluster, that you have to die sooner or later anyway. On the boardwalk's flagpole, the American flag is pulsing in an intermittent wind from the sea.

My father and mother go to the rail of the boardwalk and look down on the beach where a good many bathers are casually walking about. A few are in the surf. A peanut whistle pierces the air with its pleasant and active whine, and my father goes to buy peanuts. My mother remains at the rail and stares at the ocean. The ocean seems merry to her; it pointedly sparkles and again and again the pony waves are released. She notices the children digging in the wet sand, and the bathing costumes of the girls who are her own age. My father returns with the peanuts. Overhead the sun's lightning strikes and strikes, but neither of them are at all aware of it. The boardwalk is full of people dressed in their Sunday clothes and idly strolling. The tide does not reach as far as the boardwalk, and the strollers would feel no danger if it did. My mother and father lean on the rail of the boardwalk and absently stare at the ocean. The ocean is becoming rough; the waves come in slowly, tugging strength from far back. The moment before they somersault, the moment when they arch their backs so beautifully, showing green and white veins amid the black, that moment is intolerable. They finally crack, dashing fiercely upon the sand, actually driving, full force downward, against the sand, bouncing upward and forward, and at last petering out into a small stream which races up the beach and then is recalled. My parents gaze absentmindedly at the ocean, scarcely interested in its harshness. The sun overhead does not disturb them. But I stare at the terrible sun which breaks up sight, and the fatal, merciless, passionate ocean, I forget my parents. I stare fascinated and finally, shocked by the indifference of my father and mother, I burst out weeping once more. The old lady next to me pats me on the shoulder and says "There, there, all of this is only a movie, young man, only a movie," but I look up once more at the terrifying sun and the terrifying ocean, and being unable to control my tears, I get up and go to the men's room, stumbling over the feet of the other people seated in my row.

IV

When I return, feeling as if I had awakened in the morning sick for lack of sleep, several hours have apparently passed and my parents are riding on the merry-go-round. My father is on a black horse, my mother on a white one, and they seem to be making an eternal circuit for the single purpose of snatching the nickel rings which are attached to the arm of one of the posts. A hand-organ is playing; it is one with the ceaseless circling of the merry-go-round.

For a moment it seems that they will never get off the merry-go-round because it will never stop. I feel like one who looks down on the avenue from the 50th story of a building. But at length they do get off; even the music of the hand-organ has ceased for a moment. My father has acquired ten rings, my mother only two, although it was my mother who really wanted them.

They walk on along the boardwalk as the afternoon descends by imperceptible degrees into the incredible violet of dusk. Everything fades into a relaxed glow, even the ceaseless murmuring from the beach, and the revolutions of the merry-go-round. They look for a place to have dinner. My father suggests the best one on the boardwalk and my mother demurs, in accordance with her principles.

However they do go to the best place, asking for a table near the window, so that they can look out on the boardwalk and the mobile ocean. My father feels omnipotent as he places a quarter in the waiter's hand as he asks for a table. The place is crowded and here too there is music, this time from a kind of string trio. My father orders dinner with a fine confidence.

As the dinner is eaten, my father tells of his plans for the future, and my mother shows with expressive face how interested she is, and how impressed. My father becomes exultant. He is lifted up by the waltz that is being played, and his own future begins to intoxicate him. My father tells my mother that he is going to expand his business, for there is a great deal of money to be made. He wants to settle down. After all, he is twenty-nine, he has lived by himself since he was thirteen, he is making more and more money, and he is envious of his married friends when he visits them in the cozy security of their homes, surrounded, it seems, by the calm domestic pleasures, and by delightful children, and then, as the waltz reaches the moment when all the dancers swing madly, then, then with awful daring, then he asks my mother to marry him, although awkwardly enough and puzzled, even in his excitement, at how he had arrived at the proposal, and she, to make the whole business worse, begins to cry, and my father looks nervously about, not knowing at all what to do now, and my mother says: "It's all I've wanted from the moment I saw you," sobbing, and he finds all of this very difficult, scarcely to his taste, scarcely as he had thought it would be, on his long walks over Brooklyn Bridge in the revery of a fine cigar, and it was then that I stood up in the theatre and shouted: "Don't do it. It's not too late to change your minds, both of you. Nothing good will come of it, only remorse, hatred, scandal, and two children whose characters are monstrous." The whole audience turned to look at me, annoyed, the usher came hurrying down the aisle flashing his searchlight, and the old lady next to me tugged me down into my seat, saying: "Be quiet. You'll be put out, and you paid thirty-five cents to come in." And so I shut my eyes because I could not bear to see what was happening. I sat there quietly.

V

But after awhile I begin to take brief glimpses, and at length I watch again with thirsty interest, like a child who wants to maintain

7

his sulk although offered the bribe of candy. My parents are now having their picture taken in a photographer's booth along the boardwalk. The place is shadowed in the mauve light which is apparently necessary. The camera is set to the side on its tripod and looks like a Martian man. The photographer is instructing my parents in how to pose. My father has his arm over my mother's shoulder, and both of them smile emphatically. The photographer brings my mother a bouquet of flowers to hold in her hand but she holds it at the wrong angle. Then the photographer covers himself with the black cloth which drapes the camera and all that one sees of him is one protruding arm and his hand which clutches the rubber ball which he will squeeze when the picture is finally taken. But he is not satisfied with their appearance. He feels with certainty that somehow there is something wrong in their pose. Again and again he issues from his hidden place with new directions. Each suggestion merely makes matters worse. My father is becoming impatient. They try a seated pose. The photographer explains that he has pride, he is not interested in all of this for the money, he wants to make beautiful pictures. My father says: "Hurry up, will you? We haven't got all night." But the photographer only scurries about apologetically, and issues new directions. The photographer charms me. I approve of him with all my heart, for I know just how he feels, and as he criticizes each revised pose according to some unknown idea of Tightness, I become quite hopeful. But then my father says angrily: "Come on, you've had enough time, we're not going to wait any longer." And the photographer, sighing unhappily, goes back under his black covering, holds out his hand, says: "One, two, three, Now!", and the picture is taken, with my father's smile turned to a grimace and my mother's bright and false. It takes a few minutes for the picture to be developed and as my parents sit in the curious light they become quite depressed.

They have passed a fortune-teller's booth, and my mother wishes to go in, but my father does not. They begin to argue about it. My mother becomes stubborn, my father once more impatient, and then they begin to quarrel, and what my father would like to do is walk off and leave my mother there, but he knows that that would never do. My mother refuses to budge. She is near to tears, but she feels an uncontrollable desire to hear what the palm-reader will say. My father consents angrily, and they both go into a booth which is in a way like the photographer's, since it is draped in black cloth and its light is shadowed. The place is too warm, and my father keeps saying this is all nonsense, pointing to the crystal ball on the table. The fortune-teller, a fat, short woman, garbed in what is supposed to be Oriental robes, comes into the room from the back and greets them, speaking with an accent. But suddenly my father feels that the whole thing is intolerable; he tugs at my mother's arm, but my mother refuses to budge. And then, in terrible anger, my father lets go of my mother's arm and strides out, leaving my mother stunned. She moves to go after my father, but the fortune-teller holds her arm tightly and begs her not to do so, and I in my seat am shocked more than can ever be said, for I feel as if I were walking a tight-rope a hundred feet over a circus-audience and suddenly the rope is showing signs of breaking, and I get up from my seat and begin to shout once more the first words I can think of to communicate my terrible fear and once more the usher comes hurrying down the aisle flashing his searchlight, and the old lady pleads with me, and the shocked audience has turned to stare at me, and I keep shouting: "What are they doing? Don't they know what they are doing? Why doesn't my mother go after my father? If she does not do that, what will she do? Doesn't my father know what he is doing?"—But the usher has seized my arm and is dragging me away, and as he does so, he says: "What are *you* doing? Don't you know that you can't do whatever you want to do? Why should a young man like you, with your whole life before you, get hysterical like this? Why don't you *think* of what you're doing? You can't act like this even if other people aren't around! You will be sorry if you do not do what you should do, you can't carry on like this, it is not right, you will find that out soon enough, everything you do matters too much," and he said that dragging me through the lobby of the theatre into the cold light, and I woke up into the bleak winter morning of my 21st birthday, the windowsill shining with its lip of snow, and the morning already begun.

THE WORLD IS A WEDDING

To Juliet Barrett

ONE: "WHAT DOES SHE HAVE THAT I DON'T HAVE?"

In this our life there are no beginnings but only departures entitled beginnings, wreathed in the formal emotions thought to be appropriate and often forced. Darkly rises each moment from the life which has been lived and which does not die, for each event lives in the heavy head forever, waiting to renew itself.

The circle of human beings united by need and love began with the graduation or departure of Rudyard Bell from school, just at the beginning of the great depression. Rudyard was the leader and captain of all hearts and his sister Laura's apartment was the place where the circle came to full being. When Rudyard graduated, he decided to devote himself to the writing of plays. His aunt had suggested that he become a teacher in the public high school system until he had proven himself as a dramatist, but Rudyard rejected his aunt's suggestion. He said that to be a playwright was a noble and difficult profession to which one must give one's whole being. Laura Bell had taken care of her younger brother since he was four and she said then that Rudyard was a

11

genius and ought not to be required to earn a living. Rudyard accepted his sister's attitude as natural and inevitable, such was his belief in himself and in his power to charm other human beings.

Thus, in a way, this refusal to become a teacher and to earn a living was the beginning of the circle.

The other boys who truly belonged to the circle were also caught in the midst of the great depression. Edmund Kish wanted to be a teacher of philosophy, but he was unable to get an appointment. Jacob Cohen, recognized by all as the conscience or judge of the circle, wanted to be a reporter, but there were few jobs for newcomers. Ferdinand Harrap tried to be an author, but none of his stories were accepted, and he supported himself by directing a business agency. Francis French and Marcus Gross were teachers in the public high school system, although this was far from their ambition, Lloyd Tyler, known as "the boy," was still a student, and Laura made the most money as the buyer for a department store.

The circle was astonished when Rudyard's first long play was rejected by Broadway, for all had been certain that Rudyard would be famous and rich very soon. Rudyard had always been the one who won all the prizes in school and did everything best. Marcus Gross spoke fondly of the day, long ago and far away, when he had first encountered Rudyard in public school. It was the beginning of the new term and after the first hour Rudyard was regarded as a genius by the teacher and the pupils. So it had always been, Rudyard had been the infant prodigy, class orator, laureate, and best student. When Rudyard's plays were refused year after year by Broadway producers the circle was perplexed, for his dramatic works seemed to them delightful and profound when he read them aloud to the circle. Edmund Kish recognized the weakness of the plays, the fact that Rudyard used character and incident merely as springboards for excursions which were lyrical and philosophical, so that the essential impression was dream-like, abstract, and didactic. But he liked the plays for just this reason, and his conversations about philosophy did much to make Rudyard concern himself with the lyrical expression of philosophical ideas.

Laura was disappointed and after a time she concealed her disappointment by speaking of her brother's plays as just trash. Yet she was patient with Rudyard, delighting in the circle as such and hoping that among the new young men whom Rudyard was always bringing to the house there would be one who would want to marry her.

After five years of the depression, the hopes of most of the boys of the circle had faded slowly like a color or were worn thin like a cloth. Their life as part of the circle was their true life, and their lower middle class poverty kept them from seeking out girls and entertaining the idea of marriage. From time to time some of them became acquainted with girls and went out with them briefly, but since no one but Rudyard was doing what he wanted to be doing, marriage was as distant as a foreign country. Disdainful from the beginning of the conventional modes of behavior, their enjoyment of the life of the circle fortified and heightened their disdain.

When Laura began to doubt that she was going to get a husband, she began to drink, hiding the gin in the pantry when Rudyard tried to stop her. She drank on Saturday nights, the nights when the circle came to her house and was most itself, so that some of the boys spoke of "our Saturday nights." When she was really drunken, she became quarrelsome and voluble, and what she said was an incoherent, but blunt utterance of the naked truth. The boys tried to seem indifferent to what she said, but the reason for her drunkenness was clear and painful. When the marriage of a boy or girl who had come to evenings of the circle was discussed, and when the news of an engagement became known, Laura cried out from the kitchen like Cassandra:

"What does she have that I don't have?" Laura uttered this question again and again during the evening, amid other and like remarks.

Laura insisted in vain that her question be answered, and sometimes she placed her hands on her breasts lightly, as if in estimation, although when sober she was ashamed of any mention of sexual desire. Each newcomer or visitor renewed her hope, Laura invited him to come to dinner. Laura was full of great goodness and kindness, a goodness hardly concealed by her disgruntled and grudging remarks. She was unable to understand what was wrong. She lent the boys money and helped them in whatever they attempted, knowing that she was used by them and used most of all by Rudyard. She made petulant remarks, she said that she was a fool, but she always pressed herself forward to be helpful, typing Rudyard's manuscripts which she declared more and more often to be just trash which she could understand less and less as Rudyard's indulgence in lyrical philosophizing grew.

Thus on a Saturday night when the circle had long been in full being, Laura spoke loudly, crying out from the kitchen or uttering her sentences in the midst of a conversation.

"Tick, tick, tick," she said as she carried a dish to the table for the midnight supper.

"What are you ticking about?" asked Edmund Kish, knowing very well that her answer would be an expression of unhappiness.

"O," said Laura, "That's just my life ticking away."

"Can't you stop being human for an evening?" asked Francis French, who did not like to hear of unhappiness.

"No, I can't," said Laura, "I never can, no matter how hard I try. I just keep thinking of the rotten truth, the dirty truth, and nothing but the awful truth."

"We ought to remember," said Rudyard, who was able to enjoy everything, "the profound insight stated in the sentence, '*Joy is our duty.*'"

"I don't feel joyous," said Laura, "and I don't feel like forcing myself to be joyous, whether or not it is a duty. I don't like life, life does not like me, and I am unhappy."

"Laura is right," said Edmund, seeking to show sympathy, "she has a right to her feelings. When I used to get peevish as a child, I would say: 'What should I do? I have nothing to do?' My mother always used to have just one answer: 'Go knock your head against the wall' was what my mother always said. She was a big help."

"Tick, tick, tick," said Laura, "that's just life passing away, second by second."

TWO: "HOW MUCH MONEY DOES HE MAKE?"

During the week, Edmund Kish had been visited by Israel Brown, the most admired of all the teachers known to the circle. Israel Brown was a man of incomparable learning. He was lean, tall, hollow-cheeked, and Christ-like in appearance. When he conversed, he spoke with a passion and rush such that one might suppose that the end of his life or of the world were in the offing. He did not seem to belong to this world and this life, although he appeared to all to know about everything in this world. He was a teacher of philosophy, but he touched upon many other subjects, ancient coins, legal codes, marine architecture, the writing of the American Constitution and the theology of the early Church Fathers. No matter whom he met and no matter where he was, Israel Brown rushed to tell his listener whatever his listener seemed to care about. He was able to correct and contradict whatever his listener said to him without offending him. He said hurriedly: "You will pardon me if I point out—," and then told his listener facts about the subject which the listener for the most part did not know existed, or were known to anyone.

Thus on this day when Israel Brown stopped at Edmund Kish's house to get the compendium he had lent Edmund, one of his most devoted students, he was introduced to Edmund's mother and he spoke to her immediately with customary pace and passion, telling her all about her generation, the generation which had come to America from Eastern Europe between 1890 and 1914. He spoke of the causes of the departure of this generation from the old world, the problems and tricks of the ocean liner agencies, the prospects of the immigrants, the images of the new world which had inhabited their minds, the shortage of labor which had drawn them, and the effect of their coming upon social and economic tensions in America.

Mrs. Kish listened to Israel Brown amazed as everyone was who heard him for the first time, amazed and overwhelmed by his eloquence, his learning, and his ravenous desire to tell all that he knew. Edmund as he listened was amused by the dumbfounded look upon his mother's face. She was an intelligent woman who had been a radical in her youth and she was not wholly bound in mind by her middle-class existence.

As soon as Israel Brown departed, Mrs. Kish breathed deeply as if in relief.

"You have just seen a genius," said Edmund to his mother.

"How much money does he make?" asked Mrs. Kish.

This was the story with which Edmund, excited, came to the Saturday evening at the Bell apartment.

He was not disappointed. The circle responded with enormous joy, and immediately Rudyard started the analysis and augmentation of any news which was a loved practice.

"Your mother's question," said Rudyard, in a tone in which gaiety and a pedagogic attitude were present, "is not only brilliant in itself, but it suggests an inexhaustible number of new versions. Your mother has virtually invented a new genre for the epigram. Thus, whenever anyone is praised and whenever anything favorable is said about anyone, let us reply: *Never mind that: how much money does he make?*"

"Yes," said Ferdinand, "there are all kinds of versions. We can say: 'I am not in the least interested in that. Just tell me one thing: *What's his salary?*' Or if we want to make him look unimportant: 'What you have just told me leaves me absolutely cold. What I want to know is: *What are his wages?*' And then again '*Precisely how much cash has he in the bank?*'"

"'*How much is his yearly compensation?*'" shouted Laura from the kitchen, preparing the midnight supper, but never failing to listen to all that was said.

"It is one of the most heart-breaking sentences of our time,"

Jacob Cohen declared in a low voice, "and if it brings one to tears, the tears are obviously for Edmund's mother and not for Israel Brown."

"I don't notice anyone refusing any money," said Laura, bringing coffee, tea, and cocoa to the table, "except for Jacob." Jacob had refused to accept an allowance from his father and he had refused a job in the family business in which his older brothers prospered exceedingly. He had explained that he was going to be what he wanted to be or he was going to be nothing.

"It is easy enough to do nothing," said Jacob, seating himself at the dinner table. He did not like to have anyone's attention fixed upon what, in his being, was most intimate and most important.

"The difficult virtue," said Rudyard, "is to disregard the possibility of making money, to live such a life that making money will have no influence upon one's mind, heart and imagination." As he spoke, he was hardly aware that he was thinking chiefly of himself.

"You can't write plays for money, you just don't know how," said Laura, "so you don't have any temptation to resist: that's no virtue." Laura's love and admiration of her brother did not prevent her from attempting to overthrow the attitudes in which Rudyard took the most pride. This was the way in which she tried to defend herself from the intensity of her love and the profundity of her acceptance of him.

Rudyard did not answer her. His mind had shifted to his own work, and he took from the shelf the manuscript book in which his last play was written, seated himself upon the studio couch, and studied his own work, a look of smiling seriousness upon his face.

The other boys were seated at the dinner table, slowly eating the midnight supper and rejoicing in Mrs. Kish's question. Laura pampered each of them in his stubborn idiosyncrasy of taste. Edmund liked his coffee light, Rudyard liked his very strong, Ferdinand would only drink Chinese tea, Edmund insisted on toast, although most of them liked pumpernickel bread best of all. Laura provided what each of them liked best, which did not prevent her from being ironic about their preferences and assuming the

17

appearance of one who begrudges and denies all generous indulgence and attention.

"How beautiful," said Rudyard loudly without raising his gaze from his manuscript book, "and yet no one likes this play, not even my intimate friends. But in a generation or in fifty years, it will be cheered as the best dramatic work of the century!"

Marcus Gross strode in, his entrances being at once loud and founded on the assumption that he had been present all evening.

"The theatre in which your plays are performed," he said, "ought to be named, *Posterity*."

"Very good," said Rudyard, "you may think that you are attacking me, but I regard that as one of the finest things ever said about an author!"

It was felt that this was a perfect reply.

Between Rudyard and Marcus an antagonism had long existed, excited for the most part by Rudyard's open contempt for Marcus, who admired Rudyard very much, but was forced to conceal his admiration.

"You are absolutely safe," said Marcus, responding to the laughter, "you are taking no risk whatever. We will all be dead before anyone knows if you are right or wrong."

"I know now," said Rudyard serenely, never admitting the small doubts which on occasion overtook him and suppressing his anguish at not being recognized as a great playwright.

"The fact is," said Jacob half-aloud, thinking of the life which they lived, "we do not have very much of a choice. It is a question of your money or your life, the Mexican bandit's question. We have a choice between doing what we don't want to do or doing nothing."

"Last week," said Lloyd Tyler, the boy of the circle, and the most silent one, "my father bought his yearly ticket in the Irish Sweepstakes, and it all began again, just the same as every other year."

He told them of the new dialogue between his parents, discussing the Irish Sweepstakes.

"What would you do, if you won one hundred and fifty thousand dollars?" Mrs. Tyler had asked her husband. The cruelest irony was in her voice, for she resented her husband very much because her life had not been what she had expected it to be. What she was saying was that he would not know what to do with a great deal of money.

"What would you do with it?" she said again for emphasis, disturbing Mr. Tyler's careful examination of the evening newspaper.

"I would sleep," said Mr. Tyler flatly and strongly, for he recognized this as a criticism of his powers and his way of life.

"But you sleep now," said Mrs. Tyler, unwilling to be put off, "I never saw anyone sleep as much as that man," she said to Lloyd who was trying to keep out of an interchange in which he recognized twenty-five years of feeling.

"It would be a different sleep," said Mr. Tyler. "If I had one hundred and fifty thousand dollars, it would not be the same kind of sleep."

"No one sleeps better than you do," said Mrs. Tyler, but weakly, knowing that she had been worsted.

"What a triumph!" cried Edmund joyously. "Not even Swift would have made a better answer."

"Yes," said Rudyard, "we ought to strike a medal for your father, Lloyd. He has justified all of us."

"I wonder what he would do with one hundred and fifty thousand dollars," said Marcus.

"He would sleep the sleep of the just and the self-fulfilled," Jacob answered. "What does he have to show for his thirty years of work? He has nothing."

"He has himself," said Rudyard, who often chose to regard all things in an ideal light.

"He does not like himself," said Lloyd, "he does not care very much for himself."

"It is his own fault if he does not care very much for himself," answered Rudyard.

"Is it his own fault?" asked Lloyd sadly, for he liked his father very much, "He thinks that he would see my sister and her husband and his grandchildren more often, if he had money, and if he had given my sister a dowry. He thinks that his son-in-law would think more of him and ask him to dinner more often."

"In my opinion," said Rudyard, using the phrase which was always the introduction of a dogma, "money has nothing whatever to do with the matter. Pardon me for being intimate, but I would say that the real cause of all the difficulty is that your father did not know how to make love, or your mother has never wanted to have your father make love to her. This is the true meaning of the fact that she is dissatisfied with him. Love is always the beginning of everything, that's obvious. And perhaps we may go so far as to say, that *if* there had been satisfied love between your parents, your father would have prospered and made as much money as your mother wanted him to make."

"That's just an *idea,* that's nothing but an *idea*. Money is the root of all good!" shouted Laura from the kitchen, helping herself to one more pony of gin as the visitors arose to depart.

"Everything is mixed in everything else," said Jacob to himself, thinking of how much Laura desired to be loved.

THREE: "NO ONE FOOLS ANYONE MUCH, EXCEPT HIMSELF"

The human beings of the circle and the circle as such existed for Jacob Cohen in a way private to him. The other boys of the circle often discussed each other, but seldom thought about each other when they were alone. They came together in order not to be alone, to escape from deviceless solitude. But Jacob enjoyed the solitude of the morning and the early afternoon, during which he strolled through many neighborhoods, inspected the life of the city, and thought about his friends of the circle. They were objects of his consciousness during his solitude and in this way they existed in his mind like great pictures in a famous gallery, pictures which, however, were studied not merely for curiosity and pleasure, but as if they contained some secret of all pictures and all human beings. Jacob, thinking about his friends and walking many city blocks, was borne forward by the feeling that through them he might know his own fate, because of their likeness, difference, and variety.

This day of September as Jacob set forth was a day of profound feeling because the children went to school again for the first time. Jacob and his friends had prospered in school, and most of all at the university, in a way they never had since then. Now five years had passed and were used. All of them were in some way disappointed as they had not been in school, where each had been able to do what he truly wanted to do. The school had been for them a kind of society very different from the adult society for which it was supposed to prepare them.

Jacob had arrived at Central Park. To the west was a solid front of expensive apartment houses, in front of him was a grove of trees and an artificial lake, next to which were empty tennis courts. Jacob decided to sit down on a park bench and let the emotion inspired by the first morning of school in September take his mind where it would.

He soon found himself thinking, as often before, of the character and fate of his friends of the circle.

Francis French, who now belonged to the circle less and less, had been at first the most fortunate one and the one who impressed the official middle class most of all. He was an extremely handsome young man who spoke English with a perfect Oxonian accent which he had acquired without departing from the state of New York. His presence, his manners, and his accent had secured for him immediately after graduation an appointment as a teacher of English literature in the best of the city universities. He was clearly marked out as a young man with a brilliant academic future.

At the end of the first term, however, the head of the department, who had chosen Francis from among many, found it necessary to summon him and ask him about an anonymous note which accused Francis of immoral relationships with some of his students. In this interview Francis had need only of the good manners and tact which he had cultivated for long and with easy success. But in the shock of the confrontation, he did not reply that the note was untrue and that his friendships with his students had been misinterpreted. Instead of making this nominal denial, which was all that was required, he replied with pride and hauteur. He declared that his sexual habits were his own concern and he said that he refused to recognize the right of anyone to question him about his private life. The head of the department liked Francis very much and he did not care very much what Francis' habits were, for he was an excellent teacher. But he felt that the refusal to make the conventional denial suggested the likelihood of future difficulty, and being concerned about his own position, he felt he had no choice but to dismiss Francis. He tried again to suggest to Francis that a nominal denial would be sufficient, but Francis would not be moved. His stand gave him the pleasure of being self-righteous. For long he had felt strongly that homosexuality was the real right thing, the noble and aristocratic thing, a view he supported by citing the great authors and artists who had been as he was.

To Jacob, looking back, Francis seemed to have been involved in a failure of the imagination. He had been unable to imagine the feelings of the head of the department which were complex and yet also convenient enough. This failure was important because in so many ways Francis had devoted his will to making himself impressive to other human beings.

Now Jacob bore in mind how Rudyard had applauded Francis' stand, although it had cost Francis the status in life he desired so much. Rudyard had declared that no other answer was possible without an absolute loss of self-respect. Yet had Rudyard been confronted with the same choice, Jacob was sure that he would not have hesitated in making the answer which was convenient and profitable. Whether Rudyard knew this to be true of himself or not, he too was involved in the same loss of imagination, for he did not recognize how much Francis had hurt himself. "No one fools anyone much, except himself," said Jacob to himself. "How do I fool myself?"

Francis had soon become a teacher in the public school system, and devoted himself with energy and concentration to his sexual life. For five days each week he taught from nine until three and then from four until midnight his obsession with sexual pleasure took hold of him and in time preoccupied him so much that all the other things which had interested him were forgotten. The drudgery of teaching in a high school was the basis of the intense system with which he dealt with actuality, performing his duties as a teacher with thoroughness because this made him feel secure and full of control when he let himself go after school.

He let himself go more and more. He came less frequently to the Saturday evenings of the circle, and when he did come, he conferred most often with Rudyard, discussing his adventures and conquests. He told Marcus Gross, who was boisterous and ebullient about his own orthodox desires, that no one knew what sexual pleasure was until he became homosexual. He said also that everyone was really homosexual. Only fear, ignorance, foolishness, and shame kept all human beings from being aware of true passion and satisfaction.

Yet Jacob wondered if Francis did not permit himself passages of intellectual doubt. His sexual preoccupation had become not only a fixed idea which annihilated all other ideas, as one addicted to opium withdraws more and more from all other things; it had become a kind of sunlight: Francis had at first regarded all things in that light and he had come at last to see only the sunlight and nothing else.

"Perhaps one ought not to praise love too much," Jacob said to himself, "what will become of Francis in ten years or when he is middle-aged? He will have no wife, no house and no child. He has made an absolute surrender to one thing and in the end he may have nothing."

Jacob arose from the park bench and began to walk through the park, paying attention only to the movements of his mind.

"On the other hand," he said to himself, "I can't say for certain that anyone else has or will have more than Francis who at least has what he wants most of all."

He thought of Marcus Gross, who like Francis taught in a public high school, but was otherwise unlike him. Marcus was the scapegoat and butt of the circle, a part which he often seemed to enjoy. He was extremely serious about everything, even the prepared jokes by means of which he attempted to show his sense of humor, and he was protected by an impenetrable insensitivity from the epithets and the insults directed at him. In fact, he rejoiced in the insulting remarks made about him and to him, for he felt that such attention showed him as an interesting and rich character. Thus when the story of his visit to a house of prostitution was discussed in his presence, after he had been betrayed by the boy who had taken him, when the very choreography of his visit, his awkwardness, his disrobing, his gestures of affection were enacted before him, he was delighted. And he laughed as at another human being when the comedians came to the moment when the girl was said to have said to Marcus: "You like it buck naked, big boy?" When this quotation was reached, Marcus laughed more loudly than anyone else.

Attacked with a cruelty untouched by pity or compunction, Marcus often provided unbearable provocation. Often in the unpleasant, sodden New York summer, he entered the Bell household and went straight to the bathroom without greeting or explanation, bathed and returned in his bare feet to the living room, unable to understand why his behavior was regarded as boorish and self-absorbed. He was disturbed and hurt only when he was not kept acquainted with all that had occurred in the life of the circle, or when Rudyard attacked him, and even then he was often able to defend himself by answering Rudyard in ways which he regarded as hilarious. When Rudyard looked merely perplexed, Marcus only repeated what he had said, adding: "The trouble with you is that you have no sense of humor!" To the astonishment of all, he was offended at unexpected times, for no principle or consistent region of sensitivity could be discerned in his hurt feelings. Yet when Marcus stalked from the house at a remark which was no different from many at which he had smiled complacently, and when he did not return for weeks, an effort was made to discover what had offended him. When he returned, he behaved as if he had not been absent, he took part in the conversation as if he had been present all the while, and when Rudyard, annoyed, said to him: "How do you know?" moved by Marcus' authoritative participation in the discussion, Marcus replied briefly: "I heard," for he refused no matter what effort was made, to discuss his absences.

Unlike as were Francis and Marcus (they were extremes, the one courtly, the other uncouth) they were also very different from Edmund Kish and Ferdinand Harrap.

"And what about myself?" Jacob asked himself. "And Rudyard and Laura?"

Edmund had for four years been a student of philosophy, waiting to be asked to be a teacher. There were not many jobs to be had, but when there was one, some other student, not Edmund, was given the job. Yet Edmund was clearly superior to the others. The professors, the higher powers who possessed all the favors, at first had been enchanted with Edmund. He was energetic, original and impressive. He was learned and in love with his subject. But he loved to argue and argument excited him always until he betrayed his assumption that the other human being was a fool.

"Yet he does not think that everyone else is a fool," thought Jacob. "Not at all: he only thinks that he is smarter. Then why does he act like that? Perhaps he is trying to prove to himself that he is smart, perhaps he is never sure of that."

Triumphant in his arguments with other students, Edmund sought to be full of deference when he spoke with his teachers, especially after he had been passed by for years. But as soon as a qualification or reservation was suggested, Edmund forgot the politeness he had promised himself. He rehearsed to his teachers the ABC's of the subject and raised objections, which clearly implied that the teacher knew nothing whatever.

His teachers in the end feared and disliked him, and although they were unable to condemn him directly, they spoke of him in letters of recommendation as "a gifted but difficult person." This satisfied them that they were just and was sufficient to keep him from getting any job he wanted.

"What is it?" Jacob asked himself. "Is it something in the darkness of the family life from which we have all emerged which compels Edmund to assert himself like that? Is it his two brothers, his father's tyranny, or his mother's unequal affections? That's just one more thing we don't know."

Jacob paused to have a modest lunch. And the choice of food made him think of Ferdinand Harrap.

As Rudyard sought to be a dramatist, Ferdinand had tried to write stories. He did not lack the gift of experience, as did Rudyard, who found in all circumstances only a backdrop before which to manifest what he already possessed, his charm, his wit, and his delight in himself. Ferdinand was reserved. He held himself back and he was very much interested in whatever was before him. His stories, however, belonged to a small province, the province of his own life with his mother and his mother's family. The essential motive of his stories was the disdain and superiority he felt about these human beings of the older generation, and his stories always concerned the contemptuous exchanges of the characters, the witty quarrels which revealed the cruelty and the ignorance of their relationship to each other.

"You have to love human beings," thought Jacob, "if you want to write stories about them. Or at least you have to want to love them. Or at least you have to imagine the possibility that you might be able to love them. Maybe that's not true. But it is true that Ferdinand detests everyone but his friends of the circle."

None of Ferdinand's stories were published. Unlike Rudyard,

he did not persevere, lacking Rudyard's joy in the process of composition and Rudyard's belief in himself. For a time he did nothing at all, and then, in helping one of his uncles, Ferdinand perceived the need of an agency which would arrange matters between manufacturers and retail stores. This perception of the usefulness of such an agency required an acute but peculiar intelligence, an intelligence like a squint. Ferdinand was not concerned about becoming rich, as business men were, and thus in helping his uncle, his indifference and his sense of superiority soon made obvious to him what no one else saw. Soon, with a small office and a girl to handle the mail, Ferdinand was making five thousand dollars a year, and had only to go to the office briefly each day to see that the girl was handling matters properly.

As soon as he prospered, Ferdinand's sense of what was good taste became active. His manners became more stiff and more pointed, and he dressed like a dandy, but strangely, as if he were a dandy of the past. And when he had money to spend, his feeling that he must have the best of everything, or nothing, had to be satisfied. He had to have the best orchestra seats at the theatre and he had to have the best dinner at the best restaurants.

"An only child," said Jacob to himself, "and the child of a mother divorced from her husband since he was four years of age."

The best of anything was truly a necessity to Ferdinand and he suffered very much when he was deprived of it. He insisted also that his friends of the circle join with him, accepting his criterion. This was difficult because they had little money or no money at all. Often Ferdinand paid for them, and he always paid for Rudyard, whom he admired very much. But when he did not care to pay for one of the boys, at dinner or at the theatre, and when they suggested that they come at less expense, Ferdinand strictly forbade their coming. He refused to go or he went by himself to the best restaurant and sat in the best seat at the Broadway play. When he was asked by a stranger the reason for his concentration upon dining well, Ferdinand replied in the curt and stern tone he so often used that dinner was extremely important: if one dined well, one felt good; otherwise, one did not.

A severe, private, hardly understood code ruled Ferdinand in all things. He regarded certain acts as good behavior and everything else, every difference, change, or departure as infamous and to be denounced. It was often necessary to prevent Ferdinand from making remarks of virtually insane cruelty to newcomers and strangers who visited the circle, for if they behaved in a way of which he disapproved or in a way indifferent to what he regarded as proper, he was likely to tell them that they were unpardonable fools. Visitors and strangers did not know what it was impossible for them to know, the strict and personal standard by which Ferdinand judged all acts and all remarks. Fortunately Ferdinand's constraint and stiffness made him speak in a very low voice, so that often enough the most extraordinary insult was left unheard. It was then necessary for Rudyard or Jacob to translate the sentence of final condemnation into a mild euphemism. When Ferdinand said to a stranger: "You must be out of your mind!" Rudyard explained that Ferdinand disagreed with what the stranger had just said, while Ferdinand turned aside, indifferent to the reduction of his insult and feeling that he had made his stand.

Jacob had arrived at Riverside Drive. He looked down on the Hudson River and, feeling the overwhelming presence of the great city, he thought of his friends as citizens of the city and of the city itself in which they lived and were lost.

"In New York," he said to himself, often concluding his slow tours with such monologues, "there are nineteen thousand horses, three hundred thousand dogs, five hundred thousand cats, one million trees and one million sparrows: more than enough!

"On the other hand, there are at least six million human beings and during holidays there are more than that number. But, in a way, these numbers hardly exist because they cannot be perceived (we all have four or five friends, more or less). No human being can take in such an aggregation: all that we know is that there is always more and more. This is the moreness of which we are aware, no matter what we look upon. This moreness is the true being of the great city, so that, in a way, this city hardly exists. It certainly does not exist as does our family, our friends, and our neighborhood."

Jacob felt that he had come to a conclusion which showed the shadow in which his friends and he lived. They did not inhabit a true community and there was an estrangement between each human being and his family, or between his family and his friends, or between his family and his school. Worst of all was the estrangement in the fact that the city as such had no true need of any of them, a fact which became more and more clear during the great depression.

"Yet," thought Jacob, seeking to see the whole truth, "there is the other side, which always exists. They say of New York that it is like an apartment hotel. And they say: 'It's fine for a visit, but I would not want to live here.' They are wrong. It's fine to live here, but exhausting on a visit.

"Once New York was the small handsome self-contained city of the merchant prince and the Dutch patroon's great grandsons. And once it was the brownstone city ruled by the victors of the Civil War. Then the millions drawn or driven from Europe transformed the city, making the brownstone mansions defeated rooming houses. Now, in the years of the great depression, it is for each one what he wants it to be, *if he has the money*. If he has the money! Coal from Pennsylvania, oranges from California, tea from China, films from Hollywood, musicians and doctors of every school! Every kind of motion, bus and car, train and plane, concerto and ballet! And if the luxuries of the sun and the sea are absent, if life in this city seems brittle as glass, every kind of vehicle here performs every kind of motion to take the citizen away from the city, if he has the money! The city in its very nature contains all of the means of departure as well as return. Thus the city gives to the citizen a freedom from itself, and thus one might say that this is the capital of departure. But none of my friends will go away: they are bound to each other. They have too great a need of each other, and all are a part of the being of each."

Jacob Cohen was through for the day. He had said to himself all that he wanted to say. Thus he had conversed with himself during the years that he had dedicated himself to being the kind of a citizen that he thought he ought to be. And if he seldom uttered these thoughts to anyone, nevertheless their feeling was contained and vivid in all that other human being saw of him. This was the reason that he seemed to some, strange; to some, preoccupied; to some, possessed by secrecy and silence.

FOUR: "TEARS FOR THE HUMAN BEINGS WHO HAVE
NOTHING TO SAY TO EACH OTHER"

Jacob Cohen for long had been the conscience and the noble critic of the circle. No one knew precisely how this had come about. In school, as editor of the university daily, the students too had felt an incomparable devotion and loyalty to him. It was said that they would do anything for him. And in his family, when he refused to become part of the family business, his father and his brothers were not distressed. They did not think that he was wasting his time when, except for his tours of the neighborhood and the city, he did nothing at all, although in all other families there was concern and anger when the young man appeared to be making no effort to earn a living and to get ahead. It was felt that what Jacob did was right, no matter what he did. No one was surprised when Jacob refused to be a reporter on a Hearst newspaper because he felt that the Hearst newspapers were in sympathy with Fascism. No one was surprised although to be a reporter was Jacob's dear vocation because of which he refused to be anything else.

So too in the circle itself, Jacob's moral preeminence was absolute, although no one in the least understood it. Jacob's judgment, approval or disapproval were accepted as just. It was felt spontaneously that his judgment flowed from principles independent of personal desire or distortion. It is true that all knew a hardly conscious desire that such a person as Jacob should exist, but this did not explain their spontaneous recognition of him as that person.

No one but Jacob knew how much hopelessness and despair he felt at times, emotions bottomless and overpowering which made him lose all interest or power to be interested in anything outside of himself. Jacob did not understand these emotions which persisted for months and made him withdraw from others. Yet these emotions made possible Jacob's noble indifference, an important part of his moral authority.

It was natural that Rudyard and Laura should turn in the end to Jacob for his opinion about an argument which they had disputed for weeks. This argument concerned Rudyard's habit of reading the newspaper at the dinner table when no one was present but Laura.

"You ought to talk to me," said Laura, and there were periods when Rudyard enjoyed conversation with Laura. But often he wanted to read and he did not want to converse when he ate the dinner Laura had prepared when she returned from work. To Laura this seemed an unnecessary affront precisely because she had returned to make his dinner.

"First of all," said Rudyard, to defend his reading, "when I read at dinner it is a manifestation of the truly human. You know very well that if I were an animal, I would take my food somewhere and eat it alone. I would eat it very fast and I would be afraid that some other animal might take it away from me. But since I am a human being and since I have a head," he touched his head as he said this, "eating does not satisfy the whole of my being and it is necessary for me to read."

"How about conversation?" said Laura, disgruntled and knowing that she had no hope of persuading Rudyard since she never persuaded him of anything. "I suppose conversation is not a purely human activity?"

"It is, it is!" Rudyard replied. "But reading is superior to it, in general, as authors are superior to other human beings. And as for me, my being is such that to satisfy the rational part of it, I must regard the great works of thought and literature."

"Half the time you just read the newspaper," said Laura.

"Yes," said Rudyard serenely, "but not as others do, for I read the newspaper to rejoin the popular life of this city."

These grandiose answers, which Rudyard delivered in a tone at once superior and coy, angered Laura, but at the same time impressed her and made her remember that she had long since decided that Rudyard was a genius.

Arriving at the Bell household just after dinner, Jacob was asked his opinion.

"If a brother and sister don't have a great deal to say to each other," answered Jacob, "who does? We might as well be deaf and dumb! As a matter of fact, I'd say that we might as well be dead. Conversation is civilization."

Rudyard bowed to Jacob's judgment in general, making an exception of himself in that his sister was not as all sisters should be. But he did not say this for he was much interested in the idea of the truly human at the moment. As the other boys arrived at the apartment, he took them aside and explained it to them, and they too took pleasure in it, as well as being flattered by the appearance of intimacy which Rudyard conferred upon each of them when he took each one aside.

This discussion, which Rudyard conducted in a comic manner since he did not like to be serious about any ideas, much as ideas were dear to him, was halted when Edmund Kish entered with exciting news about the fate of the marriage of B. L. Rosen and Priscilla Gould.

"They have been seen for two weeks at dinner in the same restaurant," said Edmund breathlessly.

This far-off marriage had first astonished and then fascinated the circle. Some of the boys had been acquainted with B. L. Rosen at school, and they had been contemptuous of the way in which he had continued to be a leader of student political movements long after graduation.

"He wants to be an *official* youth," Edmund had remarked.

"He wants to be a *permanent* youth," Rudyard had added.

B. L., as all who knew him called him, feeling the nascent executive in him, had become in the end the head of all the radical student movements in all the city universities. He spoke for youth and for students. No one, however, knew of Priscilla Gould until her father, a successful Broadway playwright, wrote an article in one of the national weeklies in which he said that his daughter had been taught to believe in Communism, atheism and free love by her teachers at the university. It was B. L.'s task to see Priscilla and to persuade her to defend the university and her teachers. B. L. had succeeded very well. Priscilla had been bewildered and enchanted by the attention she suddenly received. The truth was that she had been a shy and withdrawn student and she had joined the radical student society as a way of being part of the school life, for she was afraid that she would never be anything but a wallflower. B. L. persuaded Priscilla to write an answer to her father in which she said: "My father is dishonest," a kind of choral sentence uttered repetitively throughout the detailed exposition of her father's other shortcomings as a father, such as that he had never given her the attention a child required.

This answer was an overwhelming success and B. L. was credited with a stroke of political genius. But as B. L. had helped Priscilla to write her answer, he had made love to her, almost as if from habit, for he had always absentmindedly courted some girl during his career as a student leader. When Priscilla shyly proposed to him that they get married, B. L. was much too amazed to ask for time to think about such a marriage. His prudence and circumspection had for long been concentrated on matters which were impersonal if not international. His manners and his essential kindness were such that he felt that he had to answer Priscilla immediately. When he saw the fearful and pathetic look upon Priscilla's face, he had assented immediately, telling himself that she might be as good as anyone else and perhaps better. Moreover, if he were married he might have more time for the concerns which truly interested him.

The news of the marriage was first received by the circle as a thunderbolt, but soon it awakened as much passionate interpretation as any other episode of these years.

It was suggested that some pathological feeling had compelled B. L. to marry Priscilla, either sexual feeling for his own sex, or a desire to possess an utterly passive wife. Francis French suggested that Priscilla might resemble B. L.'s mother when he was an infant at the breast. Rudyard thought it far more likely that Priscilla was seeking to escape from an incestuous desire for her father, since B. L. was truly as far away from her father as she could get. Rudyard also dismissed as banal, trite, obvious and hence untrue the view that B. L. might have married Priscilla because he wished to ascend in the social scale. Edmund, on the other hand, declared that whatever motives might have inspired the newly-wedded couple, the marriage was in actual fact an attack on the ruling class. It was somewhat far-fetched to suppose that Priscilla belonged to the ruling class, but the match had an unequivocal symbolic meaning: it was the beginning of the disappearance of the Anglo-Saxon. Ferdinand regarded the union as a striking example of the degradation which overtook all who were interested in social problems and in politics. The underlying reason for all these speculations was that marriage for all of the circle was far-off, and when Laura said: "Maybe she just likes him and he just likes her," she was regarded as superficial.

Edmund's exciting news about the distant marriage was that B. L. and Priscilla had been seen at dinner for two weeks in the same Italian restaurant, and on each night the husband and the wife had been reading two copies of the same newspaper, saying nothing to each other from start to finish.

"It's too good to be true," said Edmund joyously, "after all, they have only been married for six months. But probably they no longer can imagine a period when they were not married."

"Here we see," said Rudyard, declamatory, "in this reading of the same newspaper, a noble effort on the part of a wife to share her husband's intellectual interests!"

"This behavior," said Ferdinand, "is of a matchless vulgarity!"

"If we had any sense," said Jacob, "we would burst into tears for all the husbands and wives who have nothing to say to each other."

"How many months," said the delighted Edmund, "have passed since last they exchanged the time of the day?"

"How about you," said Laura to Rudyard, "don't you read the newspaper at the dinner table?"

"It's not the same thing," said Rudyard, "I did not marry you."

The insensitivity of this remark would not have passed unnoticed, had not Francis French entered on one of his rare visits. He too had a story in which he was very much interested. He had encountered during the previous week-end a youthful teacher and critic, Mortimer London, who was reputed to be brilliant.

"I have long believed," said Francis, "that everyone himself tells the worst stories about himself. London told me (keep in mind that fact that London himself tells this story about himself) that when he was in England last year, he had paid a visit to T. S. Eliot who had given him a letter of introduction to James Joyce, since he was going to Paris also. Now London says that he was confronted with a cruel choice, whether to use the letter and converse with the author of *Ulysses* or to keep the letter in which a great author commends him to a great author. He decided to keep the letter!"

"What a dumb-bell," said Edmund, the veteran scholar, "he should have known that the choice might be forestalled. He might have made a photostat copy!"

"Never mind that," said Rudyard, who did not like to be concerned with practical considerations, "what's really interesting is the extent to which this Mortimer London is insane. For obviously he tells this story because of great pride in himself. He *does not know* that there is nothing worse that he can say about himself: he would rather possess the letter than converse with the great author."

"Never mind," said Laura to Rudyard, "I never saw you hiding your light in a dark closet."

Rudyard did not reply, fascinated by this example of egotism as only an egotist can be.

"I wonder," said Jacob, "what are the worst stories each of us tells against himself."

"Once in a while," said Laura, "just for a change, we ought to try saying something good about anyone. Anyone can run down anyone else, it is as easy as sliding off a chute. What's hard is to love other human beings and to speak well of them."

"You are being sententious," said Rudyard, "it is obviously true that human beings are more evil than good, and thus it would be false to speak well of other human beings very much, although I am willing to try anything once," concluding as often with an irony which, directed against himself, defended him against what anyone else might say.

"The fact is" said Jacob, as the visitor arose to depart, "I can't think of what the worst story I tell against myself is, and that is nothing, if not alarming. We are all living in a world of our own."

"Yes," said Rudyard, chortling because the idea delighted him, "in a certain sense, we are all cracked!"

FIVE: "IT IS GOOD TO BE THE WAY THAT WE ARE"

During the day, after he had labored at his new play in the morning in the glow of after-breakfast, Rudyard participated in a life apart from the circle, a life in which a different part of his being showed itself. This life was concerned with the children and the adolescents of the neighborhood, and it was an intrusion, which annoyed Rudyard, if he encountered an adult. If the adult, the parent of one of his friends, met Rudyard, he said with the politeness and interest of the middle class:

"What are you doing now?" meaning, how are you trying to make a living? How are you trying to get ahead?

"I am helping my father," Rudyard always answered, having nurtured this answer until it was automatic.

"What is your father doing?" the helpless adult often inquired, never having heard of Rudyard's father because he had been dead for twenty years.

"My father is doing nothing!" was Rudyard's stock answer, followed by harsh and triumphant laughter that the questioner had walked into the trap, although in all truth Rudyard was ashamed that he had nothing impressive to announce.

Among the children and the adolescents of the neighborhood Rudyard was at his best, however. In the schoolyard near the apartment house, between bouts of handball, Rudyard conversed in the fall and in the spring with those who were to him the pure in heart and the wise just as he seemed to himself to be to them one of the wise and the pure in heart.

As he sat upon the asphalt court, after a game of doubles, he discussed with his friends Chester and Jeremiah, the star of the school, a boy named Alexander, twelve years of age, who was best in handball, basketball, high jumping, and the hundred yard dash. It was felt by all that Alexander had a great future.

"Suppose," said Rudyard to his friends, "Alexander was at least a hundred times better than he is. Then he would win all the time in all the games. But if he was as good as that, if he won all the time, if every contest was a victory, if he was sure of winning every game, then he would not enjoy the game very much."

Chester suggested that Alexander might then join the New York Yankees and earn a fabulous salary, more than the President's. Jeremiah added that his picture might appear in all the newspapers and he might marry a moving picture actress.

"Yes," said Rudyard patiently, brushing aside these ideas of the glory of this world, "suppose he hit a homer every time he came to bat? Suppose he was sure of hitting a homer? Don't you think he would get bored with playing baseball?"

"Yes," answered Chester and Jeremiah, "but he can't and he won't."

Rudyard was not in the least concerned or disturbed by any pointing to an actual fact.

"This is how we can see," he continued, "that it is good to be the way that we are. It would be no good, if we were unable to play any games at all. But just because we don't know if we are going to win or lose, just because our powers are limited and the other boys have powers not unlike our own, the game is exciting to play. So you can see that we are all what we ought to be."

"Just the same," said Chester, "I would like to hit a homer every time I came to bat."

"Me too," said Jeremiah, "for a year, anyway."

From such interviews Rudyard returned refreshed to his dramatic works. The volley of the conversation, as at a tennis match, was all that he took with him. For what he wanted and what satisfied him was the activity of his own mind. This need and satisfaction kept him from becoming truly interested in other human beings, although he sought them out all the time. He was like a travelling virtuoso who performs brilliant set-pieces and departs before coming to know his listeners.

An old teacher, meeting Rudyard after not seeing him for years, said to him that he showed no little courage in continuing to write works which gained for him neither fame nor money nor production.

"O, no," said Rudyard, "it requires no courage whatever. I write when I feel inspired. When I don't feel like writing, I don't. Thus I am not like other authors. It is not a career, it is like playing a game, and it is not courage, but inspiration, a very different emotion."

This reply was made in the style which Rudyard felt to be noble and necessary. But after this exchange, Rudyard asked himself if he had spoken truly. He knew very well a passion in himself to be applauded and to be famous, the same as other authors. Triumphant and delighted with himself, Rudyard decided that he did not want to be *regarded* as a playwright, he truly desired and enjoyed the activity of writing plays. This activity was enough to satisfy him.

The question and the answer inspired Rudyard to write a play in one act which resembled many of his previous dramas. This play contained only one character, a famous lyric poet, and only one scene, his study, in which he is surrounded by books, photographs, objects of art, and the black souvenir album in which are fixed essays and reviews of his poems which testify to his fame. The shades have been drawn down to bar the light of the living street.

The famous poet holds his head in his hands as he sits at his desk. In a monologue full of blank despair, he speaks of the fact that he has been unable to write a poem for two years.

"What difference does it make if I write a poem or I do not write a poem?" he says.

He holds in his hand a volume of his poems and he says:

"If I have done something worth doing, what good does it do me now? What good if I have drawn from the depths of my mind a good poem, if I do not enjoy now the sense of accomplishment and fruitfulness. One might as well tell a singer who has lost his voice that he was incomparable in all the great parts or equally tell a starving man that he was at a banquet two months before."

He reads aloud passages by critics in which he is awarded the highest praise:

"How can I be sure that they are right?" he says. "Many have been wrong. No poet is ever sure that he has written an important work. The famous in their lifetime are forgotten and nonentities long since in the grave appear as the true poets."

"And if this praise is true," he says, after he reads a new passage of praise from the album, "it does not lessen in the least the pain, the boredom and the emptiness which weigh me down now. If it is untrue, I have been deceived like a drunkard by passing imagination?"

He arises and stands before his long looking-glass:

"I might have acquired a great deal of money. I might have tasted the pleasures of the rich or the satisfactions of the normal. I might have enjoyed myself like a child at the seashore, near the breaking waves all through the glittering day. Instead I have grown warped, narrow and weak in this room at this table."

With his hand, he presses back his brow, looking closely at himself.

"I am too old to turn back and too young to forget my brilliant hopes. I am too intelligent to be uncritical of my fame, and the present is too important to me for me to be at peace because of the laurels I have gained in the past. Praise is worthless, but since praise is worthless, now that I cannot compose new works, I see for the first time, as if this were the first morning of my life, that there is only one reason to write poems: the only reason to write poems is for the sake of the activity of the whole being which one enjoys when one writes poems. This is the only justification."

He seats himself at his desk again, and he says:

"The silence surrounds me like four o'clock in the morning."

He draws forth a sheet of paper and takes a pencil from a cup.

"The silence of the white paper is my everlasting place. There is nothing else for me. Everything else is for the sake of this activity. When I cannot write a poem, when I have nothing in my mind but emptiness, then nothing else is good. When, on the other hand, a blazing excitement leaps in my mind, then I do not have happiness, for then all labor, all hope, all illusion are once more loaded on my back, as I sit here in my solitude surrounded by the silence which is like the night before the creation of the world."

And then, as the curtain falls, the famous poet begins to write upon his sheet of paper.

When this short play was read to the circle, it was received like many other recent plays by Rudyard. They had heard these ideas from Rudyard in conversation and were not much interested or impressed by the dramatic version.

Rudyard was distressed by this reception of his play, for he expected that the admiration of his friends would continue with equal intensity. For some time he had been annoyed with Edmund because Edmund, seeking to please him, would say:

"This new play does not seem to me as good as the first-rate plays you wrote last year."

"It is the best piece I have ever written," Rudyard had declared flatly, to vanquish his disappointment.

And when Rudyard had read aloud two plays and Edmund had said:

"I like the second more than the first," Rudyard also became angry, perceiving the criticism in this judgment.

"Now you can see," he said to Ferdinand, "the reason I have for reading two plays instead of just one. Then it can always be said that the first is better than the second. Perhaps I ought to read three plays each time. Then it will be possible to say, I like the first better than the second, but I like the third better than the first. Meanwhile I have made it possible to refuse to answer the question of whether any of them are any good! To what infinite limits I go for the sake of making my friends full of tact."

But when Edmund said of this new play that it was perhaps the best Rudyard had written, Rudyard was disturbed by this praise also, for it seemed to him to suggest a condemnation of his previous works. It was at this moment of annoyed disappointment, that Marcus Gross entered loudly.

"As for your plays," he said to Rudyard, "what have they to do with anything else? No wonder they are not produced. If you were any good, you would be successful."

"You are just a Philistine," Rudyard replied in fury. "Minute by minute, you become more stupid. You can't tell an idea from a hole in the ground!"

"Your feelings are hurt," said Marcus with solemn calm, as if he had made a discovery.

"You did not hear this play from the beginning ..." Lloyd Tyler began to say.

"It's not necessary," said Marcus, interrupting him, "they are all alike."

"In all the evenings I have been here," said Lloyd because he had been interrupted, "I have yet to succeed in uttering a complete sentence."

Ferdinand was delighted with this remark. "Do you know what Lloyd just said?" he asked loudly and then quoted Lloyd's remark which seemed to all but Lloyd to be a remark of extraordinary brilliance.

"I have not uttered a complete sentence since 1928," shouted Laura from the kitchen where she was drinking. This declaration caused an immediate uproar.

"Has Laura been drinking again?" Marcus inquired. And when she began to set the table, he regarded her carefully.

"Why don't you get married?" he said to her. "It might do you a lot of good."

Edmund told Marcus to shut up and stop being such a boob, and when the evening was over, Marcus, still astonished by being reproved, asked Edmund what he had done that was wrong and how he had offended Laura. When at last he understood, he said to Edmund pensively: "Do you know, I never thought of that. It never occurred to me."

SIX: "LOVE THE DARK VICTOR WHOM NO ONE
        OUTWITS"

Edmund thought he had made a most important discovery.

Bringing it with him to the Bell household on a Saturday evening, he was hardly able to wait for everyone's attention. And he would not speak until everyone was ready to listen to him.

"A revolution has occurred," said Edmund, "but it is subject to silence, since love is subject to shame. Love has been purified, as never before. Love has been made to be just love and and nothing else but love."

"How?" asked Rudyard.

"By the druggist," said Edmund, "by the sale of contraceptives."

Rudyard and Ferdinand exchanged looks which each understood very well. Was it possible, they said by looking at each other, that Edmund, the withdrawn scholar, had at long last suffered the loss of his innocence, an actual innocence, which existed with complete knowledge?

"The contraceptive," Edmund continued, "has purified love by freeing it from the accident of children. Now everyone with any sense can find out whom he truly loves. Children can be chosen beings, and not the result of impetuous lust or impatient appetite. Now love is love and nothing else but love!"

"Yes," said Rudyard, "a mere material device has utterly transformed the relationships between men and women: a mere material thing!"

"On the other hand," said Francis French, "it also makes possible adultery, and promiscuity, not that I have anything against promiscuity."

"I love my wife, but oh you id," said Ferdinand, who had studied Freud and Tin Pan Alley.

"Yes," said Jacob, "it makes everything too easy, which is always a good reason for suspicion and doubt. Love is more difficult than anything else. Love is the dark victor whom no one outwits."

"Exactly," said Edmund, "this device, so small and inexpensive, assures the victory of love. Love cannot be prevented, love cannot be set aside, no thoughts of utility or shame can intervene."

"There is nothing in it," said Laura, "you still have to find someone to love who loves you."

Jacob, somewhat apart, saw that on this subject opinion was absolute and speculation infinite precisely because they were so far from the actuality of love.

"How far is it to love?" he said to himself. "Love the dark victor whom no one escapes."

Edmund felt that this balloon of an idea, of which he had expected so much, had collapsed. Rudyard, who expected a visitor he had never seen before, was preoccupied, Jacob was withdrawn, Laura was sad, Ferdinand was attempting to produce a new witticism. Yet Edmund felt that he must try again.

"The Pope in Rome," said Edmund, "ought to be told of this. Yes, I will write him an epistle. Does he not know that God looked at Adam, in Eden, and remarked: 'It is not good for man to be alone.' By banning the use of the pure and purifying contraceptive, the Pope misunderstands the word of God which says that the reason for marriage is that man should have children. For it is not necessary to have marriage in order to have children, but if we are not to be alone, marriage alone is sufficient."

Rudyard and Ferdinand again exchanged glances of wonder concerned with Edmund's private life, what was new in it.

Marcus, ever late, entered loudly and demanded to know what was being discussed.

"It is not easy to say," said Jacob, "but on the surface, at least, it is an academic discussion of love."

"Speaking of love," said Marcus, who had need only of a slight pretext to brim over with his own thoughts, "I read a fine story today about Flaubert—"

"The promising French novelist, no doubt," asked Ferdinand.

"Flaubert," said Marcus, ignoring Ferdinand, "made a bet with two of his friends that he would be able to make love, smoke a cigar, and write a letter at the same time. They went to a house of prostitution and found the best girl, and Flaubert wrote the letter, smoked the cigar, and made love to the girl."

"What he really enjoyed," said Rudyard, "was the cigar."

"Speak for yourself," said Marcus, "what I want to know is, What did he say in the letter? And to whom was it written? And what was the tone? and what kind of cigar was it? and did he have time to finish it?"

"Speaking of letters," said Rudyard, who felt that this topic was exhausted, "I am being visited tonight, by a stranger who wrote me a letter."

The letter was from a true stranger, a being from a foreign

country, Archer Price, a young man of thirty who directed a little theatre in San Francisco. He had seen two of Rudyard's plays in manuscript, and now that he had come to New York, he wanted to meet Rudyard.

Rudyard was delighted by his letter, but nevertheless made fun of it.

"How can human beings of the Far West understand my play?" he asked. "Their idea of drama is the thrilling final match of a tennis tournament."

Yet Rudyard looked forward very much to the visit of the stranger.

Archer Price arrived at the Bell household with Pauline Taylor, a pretty young woman who lived in New York City, but had come to know Archer during a visit to California. When the strangers entered the house, the discussion of love stopped. In the midst of the introductions, as all were standing up, Archer, who was seldom at ease, said to Rudyard what he had decided to say before he arrived.

"I am very glad to meet you," said Archer, "because I admire your plays very much."

"What a remark!" said Rudyard, who appeared to be astounded by it and who looked to Edmund, as if to see if he too did not suppose this sentence to be outlandish.

"Says he admires two of my plays very much," said Rudyard to Edmund, and then pouted and placed one finger under his chin, as if he were about to curtsey.

"I really admire your plays very much," said Archer, bewildered and offended.

"I know you do," said Rudyard, as if this repetition were unnecessary, "otherwise you would not be here."

Archer seated himself on the studio couch and glanced at Pauline to see what her impression was. She glanced back in sympathy, for she was concerned not with Rudyard, but with Archer, and she knew how distressed he was by Rudyard's way of responding to his utterance of admiration. Neither of the newcomers knew that Rudyard's behavior had been inspired by his extreme pleasure, for he had so long desired the admiration of strangers that his self-possession teetered and he tried to regain his balance by regarding this admiration as peculiar. Both newcomers understood such emotions and attitudes very well, but they did not recognize Rudyard's version, because it was extreme, private, and directed not at the visitors, but at Edmund and Laura.

"What an obnoxious human being," thought Pauline Taylor.

Archer remained curious and open to persuasion. He regarded the apartment and saw that the furniture was worn and second-hand, making a picture of the second-hand and the used cultivated as an interesting background and decor. Against the wall stood an upright piano, next to which was a phonograph, and upon the wall was a bulletin board, tacked with newspaper clippings and letters. Archer had never seen just such a place before, but although it seemed strange to him, he recognized in it the unity which comes of the choices and habits of one human being.

Rudyard seated himself next to Archer to converse with him and Archer remarked upon his surprise that none of Rudyard's plays had ever been produced. Rudyard told him how each month for more than a year he had submitted a new play to a famous company and received each play back before a week had passed.

"I must be on the black list. They hardly have time to get the manuscript from the top manila envelope to the enclosed one, self-addressed and stamped!" said Rudyard, with a joyous look upon his face.

"Soon I will send them a letter of resignation," he said vivaciously, looking up at the ceiling coyly, "that will puzzle them!"

Archer laughed in relief, for here at last was a remark which he was able to understand as comical.

Edmund and Marcus were full of a story which they wished to communicate immediately. During the week they had heard a debate at Madison Square Garden about religion and Communism. The opponents had been Professor Suss, a famous teacher of Marxist doctrine, and Professor Adam, a theologian. The chief dispute had been about the authority of a socialist state to dictate or deny the teaching of religion to children. Professor Suss had affirmed the right of the socialist state to decide about religious education and Professor Adam had said that this was a denial of freedom of thought and belief, and thus fascist, declaring triumphantly that he was ninety-nine and one-half per cent Marxist, but reserved one-half of one per cent for God, for if one did not reserve anything for God, then the state became the deity.

Rudyard and Edmund were delighted with this story and interested especially in the one-half of one per cent reserved for God.

"How did he decide just how much God deserves?" asked Edmund.

"Perhaps he used a slide rule?" said Rudyard. "Or perhaps he made deductions for dependents, as when one computes the income tax?"

This analysis and commentary continued until Rudyard became aware that no attention whatever was being paid to the visitors who remained silent on the studio couch, looking uncomfortable and perplexed. He arose and went to his room to get the manuscript of a new play for his visitors to read, and when he returned, he placed himself next to Archer again and looked over his shoulder, the while he also cocked an ear to the conversation which remained concerned with the fraction reserved for God by Professor Adam.

"This passage is superb!" Rudyard said suddenly, after Archer had read for some time, and as he spoke, he grinned like a child who has just been given candy.

"Here, in this scene," said Rudyard, after a time, "the ignorance and irony is such that I am supreme among the dramatists who write in the English tongue." And as he spoke, he looked as if he licked an ice cream cone.

"This has not been equalled during the present century," Rudyard said again. Pauline was annoyed by these declarations, but to

Archer they seemed to be made with such certainty, such a lack of self-consciousness, such joy and aplomb, that they were delightful. It was clear that Rudyard did not expect his listener to make any comment. He enjoyed uttering such sentences for their own sake. Yet Archer thought also of how such remarks would sound to anyone who heard them apart from Rudyard's gestures, smiles, and look of self-assurance.

"You must take this play with you," said Rudyard, drawing forth a new manuscript, "it is to me the best play in the English language!" And then he giggled.

"To you," said Laura, "and to no one else." She had seen the new look of perplexity on the visitors' faces at this fabulous superlative.

Archer looked at his wrist-watch and arose.

"He lives by the clock," said Rudyard, as if he spoke of one who was absent. "Perhaps I will never see you again," he giggled.

"I don't like Rudyard Bell," said Pauline, as the two strangers departed from the house.

"He is certainly difficult," said Archer, "perhaps it is because he is gifted and has gained no recognition."

But when Archer Price returned to California, he decided that he would not attempt to visit Rudyard Bell when he next came to New York. He felt in the end distressed and perplexed by the visit. It seemed to him that the human beings of this circle existed in a private realm which did not permit the visiting stranger such as himself a true view of what they were and their life. He never saw them again.

SEVEN: "THIS KINGDOM OF HEAVEN IS WITHIN YOU;
BUT ALSO THE KINGDOM OF HELL"

"What we need is an Ark," said Rudyard to one and all, "not an island, not a colony, and not a city state, but an Ark."

Once again a play to which he had devoted much thought and

hope had been rejected. Silent and angry in the morning, he was full of the future by afternoon, and by night—this was a Saturday night and most of the circle had come to the apartment—he had bounced back to the attitudes he enjoyed amid the circle. But anger and disappointment remained in him like sores and were transformed and expressed by the idea of an Ark.

"It's an ancient and classic expression," said Rudyard, "it's about time that we thought of it. We will get a houseboat or a barge, announcing that this society is evil and we are going to depart."

Ferdinand, ever close to Rudyard, was delighted.

"We will say, *'We're through!'*" he added in a curt tone. "We will have an enormous poster in huge capitals and on it will be printed: *'We have had enough.' 'We do not like this age.'*" His voice became louder and stronger, "*'We find it beneath contempt!'*"

"This is a governing and master idea," said Edmund, equally pleased, "it is a conception so inclusive that by means of it we can make clear our judgment of the past and the future, of experience and possibility."

It was almost midnight. They sat about the midnight supper, drinking more and more coffee, and the idea of the Ark took hold of them like the excitement before a holiday.

"What will we take with us?" Rudyard continued, "I mean to say, what and who will we *permit* to enter the Ark?"

"Precisely," said Francis French, "discrimination is of the essence of this idea. There is no Ark unless we exercise the most pure, exact, and exacting discrimination."

"This is far from a joke," said Jacob, who had remained silent, although moved, "only an absolute fool would suppose that this is a laughing matter."

"Who will be elected," asked Francis, "to this elite?"

"And who will be rejected," Marcus added, "we don't want the riff-raff, the trash, the substitutes, the second-rate, the second best, and the second-hand."

"The best is none too good for us," said Rudyard, "I mean, for the Ark," he smiled with mock humility.

"It is necessary to criticize and evaluate all things," said Edmund.

"What else do you think you have been doing all these years?" said Laura, but she too was enthralled.

"Exactly, this is exactly what we have been doing," Rudyard replied, "and this is the fulfillment which was inevitable."

"And what makes you think," said Laura, "that you're the one to be the judge and the critic? You're no Noah."

"Just the fact," answered Rudyard serenely, "that the conception of the Ark occurred to me. That *such* a conception should have been born among us shows that we are worthy of it. This is not true of *any* conception, but it is true of one so noble."

"Maybe you're just disgruntled," said Laura in vain.

"Noah invented the gong," said Edmund pensively, "and Noah was the first to make wine."

"No wonder," said Laura, "he needed a drink. Anyone would need a drink, after what he went through."

"But for us," said Rudyard, disregarding his sister, "it is not so much what we accept as what we reject that is important."

"You can't have everything," said Jacob, "and you certainly can't have too much."

"We have had enough," said Ferdinand, "and more than enough."

"If you ask me," said Laura, "none of you have what you want, and that's what makes you mad."

"Anger is the vice of gentlemen," said Rudyard, "but the abounding strength of the truly noble. Let us begin with what we reject." He took notebook and pencil in hand.

"We reject automobiles," said Edmund, "I never liked them, anyway. Any boob thinks he is a king when he drives a car."

"An automobile would be useless on a boat, anyway," said Marcus.

"Too many human beings get killed in cars," said Edmund. "A fine thing for a rational being: to die for an automobile!"

"And no more marriage," said Rudyard. "Marriage is the chief cause of divorce and adultery. There are no marriages in heaven and if there are no marriages in heaven, why should we have them?"

"After all, there is something to be said for the family and family life," said Jacob.

"We will have the family," said Rudyard, "we will just not have any marriages."

"How about the phonograph?" asked Jacob, already somewhat apart. "If you reject the automobile, then you can't have the phonograph, and if we don't have the phonograph, how will we be able to hear great music?"

"We don't have to be consistent," said Rudyard, "it is an overrated virtue used chiefly to defend the fearful from the beautiful possibilities with which their imaginations might become infatuated. We will reject the automobile and accept the phonograph."

Apart from Jacob, it was felt that this was just, reasonable, and full of insight.

"How about the animals?" said Edmund. "Don't forget that we have to have two of each kind, male and female."

"Animals are fine," said Francis, "I like animals. They are interesting, spontaneous, and sincere."

"Animals and also children," said Rudyard. "We will have a new education for them, the education of the Ark. They will not be taught the skills which crush their natures and prepare them to be desperate citizens of the middle class. We will teach them every kind of virtue and vice, and by this true education, they will be made truly free. For in what sense can a human being be said to be free, if he is not possessed by the knowledge of every possibility, famous and infamous?"

"You want the children to be just like you," said Laura.

"I suppose you like the world as it is?" said Rudyard passionately. "Are you happy? Is anyone happy?"

Laura had no answer, but felt that Rudyard was wrong.

"As for me," said Ferdinand, "I spit on this life."

This declaration was acclaimed.

"This life," added Ferdinand, "can go and take a flying La Rochefoucauld for itself."

The addition was also acclaimed.

"Say what you will," said Jacob, when the applause had ended, "there is something that must be said for this life. This idea of the Ark is only an idea, and yet we all hold back. There is no flood of rejections and renunciations. We are all too much in love with many things, whether we have them or not."

"You don't like Arks," said Rudyard, knowing that a crisis had been reached, since Jacob was turning away.

"I like Arks well enough," said Jacob, "although I have never been on one, and can't be too sure. But I like many other things, even if they are not as good as they might be."

"No," said Rudyard, feeling that the emotion was slipping away and that the circle was becoming bored with the idea of the Ark.

"The kingdom of heaven is within us," said Jacob, "but also the kingdom of hell."

"What kingdom?" said Rudyard. "Do you know any kings? Do you know anyone who has found any kingdom within himself? I thought once that I had, but I was wrong."

It was too late. Jacob smiled patiently and in sympathy.

"This is where we are," said Jacob, "and this is where we are going to stay, waiting in hope and fear for what comes next in this life."

"As for me, I am going home," said Ferdinand, and all the visitors arose to depart, for they had had enough of the idea of the Ark.

EIGHT: "PRACTICALLY EVERYONE DOES WHAT HE
         WANTS TO DO IF HE CAN"

During a period when Rudyard was absent on a long visit, a celebrated cause and scandal broke out.

The scandal began with Marcus Gross. During the difficult

winter of the year, he had paid much attention to a plump and pretty girl named Irene. She was active, efficient, interested in many things, especially radical politics. Marcus met her at meetings of the radical party to which both belonged, and he courted her not only because she was pretty, but also because he had already heard about her from a friend of his, Algernon Nathan. Algernon was a certain well-known type, the perfect student who gets the highest grades in all his classes. He was precise, thin-lipped, tormented by pride, and as humorless as a public monument. He earned a handsome salary and he felt unable to understand why he was not the perfect success in the great world that he had been in school. He had succeeded very quickly with Irene. His parents owned a store and it was simple for him to bring Irene home, either in the afternoon or in the early evening, when his parents were at the store. When his parents came home unexpectedly one day, Algernon left his bedroom, attired himself in his dressing gown, and halted his parents in the hallway, asking them to depart from the house because he was having sexual intercourse. The adoration, and awe of his parents were such that they left the house immediately and hurriedly, supposing that if Algernon, the perfect student, thought that this was right, it must indeed be right.

Algernon provided Marcus with a comprehensive description of his sessions with Irene, who was, he affirmed, "passionate to a satisfactory extent," but with whom he did not like to be seen by his friends. Irene, however, wanted Algernon to take her out and to visit his friends with him. And Algernon found that what he really wanted from Irene, she did not really like. What he really wanted to do when he made love was to whip Irene. He had not gone so far as to propose this exercise to her, but had restricted himself to squeezing her and pinching her while he regarded the pain upon her face. This had been endured by Irene only upon occasion, when she was eager to please him. Her attitude was a blow to Algernon's pride, for he felt that if a girl truly loved him, she ought to want whatever he wanted.

After a time, Algernon decided that it would be more sensible and more efficient to pay for such satisfactions and not to become involved with a girl whom he had to take out and be seen with by his friends. He had made the proper inquiries and found that there were establishments where what he wanted was available, and he had gone to them with system, twice a week, taking with him a book to study on the subway, a book which extended his knowledge about such subjects as some period in history, relativity physics, or mathematical logic.

"Often, however," he explained to Marcus who admired him very much because he was a conventional success, "I merely study the faces in the subway, wonder what lives have produced such faces, and write sonnets about them when I get home."

Marcus blazed with desire when he heard Algernon's somewhat off-hand account of Irene. His own desires were orthodox and straight-forward, and such a girl was just what he longed for. He paid expensive court to Irene and took her to theatres, to the opera and to the ballet, night after night, being impatient. At the conclusion of two weeks, he proposed to Irene that she go to Atlantic City with him for the week-end. She refused flatly, and when he asked if she thought she might feel differently after six months, she said she was sure she would not, she was sorry, but to be perfectly frank, she found him unattractive. Marcus in anger replied that she had a capitalist and Hollywood conception of what was handsome, for he had been told by some girls that he was extremely attractive. He did not add that it was a colored girl to whom he had just paid ten dollars who had said: "Boy, are you handsome!"

No sooner had Marcus stopped seeing Irene than she began to go out with Ferdinand to whom she had been introduced by Marcus. The truth was that Marcus suspected Ferdinand of interviewing and seeking out Irene before his rejected week-end proposal.

Marcus was hurt, as if he had been betrayed. He saw no reason for Ferdinand's being successful where he had failed, and he felt also that such a one as Ferdinand, precious and finicky, had been unfaithful to himself in going with a girl like Irene. He protested long, as if obsessed, to Edmund and Jacob. Both of them, perverted by Marcus' stolid foolishness, provoked Marcus all the more.

Ferdinand hated Algernon and refused to acknowledge his existence when they passed on the street. The year before, Algernon's father had hanged himself because of losses in the stock market, and the circle had had a merry time about this event, for none of them liked Algernon, whom they had known as a student. They had discovered that when they asked most acquaintances if they had heard about Algernon's father, most of them said:

"Yes, he hanged himself!" and broke out laughing. The laughter was directed at Algernon as a prig, and not at the father, a small, quiet, extremely nervous man whom no one knew very well.

The outlandish answer and laughter continued so that as each newcomer was asked the question and broke into laughter, Ferdinand said:

"Look, everyone breaks out laughing," and he was pleased.

And this had also been the inspiration of the most notorious instance of an incapacity to make conversation and engage in small talk, for one day Harry Johnson, an acquaintance of the circle and of Algernon, one renowned for shyness and insensitivity, had encountered Algernon soon after his father's death. After several abortive efforts to make conversation with Algernon, who was no help whatever, Harry tried to break the silence between sentences.

"Say, what's this I hear about your father hanging himself?" he inquired.

This question had been discussed for six months, especially by Rudyard who maintained that it was a direct expression of Harry's hatred of Algernon.

Knowing how Ferdinand detested Algernon, Marcus felt that the one thing which would make him abandon Irene was the knowledge that she had been intimate with Algernon. This would certainly waken the finicky dandy in him.

Jacob was consulted by Marcus.

"Go ahead and tell him, if you like," said Jacob, "but if you tell him, you may not take much pride in yourself hereafter."

"After all, I am a friend of his," said Marcus. "Perhaps it is my duty to tell him?"

"Who do you think you are making that remark to?" said Jacob. Marcus grinned in guilt and recognition. Then he suggested that perhaps Jacob, also a good friend of Ferdinand, ought to tell him about Irene and Algernon, since he had no personal stake.

"You ought to be dead," said Jacob.

Meanwhile the news of the courtship grew. Ferdinand, who hardly ever lent a book to anyone, was lending certain selected works, long sacred to him, to Irene.

"This surely is serious," said Jacob to Edmund.

Stiffly and shyly, Ferdinand was seen bringing Irene to see other treasures and curios of his private cult. It was like the loving son who for the first time brings his intended to see his mother and his father.

"This must mean marriage," said Jacob.

Ferdinand undertook to supervise Irene's habits of dress. He went with her to the dressmaker's and he quickly persuaded her to shift from the garish to the elegant. She was surprised to find that he knew so much about dress and delighted that he cared about such matters.

He explained curtly that he had had several extra-marital relationships which had provided him with an opportunity to learn about such things. He made this explanation because he felt that he must make it clear that he had committed adultery, just as in other periods chastity was deemed a necessity and a virtue.

The two united extremes; it was the union of a brash, bright, full, open, vivacious and buxom girl to a constrained, meticulous, reserved and tormented young man.

The boys of the circle observed that strange changes also occurred in Ferdinand, now that he went with Irene. He had always abhorred politics, especially radical politics. Now he spoke with a venom he had once reserved for discourteous headwaiters of the infamy of the Stalinists.

"What does she have that I don't have?" said Laura. No one answered her although conversation had concentrated upon Irene for an hour. The silence was sharp. Laura thrust her head forward.

"You're no Adonis," she said to Edmund.

"What did I do?" asked Edmund, moved at the same time to sympathy and laughter.

"She has thick ankles and her complexion is rotten," said Laura.

"Who?" said Edmund.

"This too shall pass away," quoted Laura, departing for the kitchen to get herself a fresh drink.

At that moment the door slammed like a gunshot and Marcus entered.

"Hello, hello, hello," he shouted, the image of abounding good humor.

"What now?" said Jacob.

"What next?" said Edmund.

"I hear that Ferdinand has just married Irene," said Marcus, enjoying the astonishment of this news. He drew forth the engraved card which announced that Ferdinand and Irene would be at home to their friends on Saturday night.

"You will get one tomorrow," said Marcus, "I met Ferdinand in the street and he gave me one."

"What are you so pleased about?" asked Laura. "You're not the one who married Irene."

"I have a very good reason to be pleased," said Marcus, "I know something that Ferdinand does not know."

"Shut up," said Jacob, but vainly.

"What does he know?" asked Lloyd Tyler who had not heard about Irene's intimacy with Algernon.

"This card is very fine," said Jacob, shifting the subject, "it is just like Ferdinand to send a card as well-engraved as this."

"It must have cost a pretty penny," said Marcus, grinning.

Laura returned from the kitchen where she had listened as she drank. She replied to Lloyd's question as if it had just been uttered.

"Marcus has been saying that Irene used to sleep with Algernon and he is going to tell Ferdinand."

"Who says I am going to tell him?" said Marcus, trying to look indignant, but breaking into a fresh grin.

"You had better shut up," said Jacob, all his authority in his tone. To himself he said: "Everyone does what he wants to do if he can, after paying his respects to scruple and compunction."

"I won't say anything," said Marcus, whom Jacob alone was able to persuade to be silent. "But if I drink the champagne that Ferdinand is going to have, who knows what slips of the tongue, what *lapsus linguae* may not leak out? *In vino veritas,* they say!" he chortled, pleased that he had spoken Latin.

"Thank God that Rudyard is not here," said Edmund, and all understood without a word what Edmund had in mind, how Rudyard more than Marcus would have made this marriage the subject of endless discussion until at last Ferdinand would think that his wife's past was always talked about.

Clearly Marcus took pleasure in the fact that now that the marriage was accomplished, Ferdinand was helpless against the infamy unknown to him.

At that moment the absent hero, Ferdinand, appeared in the doorway and was greeted with congratulation which soon rose to acclamation.

"Who said that I am married?" asked Ferdinand, coldly.

"I said so. You said so. It says so on the card you gave me," said Marcus, perplexed.

"I see no reason for making any unwarranted suppositions or assumptions on the basis of an engraved card," said Ferdinand.

"This is stupendous," said Edmund, for he saw that Ferdinand had a trump card up his sleeve.

"The fact is that I am not married," Ferdinand declared. "It is possible that I may marry Irene in the near future, but at present we are merely very good friends who have decided to live together."

Marcus capsized on the sofa. His dismay spread over his face as if he were at the dentist's, his mouth open.

"What do you think of Algernon Nathan?" asked Marcus.

"You know well enough," Ferdinand replied. "He is a knave and a fool. He is a coxcomb and a jackass, and he always will be, if he lives to a hundred."

It was clear then that Marcus was seeking to suppress his own desire to tell Ferdinand about Irene's intimacy with Algernon, for this knowledge was without meaning, if Ferdinand was not married to Irene.

The circle was stunned by Ferdinand's declaration. It seemed to them an incomparable exhibition. The real right thing was not to get married until one wanted to get married and in the meantime to do as one liked, frankly and openly. Ferdinand had often formulated this attitude.

"What do you think of that?" Marcus asked Laura, for she alone often expressed conventional views about marriage.

"How much money does she make?" said Laura. "What is her yearly compensation?"

"Ten years hence," said Edmund, "this evening will still be the subject of discussion and interpretation." No one knew exactly what Laura meant, but it was clear in general that Laura intended to express contempt with the implication also that nothing good would come of such an arrangement.

Laura began to bring in cups, spoons, knives, forks, bread, jam and cheese for the midnight supper.

Marcus, defeated, felt nervous and bewildered. He fell back on a practice for which he had often been denounced, that of drawing upon a store of prepared jokes and epigrams.

"Say, speaking of marriage," said Marcus, "I heard a good one the other day. A girl says to a friend of hers who is getting married soon: 'Is your torso prepared?'"

The others looked at him in a frozen-faced silence.

"What's the joke?" asked Jacob.

Marcus paled. He knew that he was being attacked. But he felt that he must attempt to justify his utterance.

"Don't you see, she says torso when she means trousseau. It is a genuine Freudian *lapsus linguae.*"

"Enough of this Latin," said Edmund, "it is a dead tongue, and your grammar would shame a Gaul of the second century."

Marcus, persevering, launched a second effort.

"You are like the Irish," he said laboriously, "it is as Dr. Johnson said, the Irish are a fair people; they do not speak well of anyone."

"Spare us your prepared epigrams and quotations," said Ferdinand, "they resemble canned music."

"The trouble with you," said Marcus, "is that you have no sense of humor. Algernon said you had none and I said that you were hilarious. But I see that I was wrong."

This spontaneous remark was also a success. Everyone but Ferdinand laughed. He did not know why they laughed, but he was too clever to ask that it be explained to him, the trap which had often undone Marcus.

And now they all sat at the table, and ate and drank, and minds and hearts arose as if they danced. Marcus, seated next to Ferdinand, put his hand on his shoulder, and said, still warm with pleasure at the unexpected success of his remark about Ferdinand as humorless:

"You are a fine fellow, Ferdinand. I always admired you and no matter what you say or do, I will continue to admire you."

"Shut up," said Edmund, kicking Marcus under the table.

Ferdinand described his purchase of furniture and how he had imposed his scorn upon the merchants of furniture. It was a very interesting story.

"Say," said Laura, returning from the kitchen where she had just taken her tenth drink, and hurling her lightning-bolt as if she spoke of the weather, "did you know that Irene slept for a whole year with Algernon Nathan?"

"Laura," said Marcus, torn between guilt and the wish to appear to be the reproachful one.

"Yes," said Ferdinand, "I heard all about it the first night I went out with Irene." His tone was matter-of-fact. "What about it?"

"This Ferdinand is without a peer," said Edmund, "he has no equal either in America or Europe."

They all saw that Ferdinand had scored an unconditional triumph. It was impossible to make out if Ferdinand had actually known about Algernon, or with quick wit and perfect control recognized that he must not admit his ignorance.

"Are you going home now?" Jacob asked Edmund. "I have had enough pity and terror for one evening."

"Yes," said Edmund, who did not want to go but who wanted to hear what Jacob had to say about the evening.

"I will go with you," said Marcus.

"You stay here or go by yourself," said Jacob, "we don't want you with us." And on that note of judgment the young men left.

NINE: "A MILLION DOLLARS ARE WORTHLESS TO ME"

After long absence, Rudyard visited the teacher who had most befriended him in school, Percival Davis. After Rudyard had been seated in the study of Professor Davis and questioned about himself, Professor Davis said in a flat, but depressed, tone:

"I am dying."

"We are all dying," said Rudyard, uneasy and trying to find something to say.

"But I am dying faster than most human beings," said Professor Davis, unwilling to permit Rudyard to extricate himself from the fact of his own death. "I may be dead in six months. The fact is, I probably will be."

"I think that it would be boring to live forever," said Rudyard, pleased by this comment, but still uncomfortable.

"Forever, perhaps: but I would like to live for at least a

thousand years," said Professor Davis passionately, "I would not be bored in the least. I would learn about every great school of painting, both in Europe and the Orient, and I would cultivate the best wines."

"Yes, you're right," said Rudyard, hoping to shift the subject, "it would be wonderful to live for a thousand years!" He felt that through agreement he was at least polite.

Two months after, Percival Davis died of the heart attack he had expected. After hearing the news, Rudyard went strolling with Jacob and told him of the interview.

"It was not proper of him," said Rudyard, "to confront me with his death. What was there to say? What a pity that we do not have formal utterances for all the important events of life."

"You might have said," Jacob remarked, " 'I hope you are wrong. I hope that you are not going to die very soon.' "

"What difference would that have made?" Rudyard replied.

They passed a church where a hearse and other cars awaited the departure for the cemetery. Jacob, as was his wont, wanted to pause to see the coffin carried from the church to the hearse, for now as ever the joys of strict observation were important to him. But Rudyard refused to stop.

"Who wants to see a funeral, anyway?" said Rudyard, and Jacob, discerning the excess of emotion in Rudyard's voice, yielded to him.

"Two years ago, when a very gifted student died suddenly," said Jacob, "Israel Brown was asked by the family to make the funeral sermon, for the family as well as the student were without religious belief. The sermon was given in the auditorium of the Ethical Culture School. Israel Brown spoke very well, as he always does. He spoke of the gifts of the dead young man, remarking upon his original gift for certain subjects and making clear the difficulty in general of mastering these subjects. Yet all felt that this might have been a classroom and not the ceremony for the death of a young man. Now what kind of a life is this, anyway? Something important and irreparable occurs and we have nothing to say."

Moved by these thoughts, Jacob told Rudyard of a recent effort which he had kept secret. Six months before, in mid-winter when tours of the neighborhood were unpleasant, he had written a short novel, although he had never before thought of being that kind of an author. The short novel had seemed good to him. He had placed the manuscript in his desk "to cool off," as he explained. When two months had passed, he had read his short novel again and decided that it was worthless. It was a Sunday afternoon in April, just before Jacob was due from habit and principle to tour the neighborhood and see what he entitled "the Sunday look."

Depressed and benumbed that his short novel was worthless, Jacob arose from his desk, went to the window, and gazed at the park, full of human beings of each generation, infants, children, adolescents, parents, the middle-aged, and the old.

Regarding them, he said to himself, "I reject one million dollars, the highest prize of our society. For if I had one million dollars, what good would it do me? It would not help me to make this short novel, which is worthless, a short novel which is good. I can say then that I have discovered that a million dollars are worthless to me, since they cannot help me to satisfy the desire and hope which was important, intimate, and dear to me."

Rudyard told the circle of this discovery when Jacob was absent, and they were very much moved and impressed. Often after that, when they were among strangers, they spoke of "the great moment," and "the great rejection." When strangers wished to know what this moment was, they were left unanswered, except that Edmund often said that Jacob had discovered the essential vanity and emptiness of our society. The success of these teasing sentences about "the great recognition," made the boys invent variations, delicious to them, of the enigmatic sentences. It was said that Jacob has renounced a million dollars; Jacob has rejected a million dollars; Jacob has recognized that a million dollars are worthless.

Thus it came about that for the wrong reasons outsiders and strangers suffered the illusion that Jacob was a fabulous heir.

Yet at this time Jacob's feeling about himself and about the circle was undergoing a change.

"We have all come to a standstill," he said to himself, "as on an escalator, for time is passing, but we remain motionless."

"What do I want?" he continued, "Do I know what I want? Does anyone know what he or she wants?"

He decided to visit Edmund, who had once again endured the period when scholarships and teaching appointments are awarded and who had once again been rejected. In seeking to find motives or reasons to explain his rejection, Edmund let himself go into a kind of hysteria, discussing the matter with anyone he found to listen, speaking of his rare and many labors, and making use of a terminology which no one but a peer in his subject could understand. This had occurred at this time for the past five years and the circle found Edmund's obsession with it boring. Consequently when Francis French had entered in the midst of Edmund's monologue with a piece of sensational news everyone had stopped listening to Edmund, and Edmund, much offended, arose and departed, and he had now been absent from the circle for more than a week.

This was the reason that Jacob, the conscience of the circle, visited Edmund, keeping silent, however, about Edmund's offended departure.

"Do you know," said Jacob, seating himself in an armchair in Edmund's study, "practically everyone is unhappy, though few will admit the fact?"

"Yes," said Edmund, pleased by the renewal of this theme, "that's just what I've been thinking. It would be hard to overestimate the amount of unhappiness in America. The cause can't be just the depression, though I don't want to slight the depression, for obviously the rich are just as unhappy as the poor, though in different ways."

"Yes," said Jacob, "it is not only the depression. The depression is as much an effect as a cause, and the amount of unhappiness was perhaps as great in 1928 as in 1934."

"I know just what you mean," said Edmund, "I saw the other day that ninety-five per cent of the bathtubs in the world are in America. Now if anyone reflects sufficiently upon this interesting fact, he will conclude with the whole story of America."

"Everyone feels that it is necessary to have certain things of a certain quality and kind," said Jacob.

"Bathtubs come from an obsession with personal hygiene, the most consummate form of Puritan feeling," said Edmund, "but the essential point is that human beings waste the best years of their only life for the sake of such a thing as a shining automobile, the latest model. Since such things are regarded as the truly important, good, and valuable things, is it any wonder that practically everyone is unhappy?"

"The fault is not this desire for things," said Jacob, "but the way in which the motive of competition is made the chief motive of life, encouraged everywhere. Think of how competition is celebrated in games, in schools, in the professions, in every kind of activity. Consequently, the ideas of success and of failure are the two most important ideas in America. Yet it's obvious that most human beings are going to be failures, for such is the nature of competition. Perhaps then the ideas of success and failure ought to be established as immoral. This strikes me as a truly revolutionary idea, although I suppose it has occurred to others."

"It has occurred to you," said Edmund, "as it has occurred to me because we are both failures, and we have to be young men in a time of failure and defeat, during the black years of the great depression."

"Yes, we are both failures," said Jacob, "but I have no desire for the only kinds of success that are available. The other day I heard the cruelest question I ever expect to hear. Two composers met at a music festival in the Berkshires last summer and one of them said to the other: 'Calvin, why are we both failures?' That's more cruel than any other question I ever heard. The other one answered him in a hurry: 'I am not a failure,' he said, 'I am not a failure because I never wanted to be a success.' That's the way I feel too. Nevertheless the fact remains that practically everyone is unhappy. Now if the idea of love supplanted the ideas of success and failure, how joyous everyone might be! and how different the quality of life!"

"You're just dreaming out loud," said Edmund to Jacob, thinking again of how he had failed once more to be appointed a teacher.

TEN: "THE BEST PLEASURE IS TO GIVE PLEASURE"

The circle altered as the great depression was stabilized and modified. The idleness which had been beyond reproach because no one was successful, because most were frustrated, because the parents' generation had lost so much of its grip and pride, ended, for now there were jobs for everyone, although not the jobs each one wanted. Some had gone to Washington to take the new Federal jobs made necessary by the New Deal, and in New York too it was no longer difficult to get a job. Rudyard refused to be employed in the Federal project for playwrights, authors, musicians, and other artists, and he defended his refusal, as from the first, by speaking of his principles. Laura was angry at this refusal, but after a time she declared once again that Rudyard was a genius and he ought not to have to earn a living.

Soon all who belonged to the circle except Rudyard and Jacob had jobs which enabled them to pay for the modest round of luxuries upon which Ferdinand insisted. The theatre began to be for Ferdinand a kind of ritual. No matter how poor the play was, the ceremonial of going to the first night of a Broadway play had for Ferdinand the rigorous and expensive qualities he had desired since he put aside his desire to be an author. His marriage became by imperceptible degrees of which no one dared to speak, a recognized union, but this did not change in the least Ferdinand's participation in the circle or his mode of life. Irene was accepted by the circle as being just like Marcus, and the circle's judgment of her was formulated by Rudyard when he said: "Personally, I like her," a statement which meant that he understood very well all the reasons for not liking Irene, and which was understood by all to mean that Irene was detestable.

Marcus went to Bermuda for the Christmas holidays, and at Easter he went to Cuba, trips paid for by his labors in the public school system. After his trip to Cuba, he spoke of the *Weltanschauung* of the cabin cruise and of the nature of time and duration on a luxury liner. Rudyard declared that Marcus had become a beachcomber and an idler. When Marcus replied that Rudyard was in no position to accuse anyone of being an idler, Rudyard told him that he was being ridiculous. "Don't be *too obvious*," said Rudyard to Marcus, "it is expected that you will be obvious, but please draw the line *somewhere.*" Roaring, Marcus answered: "Obvious, obvious! what do you mean, obvious? If I say that the sun is shining, I suppose you will say that I am being obvious." "Yes!" said Rudyard in triumph and joy. "Who discusses the weather? Who discusses sunlight? We are not peasants. The weather is an old story, it is old hat."

Soon after this exchange, Rudyard was asked if he wanted to teach the drama in a girl's school in Cleveland, Ohio. The job was excellent and Rudyard was extremely pleased. "Such is the mystery of this life," he said. "The secret missions and visits of Milady Fortune, a well-known lady of the evening, are invariably surprises. Had I sought this job, I would not have received it. Just because I did not strive for it, it was given to me. All good things are given, not gained by the effort of the will."

No one paid attention to this comment and interpretation, because more interesting by far was the topic of the effect of Rudyard's departure on the circle as such. Edmund declared that Rudyard ought not to become a teacher, since he had dedicated himself to the writing of plays. Edmund quoted some of Rudyard's best past arguments in defense of his mode of life, and concluded with the statement that Rudyard would feel unhappy and estranged when he was so far from the circle. Laura was affected the most. She was excited and pleased for a moment, and then she was terrified. She said to Rudyard repeatedly that she might well ask to be sent to Cleveland by the department store which employed her. But Rudyard felt that he had had enough of life with Laura. He told her that he did not consider such a move a wise one for her, and he suggested that she secure a smaller apartment, for he did not intend to return to the city in the summer, he was going to be in the country. Ferdinand agreed with both Rudyard and Edmund. They were both his friends and whatever they said or did was right.

Edmund and Jacob discussed the fate of the circle after Rudyard's departure. Jacob felt that the circle would continue certainly and some of the others, overshadowed by Rudyard's energy, might now realize new possibilities in themselves. He observed how year by year Rudyard's authority had diminished so that now Ferdinand truly dictated the circle's mode of life more and more, as he earned more and more money. When he said this, Jacob explained as before that he himself did not truly belong to the circle. This was a necessity to each of them, to maintain that he himself was but a visitor or stranger, although the others truly belonged to the circle.

As Rudyard prepared to depart, he said again to his sister that she surely ought to move to a smaller apartment, since it was unlikely that they were ever going to live with each other again. The other boys said nothing, but they felt it cruel and unnecessary for Rudyard to dictate to Laura. Edmund suggested to Ferdinand in private that perhaps Rudyard did not want the circle to exist when he was absent. Hearing Rudyard say petulantly to Laura for the fourth time that it was senseless for her not to move elsewhere, Lloyd said with naiveté that then they would all be deprived of their community. "Yes, that's just it," said Rudyard, his face full of annoyance and distaste, "I don't want Laura to provide a clubhouse anymore." Laura became furious. "You were willing enough for me to do that until now," she said. "Never," Rudyard replied, "I never wanted you to provide a second home for the boys." He spoke with a self-righteous tone because he was sensitive now about the fact that he had been dependent upon Laura.

The week-end before Rudyard was to depart for Cleveland, Ohio, it was decided that a farewell party ought to be given for him. Ferdinand immediately declared that as a matter of fact he was going to contribute a case of champagne to this party. As his prosperity mounted, his gestures became more and more of a systematic extravagance. Laura wanted to make dinner for the whole circle, but Edmund dissuaded her. The question of who was to be invited to this party among those on the edge of the circle, the visiting strangers and the accepted newcomers, became the subject of intensive discussion.

The whole circle dined at the best restaurant in the neighborhood and Ferdinand insisted upon paying the check. "He is beside himself," said Edmund to Jacob, "this departure means more to him than he knows."

By the time everyone had returned to the Bell household, Laura was drunk. This was no less than was expected, for Laura had been drinking every night for weeks. But no one expected the speech she began to make as soon as the champagne was opened.

"Five years ago, just about the time when we all began to see each other," said Laura, rocking and gaining the attention of all by the loudness and shrillness of her voice, "I read a story by Rilke. I think it was Rilke. It was just a very short story. It was just a page and a half, and it may have been less. It was very good. I don't remember all of it, but what I remember was very good. The story is about wandering Siberians. They are hunters and they hunt wild cows on the Siberian steppes or tundras, or something. Anyway, they hunt for wild cows."

Rudyard, annoyed, said: "Laura has established the fact that they were hunters. She has made that clear." He was obviously impatient with Laura.

"Never mind," said Laura, "the main thing is that the Siberians spear the wild cows like cowboys on horseback. And when the poor cow is bleeding to death, the hunter lays down on one side of the cow and chews big pieces of meat from the side of the cow. This is just like many other stories so far. The different part is that on the other side of the cow, the horse also lays down and chews out big pieces of meat."

"The story," said Rudyard, "is by Kafka, not Rilke, and you have distorted it." He took a book from the shelf, turned to the proper page and read aloud, pausing after each sentence.

" 'Their very horses live on meat. Often a rider lies down beside his horse. Then both feed on the same piece of meat.'

"The story," Rudyard continued in a critical voice, "is about nomads, not Siberians. It is nomads who come to the capital. They eat butchers' meat, which they have stolen from butchers' vans. The meat comes from the slaughter house and nothing is said about eating living cows who are bleeding to death. You have changed the story in a way familiar to me because I know how your memory distorts many things, making what has happened more brutal and more cruel than it was in actual fact."

"Never mind," said Laura. "Let's say that I wrote the story then. I wrote the story from my knowledge of life. But I am the cow, and you," she said pointing at Rudyard, "are the nomad, the Siberian, and you," she said, pointing to the other boys, "are the horses, chewing on the other side."

"I am not a horse," said Marcus, who was amused and thought this a witticism.

"Shut up," said Edmund to Marcus.

"If you expect too much from human beings," said Jacob, "you are bound to be disappointed."

"I never expected anything unusual," said Laura, "all I ever wanted was what everyone else has."

"This is getting hysterical," said Marcus, who was always slow. "What a party!"

"Can't you think of anything good to say about any of us?" asked Jacob in a kind voice.

"I can," said Laura, "but if I lean backwards anymore, I will fall down and injure my spine, to coin a phrase." Laura reached for a glass of champagne, which Rudyard tried to keep her from getting. But he was unsuccessful.

"I don't have what I want," said Jacob to Laura, "and I don't think that many of us have what we want."

"Yes," said Rudyard, returning to his own kind of rhetoric, "I too may say that I am disappointed. My plays are not performed, although many of them are masterpieces, if I may say so. I think I may say without immodesty that I am superior to the age in which I live. I pay for my superiority to Broadway by leading this life of obscurity. Yet I do not seek out a scapegoat, as you do, Laura. Furthermore, we ought to remember that this life is a mystery in which each of us is given by God his own gifts and shortcomings. To live is better than anything else! Let us take pleasure in life!"

"Never mind," said Laura, "if you like, go ahead and say that God gave me a plain face and made me full of self-pity. What am I going to do about it? Do you think I ought to take pleasure in it? I want a husband like all the other girls. I don't want to be left alone."

"In my late adolescence," said Edmund, "life seemed to me to be Shakespearean. But now as I get older I see that life really resembles the stories of Dostoyevsky."

"Enough of these literary allusions," said Laura. "You're no Karamazov."

This new version of Laura's famous sentence, "You're no Adonis," drew forth reminiscent laughter lacking in vigor because Laura stood before them, cold-faced.

"Marriage is not so important," said Irene, who had been silent and who, as a newcomer, had not really understood what Laura was saying.

"What do you have that I don't have?" said Laura to Irene, quoting herself again.

Jacob arose and it was natural that all should accept this moment as belonging to him.

"The fact is," said Jacob, in a low and careful voice, "we all have each other and we all need each other. Laura's story was a very good story, whether it was written by Rilke or Kafka. All of us consume each other, and life without such friends as we are to each other would be unbearable. The best pleasure of all is to give pleasure to another being. Strange as it seems, I see this truth every day when I give my cat his dinner, and I see how unbearable solitude is when I come home and he is pleased to see me, and I am pleased that he is pleased."

"I am not a cat," said Laura, unwilling to be consoled by mere analogy, "I am a girl."

"Each of us," said Jacob, "has been disappointed and most of us will continue to be disappointed. It would be foolish to try to say that the disappointment is not painful or that it is good for us or that it is necessary. Yet, on the other hand, which of us would really like to be dead? Not one of us would prefer that his life had ended in childhood or infancy, and that he had not lived through the years he has lived. Since this is true of the past, it is likely that it will be true of the future, and in the same way. By the same way, I mean that we will not get what we want; our desires will not be richly satisfied; but nonetheless we will be pleased to live through the years, to be conscious each day and to sleep every night."

"Not me," said Laura, "speak for yourself." She took another glass of champagne.

"You do not know what you are saying, Laura," said Edmund. Taking a book in his hand, he too read aloud:

" 'When one is upset by anger, then the heart is not in its right place; when one is disturbed by fear, then the heart is not in its right place; when one is blinded by love, then the heart is not in its right place; when one is involved in anxiety, then the heart is not in its right place. When the mind is not present, we look, but do not see, listen but do not hear, and eat but do not know the flavor of the food.' "

"I am wearing my heart on my sleeve," said Laura, unmoved, "all the sentences in all the books will not do away with my disappointment."

"How about your love?" asked Marcus.

"I don't have any love," said Laura.

"How much money do I make?" said Edmund.

"We can't just run on like this," said Jacob, "and yet nothing seems to do any good."

Laura had begun to cry and those who saw her tears tried to make believe that they did not see them.

"I just don't like it," she said, sobbing, "I am going to get out of this house." She started for the door. Edmund and Ferdinand took hold of her and dissuaded her.

"Have some more to drink," said Marcus in an effort to be helpful.

"I am going to try again," said Jacob, "since there is nothing else to do but try again." He said this as to himself and then he spoke loudly and clearly:

"*The world is a wedding.* I read this sentence in an old book last week. I had to think for two days before I had any conception of what this sentence *The world is a wedding* was supposed to mean. Does it mean anything? Yes, and it means everything. For example, it means that the world is the wedding of God and Nature. This is the first of all the marriages.

"It was natural that I should think of Pieter Breughel's picture, 'The Peasant Wedding.' Do you remember what that picture looks like? If you look at it long enough, you will see all the parts that anyone and everyone can have. But it is necessary to belong to a circle of friendship, such as ours, if one is to be present at the wedding which is this world."

"The world is a marriage of convenience," said Laura drunkenly, "the world is a shot-gun marriage. The world is a sordid match for money. The world is a misalliance. Every birthday is a funeral and every funeral is a great relief."

"I only went to a wedding once," said Francis. He spoke in a low voice but with an intensity which made everyone listen. "It was the wedding of my older sister at the age of thirty-six.

"The bridegroom's mother, who was eighty-five, was brought in a taxi to the ceremony. She paid no attention to the ceremony, but kept telling my mother how, at the home for the aged where she lived, she was persecuted and other old men and women pampered; but my younger sister and I listened to what she said because it was more interesting than the ceremony itself. One thing we kept noticing was that the bride was at least a head taller than the bridegroom.

"Then the old lady was sent back to the home for the aged in a taxi, after getting my mother to promise to see her. After her departure, the wedding party went to the big downtown hotel where the bride and bridegroom had taken a room for the night. My younger sister and I kept getting more and more disappointed because we had never been to a wedding before, and we thought that all weddings must be like this. Up in the hotel room where we had been sent to wash, we looked at the twin beds and giggled. Then we stopped giggling because the room looked as depressing as everything else. We had dinner in the big dining room downstairs, the bridegroom, the bride, my mother, my younger sister and myself. No one had very much to say to anyone else. It was just as if we were having dinner on a rainy Sunday. After dinner ended, we said goodbye to the bridegroom and the bride, and we went home in the subway. I had homework to do and my sister had to practice her piano lessons. We asked my mother if in honor of the occasion we might not postpone the homework and the lessons, and she said the wedding was all over."

Francis paused. He had become almost breathless as he continued his story.

"I want to ask all of you this question," he said. "Do I agree with Jacob that the world is a wedding, or don't I? What do all of you think?"

"You're right," said Laura, "and he is wrong."

"In the beautiful picture by Pieter Breughel," said Jacob, disregarding what Francis and Laura had just said, "you can see a squatting child on the floor, sucking his thumb which is sticky with something sweet. Standing by the table are two musicians, bearing bagpipes. One is young, handsome and strong; he is dressed in brown and his cheeks are puffed out. The other musician is unkempt and middle-aged. He looks far away as if he were thinking of his faded hopes. The serving men are carrying a long tray full of pies. The bride is seated beneath the red-white mistletoe and on her face is a faint smile, as if she thought of what did not yet exist. The bridegroom is leaning back and draining down the ale from a fat stein. He drinks as if he were in the midst of a long kiss. Nearby is a dwarf and at the head of the table a priest and a nun are conversing with each other. Neither of them will ever have a husband or a wife. On the right hand of the bride, an old man looks ahead at nothing, holding his hands as if he prayed. He has been a guest at many wedding feasts! He will never be a young man again! Never again will youth run wild in him!

"Opposite the bride are the fathers and the mothers, all four. Their time is passed and they have had their day. Yet this too is a pleasure and a part for them to play. I can't tell which is the suitor whom the bride refused, but I know he is there too, perhaps among the crush that crowds the door. He is present and he looks from a distance like death at happiness. Meanwhile in the foreground a handsome young man pours from a jug which has the comely form of a woman's body the wine which will bring all of them exaltation like light. His bending body is curved in a grace like harps or violins. Marcus, open a new bottle."

Marcus obeyed, and after the pop, the puff, the foam, and the flow, he poured the wine in glasses.

"I suppose everything is all right," said Laura, "I suppose everything is just fine."

"No," said Jacob, "I don't mean to say that this life is just a party, any kind of party. It is a wedding, the most important kind of party, full of joy, fear, hope, and ignorance. And at this party there are enough places and parts for everyone, and if no one can play every part, yet everyone can come to the party, everyone can come to the wedding feast, and anyone who does not know that he is at a wedding feast just does not see what is in front of him. He might as well be dead if he does not know that the world is a wedding."

"You can't fool me," said Laura, "the world is a funeral. We are all going to the grave, no matter what you say. Let me give all of you one good piece of advice: *Let your conscience be your bride.*"

Poetry

from IN DREAMS BEGIN
RESPONSIBILITIES (1938)

The Ballad of the Children of the Czar

1
The children of the Czar
Played with a bouncing ball

In the May morning, in the Czar's garden,
Tossing it back and forth.

It fell among the flowerbeds
Or fled to the north gate.

A daylight moon hung up
In the Western sky, bald white.

Like Papa's face, said Sister,
Hurling the white ball forth.

2

While I ate a baked potato
Six thousand miles apart,

In Brooklyn, in 1916,
Aged two, irrational.

When Franklin D. Roosevelt
Was an Arrow Collar ad.

O Nicholas! Alas! Alas!
My grandfather coughed in your army,

Hid in a wine-stinking barrel,
For three days in Bucharest

Then left for America
To become a king himself.

3

I am my father's father,
You are your children's guilt.

In history's pity and terror
The child is Aeneas again;

Troy is in the nursery,
The rocking horse is on fire.

Child labor! The child must carry
His fathers on his back.

But seeing that so much is past
And that history has no ruth

For the individual,
Who drinks tea, who catches cold,

Let anger be general:
I hate an abstract thing.

4
Brother and sister bounced
The bounding, unbroken ball,

The shattering sun fell down
Like swords upon their play,

Moving eastward among the stars
Toward February and October.

But the Maywind brushed their cheeks
Like a mother watching sleep,

And if for a moment they fight
Over the bouncing ball

And sister pinches brother
And brother kicks her shins,

Well! The heart of man is known:
It is a cactus bloom.

5
The ground on which the ball bounces
Is another bouncing ball.

The wheeling, whirling world
Makes no will glad.

Spinning in its spotlight darkness,
It is too big for their hands.

A pitiless, purposeless Thing,
Arbitrary and unspent,

Made for no play, for no children,
But chasing only itself.

The innocent are overtaken,
They are not innocent.

They are their father's fathers,
The past is inevitable.

6
Now, in another October
Of this tragic star,

I see my second year,
I eat my baked potato.

It is my buttered world,
But, poked by my unlearned hand,

It falls from the highchair down
And I begin to howl.

And I see the ball roll under
The iron gate which is locked.

Sister is screaming, brother is howling,
The ball has evaded their will.

Even a bouncing ball
Is uncontrollable,

And is under the garden wall.
I am overtaken by terror

Thinking of my father's fathers,
And of my own will.

In the Naked Bed, in Plato's Cave

In the naked bed, in Plato's cave,
Reflected headlights slowly slid the wall,
Carpenters hammered under the shaded window,
Wind troubled the window curtains all night long,
A fleet of trucks strained uphill, grinding,
Their freights covered, as usual.
The ceiling lightened again, the slanting diagram
Slid slowly forth.
                    Hearing the milkman's chop,
His striving up the stair, the bottle's chink,
I rose from bed, lit a cigarette,
And walked to the window. The stony street
Displayed the stillness in which buildings stand,
The street-lamp's vigil and the horse's patience.
The winter sky's pure capital
Turned me back to bed with exhausted eyes.

Strangeness grew in the motionless air. The loose
Film grayed. Shaking wagons, hooves' waterfalls,
Sounded far off, increasing, louder and nearer.
A car coughed, starting. Morning, softly
Melting the air, lifted the half-covered chair
From underseas, kindled the looking-glass,
Distinguished the dresser and the white wall.
The bird called tentatively, whistled, called,
Bubbled and whistled, so! Perplexed, still wet
With sleep, affectionate, hungry and cold. So, so,
O son of man, the ignorant night, the travail
Of early morning, the mystery of beginning
Again and again,
                    while History is unforgiven.

The Beautiful American Word, Sure

The beautiful American word, Sure,
As I have come into a room, and touch
The lamp's button, and the light blooms with such
Certainty where the darkness loomed before,

As I care for what I do not know, and care
Knowing for little she might not have been,
And for how little she would be unseen,
The intercourse of lives miraculous and dear.

Where the light is, and each thing clear,
Separate from all others, standing in its place,
I drink the time and touch whatever's near,

And hope for day when the whole world has that face:
For what assures her present every year?
In dark accidents the mind's sufficient grace.

Far Rockaway

"the cure of souls." HENRY JAMES

The radiant soda of the seashore fashions
Fun, foam, and freedom. The sea laves
The shaven sand. And the light sways forward
On the self-destroying waves.

The rigor of the weekday is cast aside with shoes,
With business suits and the traffic's motion;
The lolling man lies with the passionate sun,
Or is drunken in the ocean.

A socialist health takes hold of the adult,
He is stripped of his class in the bathing-suit,
He returns to the children digging at summer,
A melon-like fruit.

O glittering and rocking and bursting and blue
—Eternities of sea and sky shadow no pleasure:
Time unheard moves and the heart of man is eaten
Consummately at leisure.

The novelist tangential on the boardwalk overhead
Seeks his cure of souls in his own anxious gaze.
"Here," he says, "With whom?" he asks, "This?" he questions,
"What tedium, what blaze?"

"What satisfaction, fruit? What transit, heaven?
Criminal? justified? arrived at what June?"
That nervous conscience amid the concessions
Is a haunting, haunted moon.

Someone Is Harshly Coughing as Before

Someone is harshly coughing on the next floor,
Sudden excitement catching the flesh of his throat:
Who is the sick one?
                    Who will knock at the door,
Ask what is wrong and sweetly pay attention,
The shy withdrawal of the sensitive face
Embarrassing both, but double shame is tender
—We will mind our ignorant business, keep our place.

But it is God, who has caught cold again,
Wandering helplessly in the world once more,
Now he is phthisic, and he is, poor Keats
(Pardon, O Father, unknowable Dear, this word,
Only the cartoon is lucid, only the curse is heard),
Longing for Eden, afraid of the coming war.

The past, a giant shadow like the twilight,
The moving street on which the autos slide,
The buildings' heights, like broken teeth,
Repeat necessity on every side,
The age requires death and is not denied,
He has come as a young man to be hanged once more!

Another mystery must be crucified,
Another exile bare his complex care,
Another spent head spill its wine, before
(When smoke in silence curves
                            from every fallen side)
Pity and Peace return, padding the broken floor
With heavy feet.
                Their linen hands will hide
In the stupid opiate the exhausted war.

Tired and Unhappy, You Think of Houses

Tired and unhappy, you think of houses
Soft-carpeted and warm in the December evening,
While snow's white pieces fall past the window,
And the orange firelight leaps.
                                        A young girl sings
That song of Gluck where Orpheus pleads with Death;
Her elders watch, nodding their happiness
To see time fresh again in her self-conscious eyes:
The servants bring the coffee, the children retire,
Elder and younger yawn and go to bed,
The coals fade and glow, rose and ashen,
It is time to shake yourself! and break this
Banal dream, and turn your head
Where the underground is charged, where the weight
Of the lean buildings is seen,
Where close in the subway rush, anonymous
In the audience, well-dressed or mean,
So many surround you, ringing your fate,
Caught in an anger exact as a machine!

A Young Child and His Pregnant Mother

At four years Nature is mountainous,
Mysterious, and submarine. Even

A city child knows this, hearing the subway's
Rumor underground. Between the grate,

Dropping his penny, he learned out all loss,
The irretrievable cent of fate,

And now this newest of the mysteries,
Confronts his honest and his studious eyes—

His mother much too fat and absentminded,
Gazing far past his face, careless of him,

His fume, his charm, his bedtime, and warm milk,
As soon the night will be too dark, the spring

Too late, desire strange, and time too fast,
This first estrangement is a gradual thing

(His mother once so svelte, so often sick!
Towering father did this: what a trick!)

Explained too cautiously, containing fear,
Another being's being, becoming dear:

All men are enemies: thus even brothers
Can separate each other from their mothers!

No better example than this unborn brother
Shall teach him of his exile from his mother,

Measured by his distance from the sky,
Spoken in two vowels,
                    I am I.

Sonnet: O City, City

To live between terms, to live where death
Has his loud picture in the subway ride,
Being amid six million souls, their breath
An empty song suppressed on every side,
Where the sliding auto's catastrophe
Is a gust past the curb, where numb and high
The office building rises to its tyranny,
Is our anguished diminution until we die.

Whence, if ever, shall come the actuality
Of a voice speaking the mind's knowing,
The sunlight bright on the green windowshade,
And the self articulate, affectionate, and flowing,
Ease, warmth, light, the utter showing,
When in the white bed all things are made.

The Ballet of the Fifth Year

Where the sea gulls sleep or indeed where they fly
Is a place of different traffic. Although I
Consider the fishing bay (where I see them dip and curve
And purely glide) a place that weakens the nerve
Of will, and closes my eyes, as they should not be
(They should burn like the street-light all night quietly,
So that whatever is present will be known to me),
Nevertheless the gulls and the imagination
Of where they sleep, which comes to creation
In strict shape and color, from their dallying
Their wings slowly, and suddenly rallying
Over, up, down the arabesque of descent,
Is an old act enacted, my fabulous intent
When I skated, afraid of policemen, five years old,
In the winter sunset, sorrowful and cold,
Hardly attained to thought, but old enough to know
Such grace, so self-contained, was the best escape to know.

Calmly We Walk through This April's Day

Calmly we walk through this April's day,
Metropolitan poetry here and there,
In the park sit pauper and *rentier*,
The screaming children, the motor-car
Fugitive about us, running away,
Between the worker and the millionaire
Number provides all distances,
It is Nineteen Thirty-Seven now,
Many great dears are taken away,
What will become of you and me
(This is the school in which we learn ...)
Besides the photo and the memory?
(... that time is the fire in which we burn.)

(This is the school in which we learn ...)
What is the self amid this blaze?
What am I now that I was then
Which I shall suffer and act again,
The theodicy I wrote in my high school days
Restored all life from infancy,
The children shouting are bright as they run
(This is the school in which they learn ...)
Ravished entirely in their passing play!
(... that time is the fire in which they burn.)

Avid its rush, that reeling blaze!
Where is my father and Eleanor?
Not where are they now, dead seven years,
But what they were then?
                         No more? No more?
From Nineteen-Fourteen to the present day,

Bert Spira and Rhoda consume, consume
Not where they are now (where are they now?)
But what they were then, both beautiful;

Each minute bursts in the burning room,
The great globe reels in the solar fire,
Spinning the trivial and unique away.
(How all things flash! How all things flare!)
What am I now that I was then?
May memory restore again and again
The smallest color of the smallest day:
Time is the school in which we learn,
Time is the fire in which we burn.

Dogs Are Shakespearean, Children Are Strangers

Dogs are Shakespearean, children are strangers.
Let Freud and Wordsworth discuss the child,
Angels and Platonists shall judge the dog,
The running dog, who paused, distending nostrils,
Then barked and wailed; the boy who pinched his sister,
The little girl who sang the song from *Twelfth Night*,
As if she understood the wind and rain,
The dog who moaned, hearing the violins in concert.
—O I am sad when I see dogs or children!
For they are strangers, they are Shakespearean.

Tell us, Freud, can it be that lovely children
Have merely ugly dreams of natural functions?
And you, too, Wordsworth, are children truly
Clouded with glory, learned in dark Nature?
The dog in humble inquiry along the ground,
The child who credits dreams and fears the dark,
Know more and less than you: they know full well
Nor dream nor childhood answer questions well:
You too are strangers, children are Shakespearean.

Regard the child, regard the animal,
Welcome strangers, but study daily things,
Knowing that heaven and hell surround us,
But this, this which we say before we're sorry,
This which we live behind our unseen faces,
Is neither dream, nor childhood, neither
Myth, nor landscape, final, nor finished,
For we are incomplete and know no future,
And we are howling or dancing out our souls
In beating syllables before the curtain:
We are Shakespearean, we are strangers.

I Am to My Own Heart Merely a Serf

I am to my own heart merely a serf
And follow humbly as it glides with autos
And come attentive when it is too sick,
In the bad cold of sorrow much too weak,
To drink some coffee, light a cigarette
And think of summer beaches, blue and gay.
I climb the sides of buildings just to get
Merely a gob of gum, all that is left
Of its infatuation of last year.
Being the servant of incredible assumption,
Being to my own heart merely a serf.

I have been sick of its cruel rule, as sick
As one is sick of chewing gum all day;
Only inside of sleep did all my anger
Spend itself, restore me to my role,
Comfort me, bring me to the morning
Willing and smiling, ready to be of service,
To box its shadows, lead its brutish dogs,
Knowing its vanity the vanity of waves.

But when sleep too is crowded, when sleep too
Is full of chores impossible and heavy,
The looking for white doors whose numbers are
Different and equal, that is, infinite,
The carriage of my father on my back,
Last summer, 1910, and my own people,
The government of love's great polity,
The choice of taxes, the production
Of clocks, of lights, and horses, the location
Of monuments, of hotels and of rhyme,
Then, then, in final anger, I wake up!

Merely wake up once more,
                              once more to resume
The unfed hope, the unfed animal,
Being the servant of incredible assumption,
Being to my own heart merely a serf.

The Heavy Bear Who Goes with Me

"the withness of the body"

The heavy bear who goes with me,
A manifold honey to smear his face,
Clumsy and lumbering here and there,
The central ton of every place,
The hungry beating brutish one
In love with candy, anger, and sleep,
Crazy factotum, dishevelling all,
Climbs the building, kicks the football,
Boxes his brother in the hate-ridden city.

Breathing at my side, that heavy animal,
That heavy bear who sleeps with me,
Howls in his sleep for a world of sugar,
A sweetness intimate as the water's clasp,
Howls in his sleep because the tight-rope
Trembles and shows the darkness beneath.
—The strutting show-off is terrified,
Dressed in his dress-suit, bulging his pants,
Trembles to think that his quivering meat
Must finally wince to nothing at all.

That inescapable animal walks with me,
Has followed me since the black womb held,
Moves where I move, distorting my gesture,
A caricature, a swollen shadow,
A stupid clown of the spirit's motive,
Perplexes and affronts with his own darkness,
The secret life of belly and bone,

Opaque, too near, my private, yet unknown,
Stretches to embrace the very dear
With whom I would walk without him near,
Touches her grossly, although a word
Would bare my heart and make me clear,
Stumbles, flounders, and strives to be fed
Dragging me with him in his mouthing care,
Amid the hundred million of his kind,
The scrimmage of appetite everywhere.

A Dog Named Ego, the Snowflakes as Kisses

A dog named Ego, the snowflakes as kisses
Fluttered, ran, came with me in December,
Snuffing the chill air, changing, and halting,
There where I walked toward seven o'clock,
Sniffed at some interests hidden and open,
Whirled, descending, and stood still, attentive
Seeking their peace, the stranger, unknown,
With me, near me, kissed me, touched my wound,
My simple face, obsessed and pleasure bound.

"Not free, no liberty, rock that you carry,"
So spoke Ego in his cracked and harsh voice,
While snowflakes kissed me and satisfied minutes,
Falling from some place half believed and unknown,
"You will not be free, nor ever alone,"
So spoke Ego, "Mine is the kingdom,
Dynasty's bone: you will not be free,
Go, choose, run, you will not be alone."

"Come, come, come," sang the whirling snowflakes,
Evading the dog who barked at their smallness,
"Come!" sang the snowflakes, "Come here! and here!"
How soon at the sidewalk, melted, and done,
One kissed me, two kissed me! So many died!
While Ego barked at them, swallowed their touch,
Ran this way! And that way! While they slipped to the ground,
Leading him further and farther away,
While night collapsed amid the falling,
And left me no recourse, far from my home,
And left me no recourse, far from my home.

from GENESIS: BOOK I (1943)

Editor's note

Genesis was Schwartz's most ambitious and least successful work.
A sprawling book-length poem interspersed with narrative prose,
it was intended, through the alter ego of Hershey Green, to tell
Schwartz's life story, and by extension, the story of European
Jews in America. The poem begins as Green is interrupted in his
sleep, visited by anxious thoughts and memories, as well as by a
host of jovial if cynical spirits who egg him on to tell his tale. In
the prose sections, he begins with his ancestors' lives in Europe,
and works his way to his own seventh year in America. In verse
passages that separate the prose, the ghosts comment in sometimes gorgeously lyrical, sometimes plodding poetry.

    The narrative structure alone would make *Genesis* a hard book
to excerpt, but further complicating the matter is its uneven quality. The prose is often flat, slow, and sentimental, and the voices
of the ghosts in verse are often unbelievable or downright silly.
But there isn't a page without good, even great lines and passages.

    Genesis was deeply important to Schwartz; in phases of manic
self-confidence, he thought the poem would make him immortal,

and when despairing he thought it a complete failure. I have chosen to include these selections not because they show Schwartz
at his best, but because this work was central to his conception
of himself as a person and as a writer. Also, almost none of this
book has been available since its initial printing in 1943. A full
view of what Schwartz worked to accomplish would be incomplete without it.

I have used this symbol [~] to indicate breaks between selections. My selections begin with the poem's opening passage.

Selections

"…. Me next to sleep, all that is left of Eden,"
—The one who speaks is not remarkable
In the great city, circa 1930,
His state is not uncommon in the world,
O, by no means, sleepless and seeking sleep
As one who wades in water to the thighs,
Dragging it soft and heavy near the shore;
For now his body's lapse and ignorance
Permits his heavy mind certain loose sleeves,
Loose sleeves of feeling drawing near a drowse:
He knows of dark and sleep the unity,
He knows all being's consanguinity,
All anguish sinks into the first of seas,
The sea which soothes with softness ultimate
—Thus he descends,
                        and coughs, coughs!
                                        the old cold comes,
Jack-in-the-box, the conscious mind snaps up!
—He wakes,
                his fuzzed gaze strains the dark,
And at the window's outline looks, in shock,
To see a certain whiteness glitter there,

Snow! dragging him to the window
With hurried heart. The childhood love still lives in him,
Like a sweet tooth in grown-up married girls,
December's white delight, a fourth year wish,
The classic swan disguised in modern life,
Freedom and silence shining in New York!
But, standing by the window, sees the truth,
Four stories down the blank courtyard on which
The moonlight shines, diagonal and pale
—And high, the moon's half-cut and glittering shell
Shines like the ice on which electric shines—
Says to himself, "How each view may be false!"
And then the whole thing happens all over again,
Waking, walking to the window, looking out,
Seeking for snow in May, a miracle
Quick in the dozing head's compelled free mix
—He sees the snow which is not snow, but light,
The moonlight's lie, error's fecundity
Fallen from the dead planet near the roof—

Absolute dark and dream space fall on him,
And he through dark and space begins to fall,
At first afraid, then horrified, then calm.
Then the wide stillness in which dream belief
Begins, prepared for all. And he begins
Once more to tell himself all that he knows
Over and over and over and over again,
All of the lives that have come close to his,
All of his life, much mixed in memory
Many a night through which he cannot sleep,
Many a year, over and over again!

But now a voice begins, strange in the dark,
As from a worn victrola record, needle
Which skims and whirrs, a voice intoned

As of a weak old man with foreign accent,
Ironic, comic, flat and matter of fact,
With alternation measured, artificial,

                          moaned,
And yet with sympathy, *simpatico*

                          as if
A guardian angel sang!

                     Then other voices,
Bodiless in the dark, entered in chorus:
"He must tell all, amazed as the three Magi
When they beheld the puking child! All is
Not natural! That's Life, the Magi too
Might have remarked to one another, Life
Full of all things but what one would expect—"

And he who listened said then to himself,
"A daemon, a daemon, no doubt: who else?
Such as was heard by Socrates, perhaps,
Or an angel, the angel who struggled with Jacob,
If Jacob lived, if angels also live—"

To which one voice cried back, as if in echo,
"Rome and romance of Death, what Mutt and Jeff,
Quixote, Alcestis, Jacob, Uncle Sam,
Hamlet and Holmes look down on all of you!
What King and Queen of Hearts as playing cards?
What President or Pharaoh on a coin?
—Your mind, kept waiting by a desperate hope
For the epiphany which starlight seems
Here where Long Island like a liner slants
To the great city, Europe's last capital,
Now must suppose in Being's surprises nothing less
Than singers who have soared through many keys,
Justice, Forgiveness, and Knowledge in their cries!—"

"A number of the dead have come to you,
O Hershey Green!"
                    "Have come to me?" he cried,
He shouted out, rapt in the absolute dark,
As one who in an empty valley bound by rocks
Shouts and awaits with some hope something more
Than merely his own voice in echo bruised,
And merely his own heart,
                        "Have come to you!
Hallucination holds you by the head,
Many a night you told yourself your life,
Tell it to us, we have no more to do,
Tell it to the immortal dead in the stone
And the chill of their—O so this is it!—conclusion …"
"Is this a true thing?" Hershey Green in the dark
And stillness spoke out again, leaning to hear
If once again his speech would bring back speech,
"O it is true enough! Many are dead.
Come, with your endless story," one voice said,
"Hallucination leads you by the hand,
This is the way to freedom and to power,
This is the way to knowledge and to hope,
This is the way the world begins and ends,
Logos, man's inner being going out—"

~

The child was born late at night in the middle of winter.
   Jack Green was overwhelmed with joy, excited and exalted as
never before in his life. An hour after the child was dragged head-
first with the help of instruments
   From his mother's womb, Jack Green called his relatives and
his friends to tell them that he had a son. Snow had begun to fall
from the low-hanging sky,

Pink-grey with the city lights, when Jack Green woke relatives
and friends from the warmth of sleep: his emotion overflowed
and demanded expression and required surrounding and answering voices,

He had to tell everyone! His mother-in-law said to him, They
are sleeping, they will be angry. But he could not be stopped,

He spoke with warmth to people he had been cool to for years.
His joy placed him outside himself,

He called his brother Albert and spoke with eloquence over
the instantaneous miles, saying he had been wrong and on such
an occasion

All must be forgiven. Everyone is always wrong all the time,
answered Albert, wakened from sleep, too little awake in early
morning

To know exactly what he was saying—

"The tears are icicles upon his cheeks
As the poor boy arrives at his first breath—"

"O Life is wonderful beyond belief
Here most of all, in parenthood's great pleasure …"

"What egotism is so sharp and deaf
(Sharp as the knife and deaf as rock), which lives
That it can quite resist the infant's face,
The fresh identity, the bawling life?"

"Ravished is Everyman by the small sight!
Faced by the double face and breathing twice
—The harder that the ego pained itself (like ice,
Pressed to the skin, a heavy iron-like pain),
The greater joy abounds! joy overflows …"

"This I always find touching, that great joy
Cannot contain itself, but overflows,

The body must run up and down the stairs,
Shout the good news and kiss the passing stranger,
—Joy drives such overwhelming energy—
Any move will express, dance out, and free
The body from the terrifying pleasure—"

"The father's joy is a new class of joy,
—First Abraham, after his hopeless years—"

"Forgiveness for his brother and his friends!
Success is kind when quite secure and sure,
Success must buy the drinks, hand out cigars
(These actions are the same as sorrow's tears!),
And is in this emotion just as blind
And self-absorbed as invalids, as cruel
As disappointment!
                    At two o'clock in the morning,
Jack Green must call his relatives and friends!"

"Thus may new goodness make the evil good
—I am a hopeless optimist, I know!"

The day came when the child was to be given a name, a name
announcing the unique inimitable psyche,
    And the tiny foreskin was to be cut with the knife which
reached across five thousand years from Palestine,
    Making him with this last turn of the knife even unto coitus
fully a member of the people chosen for wandering and alienation.
    Eva wished to name him Noah, after her dead father, who had
come to America with his anger, but her mother did not want her
to use that name.
    Eva turned over a dozen names in her mind, unable to decide
which one she liked best until

She thought of the neighbor's child, four years of age, fat and happy,

Whom Eva had looked at fondly and fondled during her barren unhappy years. His name was Harold, but he called himself Hershey, a German version, because he was obsessed with chocolate, and amused adults had come to call him Hershey, Hershey Bar, struck by the quaintness,

Extending the smile of amusement at the child with this poem. And Eva had vowed in a moment of delight with the child, that if she had a child, she would name him Hershey, for, looking at him, she saw the image of what she wanted her child to be:

She decided in a moment, Baby Green was named Hershey, howling his pain and ignorance when his foreskin was cut,

And all thought twenty years in advance of the next generation—

"Lo, with what tenderness he speaks his name,
As if he spoke a scandal or a fame!"

"Why not? It is a sign of the self's darkness,
The private darkness of the individual
The anguished darkness of the struggling will,
The sound which means the ego is alone,
The bass of harbor boats, alone, alone!
The pathos of departure's fogbound moan,
The self's self-exile from the womb and home—"

"The basis of the art of poetry,
The hard identity felt in the bone—"

"The basis of the art of music, too,
The self-same darkness flows from orchestras,
The brilliant congress of the instruments
Merely goes walking in what wilderness—"

"His name might have been Noah: beautiful!
Suggests so much a boat on desperate seas—"

"Hershey, I think, is best, the Hershey Bar,
A bitter chocolate or a milk sweet chocolate
—Such is the self, knowing and gnawing the body,
When the decayed teeth of the Pleasure-Principle
Bite it, by the sweet senses' candies pained!"

"There is a joke which grows within my mind:
Here is a stadium and cheering crowd,
Pigeons pass overhead, and one lets go
(Nature's necessities are all his life),
—The one man wet amid the 70,000
Cries out, Here are 70,000 faces,
Why did that pigeon have to pick on me?
—The joke of individuality!
O what a practical joke on everyone,
Something is always new under the sun!"

"Enough, dear friend in this, the last illness,
Now let us shift the image for the boy—"

"Let us regard the deities once more,
Augment his story with our world-wide views,
He pleads for it, he looks for it himself
—Let us look down from heights, from Everest—"

"Or from a star, or from Eternity,
O from Eternity, that is, from Death:
What huge divinities move near the child,
Small as a pebble by a mountain side!"

"Lo, by a mountain range! which, lumbering,
Booming and thundering, begins to quake

—As if Creation first cracked nothingness!
Concussion's stroke rides through the city air—
No lesser trope can be as adequate,
The grandson of two Noahs, running away!
—How many other deities are near!—"

"Europe, America, and Israel,
—Israel bearing, as the boy just said,
The knife which cut the foreskin Moses knew,
Comes for five thousand years from Palestine!"

"How many other deities are near,
And soon, the Great War's shocking scrimmages!"

"—How wise in intuition of his life
The bawling baby screaming at the knife!"

"But let the obsessed boy renew his story,
So interesting, leaning to what comes next—"

~

"America, America! O Land
Whence come chiefly the poor hurt peoples
Who for a reason good or bad cannot endure
Or be endured by the old *Vaterland*
—Being a Jew, or being a younger son, being
A Quaker, or among the wise who think
The world may end on any seventh day,
A most dynamic and dramatic view of Life—"

"That Barnum knew America quite well,
He knew the gold rush which the populace
Would run to as to fires. And he knew
The love of freaks, the hatred of the norm,
The passion for monstrosity and shock!"

"Land of the failure! land of the refugee!
Land of the gold like oranges on trees,
Land of the European man who holds
St. Patrick's Day or Budapest in him
—Moving in such a crowd, Jack Green grew fat
With this world's goods!"

                              "Lo, the relation here
Between the immigrant and immigrant
New come: just as the card sharp to the hilt
Uses his victims' greed, which is in him
Sharper perhaps, but under strict control
(Knowledge of weakness is a mighty strength!)
—Self-knowledge marks the cards and takes the pot
And gives moral dominion to the soul!"

"Thus it is, thus it has always been!
The criminal like the saint needs discipline!"

"What an America! Adams and James
Return how many times to Europe's shore
As the new troops pass them, in reverse,
(O heavy irony of all such passages!)
And heartsick go to the grave, crying aloud
—We did not know the causes of our lives,
We know at last we did not know our lives!"

" 'Who is Vermeer?' asked Pierpont Morgan then,
And paid one hundred thousand dollars when
It was explained to him. He was a king!
A financier! master of many hearts!
—Mark Twain preferred cigar store Indians
To all the noble statues which he toured
In Florence and in Rome. He sneered for fun!
—'I never in my life had any fun,
I never did the things I wished to do!'

Mourned a tycoon, who owned America!
—Red caps, glass beads, and many other things
Little in value first he gave to them,
And stared for gold among most beautiful trees:
O clemens, o pia, o dulces Maria!
This was the first day of America!
All of these immigrants ruined by the ride!"

~

Hershey's ego defined itself further by means of father, mother and brother.

During these years, when the fog of infancy, blooming and booming, slowly lifted,

Hershey often sat in the window-seat which looked out on a street in the middle of which

A trolley passed, yellow and red in broad stripes, sparking the wire,

Delighting him more than any other object! It was to him a thing of inexhaustible interest, ever-renewed,

A kind of boat, sliding, skating, singing, stopping, and beginning again,

Presenting him with movement which is the beginning of drama, an obvious miracle passing at regular intervals:

And thus it was that when, one day, a middle-aged friend of Eva Green brought her son's fiancée to the apartment, and when the engaged girl, who was very pretty, drew the child to her

And kissed him! as if he were her future, his plump childness pleasing her, then did he cry out joyously,

'Trolley, trolley!" his first metaphor, the swift perception of a resemblance between different things. For he meant to say

The pretty lady who kisses me delights me like the trolley.

All the adults were delighted and applauded him and petted him,

Until his success grew warm in him, although he hardly knew why—

"Come now, this is too good, too pure a sign!
Kissed by the fiancée, the girl engaged
In going to the fête where privacies
Mix in the act which makes societies
—Too pat, too easy, and too pure a sign!"

"A fiancée; the quintessential flower:
Who better shall draw from the little boy
The first of all the many metaphors
With which he will enact his hope and fear?"

"How in this death we need the metaphor:
We go from trope to trope like acrobats!"

"Surprises, Being's surprises everywhere,
—Cumuli clouds full of ontologies!"

"We in our death enjoy this very much,
Seeing how one thing is another thing
In certain ways, a girl being a rose
In certain ways, a poet being a train
(Because he takes you where you have not been),
Painting as light, sleep as essential sin
(Being a desperate abandonment)...."

"Light is the heroine of all the paintings,
The camera is the hero of the screen!"

"Such metaphors are pleasant. But some come
Which show us with their light how much we missed
(Who were not those on whom *nothing is lost*)
When we were there and *could*; and might have loved ..."

"How much we did not see when we were there,
Walking through Life self-blinded by desire

111

—Such metaphors like the rack torture us
With utter memory and that remorse
Forever *late*, which is the greatest pain!"

~

"Now I will really know how good it is
To have the sleep of Eden, like a tree,
I will bear this in mind like a man reprieved
(O how their voices influence my voice!)
And make myself think of the horror which
I have escaped! enjoying *everything*,
Taking keen pleasure in the smallest things,
Tying my laces, or sharpening a pencil—"

Yet as he spoke, he feared it was not true,
And yet enjoyed it all as he enjoyed
Soft drinks on summer days after a game,
Gulped down to drown the throat's pulsating need—
His pride rose with these thoughts, vainglorious,
—O like a raving fire leaping up!
He told himself all that his mind might do,
Half-doubting and half hoping it was true:

"As Adam named the beasts, with careful love,
I name the animals and the divinities
Who walk about this newfoundland, America,
(Europe the greatest thing in North America!
For instance, as one voice just said to me)
—As Socrates, who questioned everything
Because his love was great, because he loved
Life very much, but not too much, and not
Enough to accept a life without the stars,
Thus now I'll flick the salt of intellect
Upon all things, the critical salt which makes
All qualities most vivid and acute—

As Joseph, I'll enact my sweet revenge
In basic psychological reviews,
Accuse the innocents who perjured me,
Me innocent: showing sublimely then,
The Justice who uncovers innocence,
Omniscient, generous, O all forgiving
And most successful brother who displays
How he was right throughout, in his conceit,
All dreams come true, and every feat performed—"

Then said a far-off singer in his style
Breaking in suddenly on Hershey's peace,
"Let go this braggadocio, young man!
… *Dunamos*, dynamite, puissance, Power,
Divinity secretly close to the will
Like May beside the leaf: listen and speak,
The chorus is an ancient well-known goodness,
Like bread and wine, although more difficult. Cause
Is the secrecy and mystery. The Seed
Is marvellous. Let us look down on it. The Star …
Everything is a part and in the pit
Of all the nexi, darkness is cat-black,
In between sleeping and waking, part by part
(And once the sun blared like a lion, and once
The starlight fell like a petal, piercing the eye—)"

And then another ghost assumed the theme,
"Lincoln is on a penny in the mind,
A canton of the spirit! Rises and speaks!
And Jeeves and Cinderella show the boat
We all are in, the rotten ship of state!
Chaplin shuffles and tips his hat! Then runs!
John Bull and Uncle Sam are not cartoons
But heavy actual bullies boxing through us!
They move through all of us, like summer fine:
Keep thinking all the time, O New York boy!

Go back,
In each, all natural being once more lives!
The subtile serpent which the apple brought
To Mamma and to Papa, starting all!
Caesar and Caesar's pal also in you,
Also the servant and the comedian,
—Lo, he has set the world in each man's heart!
And both the lamb and lion are quick in you,
The mountain and the lake, the tree and stone
All of these kinds their being must renew
—When you lie down to sleep, they rise in you!"

"Let us fly off and tour the world awhile,
Freely and frankly, going from branch to branch,
To show the boy *trouvailles* within the mind,
Many Americas found suddenly,
Surprise upon surprise upon surprise!"

"As, once I saw two nuns, like cameras;
There they were, taking pictures of modern life!"

"Remember this, young man, as we fly on,
Verdi at eighty-seven kneeled beneath
The bed to find a fallen collar-stud,
And apoplexy struck him down. Alas!
"Twas this he left out of his operas,
—Of actuality, the ragged richness!
Bend down under the bed and look for this!
O hear the children coming home from school,
And hear the gunshots of the starting car,
And hear the thin strings of the telephone,
And Sister's ennui, practising her scales,
And see the cinders and the broken glass—"

"And yet, behold the heart within these things:
Change jingled in his pocket like gay pleasure,

And his checked tie was what an attitude.
In his lapel a flower quoted Nature—"

"And more and more, behold the dialectic,
How light brings shadow, how the evil, good,
And how each eminence needs lowness near,
And how each eminence brings straining Iago,
And too much good makes too much sorrow soon—"

"The mind skates like a falling star! the mind
Speeds between heaven and earth like Light itself!"

"The gold, the vivid, and the actual
Will melt like flakes upon the open hand,
The mind in memory alone can live
(How many times I climbed on hands and knees
This Himalaya, depth on every side),
The memory alone can hold the self!
Logos alone can understand the blue—"

"If one but knew, if one knew Being-hood,
—This is as if we sat after a dinner,
And heard of many years in unity,
Or noble lords and ladies who have left
The city struck by plague, passing the time—"

"In us, all natural being once more lives,
—A skein of geese, a walk of snipe,
A murmuration of starlings, an exultation
Of larks, a watch of nightingales, a host
Of sparrows, a cast of hawks, a pride of lions,
                                    a sloth of bears,
A route of wolves, a rag of colts,
                                    a mute of hounds,
A cowardice of curs, a shrewdness of apes,
A luxury of nymphs, a lilt of mares,

A round of girls, a dark of plays, a jig
Of vaudeville, a crowd of joys
—Blue grapes and yellow pears beside a jar!
—All of this life and more, much more in us!
Later we will unmask, singing our names!"

"—Her privates we, yet ignorant in death,
We wait to see Eternity's worst views—"

Then said another singer in his style,
"*In medias res*, in the middle of Life,
In the middle of everything, sick boy,
—Where is the first of consciousness, where is
Where first-hand memory begins for you—"

"Eden, image of many complex thoughts
About beginning, hangs just like a picture
In many living rooms in the Western World;
Later, we might consider it; not now, later—"

"Begin in any place in consciousness,
Life and each part of Life is infinite,
Infinitely divisible, traversable,
And visible! seek out the motives there—"

"O seek, he means the depths of the Past from which
The soul's moves rise as grasses from the earth—"

~

And then one day Hershey played by the door of the apartment house, when three of the other boys, always friends before
now, members of the kindergarten class,
    Took up the janitor's hose, coiled serpentine on the sidewalk,
and suddenly turned it on Hershey, crying,

You are a Jew! a Jew! Hershey ran away all wet from the bap-
tismal flood of the communal mind,

He ran away to his mother, asking her what was wrong, what
was being a Jew?

But she did not answer, he did not know so well, wetly, and
sensuously, until far later years.

She took his hand and rang the doorbell where one of his opponents lived,

And protested to his mother in a loud self-righteous tone,
which made Hershey ashamed, although he hardly knew why,

But knew that more than he understood defended and offended him,

And knew with passion that laughter thrown at him by boys
pitted against him was one of the worst pains, and that other boys
turning on him

Stripped him, even if he ran to his mother, stripped him and
left him alone, naked, wet and ashamed.

And then one day when his father gave him a fountain pen, and
he lost it the very next day,

Playing in the empty lot behind the apartment house. He went
and told his mother and begged her then, securing her promise,

Not to tell his father. But when in the evening his father came
to see him go to bed, his father asked him and asking smiled,

Where his fountain pen was? When Hershey began to lie, Jack
Green smiled still more broadly, the lying child was a joke, or the
lying child was himself,

And said to the poor pajama'd boy that he knew he had lost his
fountain pen, and gave him another one, his own, a better one, the
best, and for some time admired by him,

And then Hershey knew such joy as Adam might have known,
had his father brought him back to a greater Eden,

Making his loss his gain. But in the midst of his joy, Hershey
saw that his mother had betrayed him,

He saw there was a communication between his parents which
would always betray him.

Because he was a child.

"Poor boy, how education comes to you!
Learning to be a Jew, attacked because
A Jew, born to the long habit of pain
And alienation, of the people chosen for pain...."

"Attacked for the first time because you are
A kind, a class! as you were not yourself,
The pain of the sole psyche insufficient,
The naked surd's self-torture not enough!"

"Thus to begin, in sudden dripping shock,
Abstractions' mastery, as if a teacher
Taught species, genus, higher genera,
Slapping his student's face as if to say
This is what faceness is, learn it through pain:
How better than in shock to learn of terms?"

Hershey felt now as when his hands and arms
Fell asleep, powerless, too weak in strength
To hold a cigarette, or hold a pin....

"Now of betrayal, now these far-off singers
Will speak of parents' and betrayals' first—"
Hershey prepared himself, speaking these words,
Once more in mimicry of what he heard—

"The loss of faith's virginity, the sense
That anyone might lie, as when the earth's
Flatness turned out to be a curving lie,
Falseness objective in the turning world
—The sense that always underneath the face
Many a motive hid the truth, prepared
Illusions, made the mirage, deceived!"

"Life is a lie! Life is a long long lie,"
Another far voice cried, "Death is a news

Life painted differently! What have we now
But this eternal knowledge and regret,
Not an oblivion … at best, a sweet drugged sleep
When we are lucky! the sleep of hospitals—
True, one gets used to pain as one gets used
To living near a waterfall or trains,
But I cannot believe I will become
Used to regret, return, the infinite
Apocalypse of all that might have been,
Millions of instances shown in these lives,
Every future untrue and every hope,
Even in satisfaction, vain and false,
Since no success is terminus, serene.…"

"The hanged man like a sack upon a tree
Cannot believe the freedom of the will—"

~

"Happy as some in May, in the May morning,
When sunlight stamps gold coins on the blazed gaze,
And on the river does the diamond-dance,
—These sensuous skins, alas, obsess the life—"

"O Sun of Nature! source of all the forces,
All blooms, all snakes, and Botticelli's views
Of both of these, and Nature as a dance:
(Light is the heroine of every picture—)"

"O what a glory has the turning world!
And that is why some say that God himself
Took on this flesh:

to be God was not enough
To feel in blues and greens of natural life
Immediacies they have, like any kiss—"

"I hardly know just what it means to me,
But when I hear the word, my soul soars,
Strong as a gull over the evil shores
Of this unending terrifying night—"

"Hear how he speaks like us, now more and more—"

"Again, go back, see how Christ's story lives,
Born in the winter, risen from the year
As once in Palestine—

                              "If you were wise!
Like the three Magi all your attitudes,
Expecting any kind of Paradise,
In any poverty or paradox!"

"See how the Bible rules the consciousness
Of the West for two thousand years:
                              O, what a book!"

"Bible and Ovid too! who brings to us
Leda, Medea, Psyche, she who wished
To look at Love's forbidden hidden face,
Long before Sigmund Freud looked down on it,
And saw the serpent climbing up the stairs—"

"Psyche arrived after the birth of Christ!"

"The Sistine Chapel is the Western mind!"

"The snow: obsessed with it! This we must know
And understand; his love of it unceasing
In the deep mind beneath the conscious mind
Whence many motives rise up to command!"

"The gift! the bicycle! the gift of motion,
As he had loved the street-car years ago,
Since motion, as the Stagirite once said,
Is being's deepest wish, most general form...."

"Gift from the doubted wished-for nameless *Ahhhhhhh*
—Amid snatches of sleep, dreaming of snow!"

~

"Manic-depressive Lincoln, national hero!
How just that this great nation, being conceived
In liberty by fugitives should find
—Strange ways and plays of monstrous History—
This Hamlet-type to be the President—"

"This failure, this unwilling bridegroom,
This tricky lawyer full of black despair—"

"He grew a beard, becoming President,
And took a shawl as if he guessed his rôle,
Though with the beard he fled cartoonists' blacks,
And many laughed and were contemptuous,
And some for four years spoke of killing him—"

"He was a politician—of the heart!—
He lived from hand to mouth in moral things!
He understood quite well Grant's drunken-ness!
It was for him, before Election Day,
That at Cold Harbor Grant threw lives away
In hopeless frontal attack against Lee's breastworks!"

"O how he was the Hamlet-man, and this,
After a life of failure made him right,

After he ran away on his wedding day,
Writing a coward's letter to his bride—"

"How with his very failure, he out-tricked
The florid Douglas and the abstract Davis,
And all the vain men who, surrounding him,
Smiled in their vanity and sought his place—"

"Later, they made him out a prairie Christ
To sate the need coarse in the national heart—"

"His wife went insane, Mary Todd too often
Bought herself dresses. And his child died.
And he would not condemn young men to death
For having slept, in weakness. And he spoke
More than he knew and all that he had felt
Between outrageous joy and black despair
Before and after Gettysburg's *pure peak*—"

"He studied law, but knew in his own soul
Despair's anarchy, terror and error,
—Instruments had to be taken from his office
And from his bedroom in such days of horror,
Because some saw that he might kill himself:
When he was young, when he was middle-aged,
How just and true was he, our national hero!"

"Sometimes he could not go home to face his
    wife,
Sometimes he wished to hurry or end his life!"

"But do not be deceived. He did not win,
And, it is plain, the South could never win
(Despite the gifted Northern generals!)
—Capitalismus is not mocked, O no!
This stupid deity decided the War—"

"In fact, the North and South were losers both:
—Capitalismus won the Civil War—"

"—Capitalismus won the Civil War,
Yet, in the War's cruel Colosseum,
Some characters fulfilled their natures' surds,
Grant the drunkard, Lee the noble soldier,
John Brown in whom the Bible soared and cried,
Booth the unsuccessful Shakespearean,
—Each in some freedom walked and knew himself,
Then most of all when all the deities
Mixed with their barbarous stupidity
To make the rock, root, and rot of the war—"

"This is the way each only life becomes,
Tossed on History's ceaseless insane sums!"

~

"A wise man says, Religion is what man
Does with his solitude: what a remark!
—We know, do we not know? what some men do
When left alone: Arnauld declared that Man
Was capable of any monstrous act
When left in solitude in his own room
—Pascal, his pupil, on the other hand,
Observed that all our trouble and our pain
Sprang from the failure to stay in one's room?
—*Les extrêmes se touchent*: these poles which meet
Define a circle of uneasiness,
Somewhat a swaying sea. We are but sailors—"

"The early morning light becomes a sign:
It is the snow! Even as sometimes snow
Stands for the early morning light. These shifts
Show Baudelaire and Freud were well-advised,

Saying, Man walks through a dark wood of symbols,
All his life long, no matter what he does—"

"I when I heard of God from black despair
Rose always like a bird; quickly, lightly,
Prone in the former life to utter sadness
Because my efforts fell short many times:
I said to myself, 'An infinite God!
If such a being really exists, he hears
What I am saying now. Does He not know
All, look at all, see all with perfect views?
And if He hears me, is it not possible
—Although I am not sure—that He will help me?
Is it a profanation of the pure Idea
Which makes me think that He really exists
To think that He will aid me in my pain?
                                        Can I be sure?'"

"I too would think these thoughts, also unsure,
—And yet, thinking these thoughts I always rose,
I was less desperate, I could endure
My dark body's awkward brutality,
I could endure my soul's black guilt which hoped
The world would end, and all things, screaming, *die*,
Because I was in my ambition stopped
The while my brother, friend, and enemy
Succeeds with seeming spontaneity,
And wins the girl, acclaim, the world's applause!
Yes! when I thought of God Himself *an sich*,
It was *enough*, although I knew He judged,
Judging the world in me! ... Infinite joy
Flooded me then, as if I came to the shore
Of the cold sea upon a summer's day,
And let my dear dark body be by water's silk
All over touched and known! This was my stay,

My hope, my wish, my ground, my good, my God!"

"Will Hershey Green go down this old abyss
Of thought in days to come, since now he asks
Questions and answers of the Catholic boy?
—How can he help but go, being what he is?"

"The Sunday-looking people, like big flowers,
Know many shades, however secular:
They know the heart hangs down, a Christmas stocking,
They feel strange drafts, however warm the May,
They know that Nature sails like a Zeppelin
Precarious aloft in a dark void:
The fool hath said in his heart, There is no God!
—He marks the fall of sparrows, verily!"

"Everything happens in the mind of God,
This is the play it is, ever since Eden!"

"Let me revive my passions, far from this,
Although as relevant to the agonist,
Let me go off upon a candid cadenza,
Running through memories as shuffling cards:
—Branded by parents with identity,
(Mama and Papa who with private parts
Most irresponsibly began this *crise*,)
I sailed the seven seas, I saw the Czar,
Millions of mighty men sang through my soul,
The stars stretched out senseless as alphabets,
I thought the world was anybody's fun!
Gemütlichkeit was like the sunlight then!
The golded charging and electric earth
Appealed to me, full of such plants and sweets!
I saw the infamy which made me rich,
Capitalismus native to the heart,

Nothing like that before for egotism,
Never such forms and such fine playing fields!
I saw the evil of the average man
—Clio! between your legs obscenities
Performed and pushed! Jesus and Socrates
Downed by the populace with happiness,
—I saw all modern life in Street & Smith,
Promised virility, and social charm,
Strong muscles and trapped breasts hailed in the ads,
Yet Life was wonderful, beyond belief,
Wine was a light, and all the arts were lights,
The dancers with their discipline destroyed
The chaos and the waste of Broadway crowds,
They with their limbs an inner order knew,
They took it. with an easy willingness,
I took it too, from an orchestra seat
—But when will the houselights of the universe
Go on? You! You! trapped in your childhood!
Let us go back to the past, quickly and smoothly
The dark water closes its lips on today—"

~

"O Father of all hearts, give this poor boy the power
To speak his naked heart without excessive nausea,
O Dream behind the Dream, give him the strength
To see himself with disgust full depth and full length!"

"The history of Life repeats its endless circle,
                    over and over and over again,
In the new boy, in the new city, in the time forever new,
                    forever old,
—All of the famous characters are glimpsed again,

All the well-known events; yet something new,
Unique, undying, free, blessèd or damned!"

"Everything happens in the mind of God:
                    This is all
You need for wondrous hope, and this we give,
                    Sleepless Atlantic boy!"

                    "O no!
You do not give that, but give greater darkness,
All this is but a fixed hallucination
Made by the passion of imagination:
This may be false, if I know anything,
I do not know that all is in the mind of God,
I do not have that hope miraculous,
I am more certain of all other things,
The bed, the darkness, and my dear dark body
Are with me, certain,
                    God is a dream! And this is what
I do not know and have to know. O *if*
I only knew *that!* then what other lights on all—"

Thus Hershey Green, drawn in the opera,
Thrilled and enthralled by each new aria!

"Poor New York boy, with what finality
You will in time say,—and triumphantly!—
O what a metaphysical victory
The first morning and night of death must be!"

                    END OF BOOK ONE

from VAUDEVILLE
FOR A PRINCESS (1950)

True Recognition Often Is Refused

We poets by the past and future used
Stare east and west distractedly at times,
Knowing there are, in fullness and in flower,
Chrysanthemums and Mozart in the room,
A stillness and a motion, both in bloom.

Or know a girl upon the sofa's ease,
Curved like a stocking, being profoundly round,
As rich and dark as April's underground.
We see in strict perception probity,
The lasting soil and good of all our art,
Which purifies the nervous turned-in heart.

And when we hear in music's empty halls
Torn banners blowing in the rain and shame,
We know these passages are surfaces,
Knowing that our vocation cannot be
Merely a Sunday with the beautiful.
There is pace and grace we must fulfill.

For we must earn through dull dim suffering,
Through ignorance and darkened hope, and hope
Risen again, and clouded over again, and dead despair,
And many little deaths, hardly observed,
The early morning light we have deserved.

Starlight like Intuition Pierced the Twelve

The starlight's intuitions pierced the twelve,
The brittle night sky sparkled like a tune
Tinkled and tapped out in the xylophone.
Empty and vain, a glittering dune, the moon
Arose too big, and, in the mood which ruled,
Seemed like a useless beauty in a pit;
And then one said, after he carefully spat:
"No matter what we do, he looks at it!

"I cannot see a child or find a girl
Beyond his smile which glows like that spring moon."
"—Nothing no more the same," the second said,
"Though all may be forgiven, never quite healed
The wound I bear as witness, standing by;
No ceremony surely appropriate,
Nor secret love, escape or sleep because
No matter what I do, he looks at it—"

"Now," said the third, "no thing will be the same:
I am as one who never shuts his eyes,
The sea and sky no more are marvelous,
And I no longer understand surprise!"
"Now," said the fourth, "nothing will be enough,
—I heard his voice accomplish all wit:
No word can be unsaid, no deed withdrawn,
—No matter what is said, he measures it!"

"Vision, imagination, hope or dream,
Believed, denied, the scene we wished to see?
It does not matter in the least: for what
Is altered, if it is not true? That we
Saw goodness, as it is—*this* is the awe
And the abyss which we will not forget,
His story now the sky which holds all thought:
No matter what I think, I think of it!"

"And I will never be what once I was,"
Said one for long as narrow as a knife,
"And we will never be what once we were;
We have died once: this is a second life."
My mind is spilled in moral chaos," one
Righteous as Job exclaimed, "now infinite
Suspicion of my heart stems what I will,
—No matter what I choose, he stares at it!"

"I am as one native in summer places
—Ten weeks' excitement paid for by the rich;
Debauched by that and then all winter bored,"
The sixth declared. "It is peak left us a ditch!"
"He came to make this life more difficult,"
The seventh said, "No one will ever fit
His measure's heights, all is inadequate;
No matter what I do, what good is it?"

"He gave forgiveness to us: what a gift?"
The eighth chimed in. "But now we know how much
Must be forgiven. But if forgiven, what?
The crime which was will be; and the least touch
Revives the memory: what is forgiveness worth?"
The ninth spoke thus: "Who now will ever sit
At ease in Zion at the easter feast?
No matter what the place, he touches it!"

"And I will always stammer, since he spoke,"
One, who had been most eloquent, said, stammering,
"I looked too long at the sun; like too much light,
So too much goodness is a boomerang,"
Laughed the eleventh of the troop. "I must
Try what he tried: I saw the infinite
Who walked the lake and raised the hopeless dead:
No matter what the feat, he first accomplished it!"

So spoke the twelfth; and then the twelve in chorus:
"Unspeakable unnatural goodness is
Risen and shines, and never will ignore us;
He glows forever in all consciousness;
Forgiveness, love, and hope possess the pit,
And bring our endless guilt, like shadow's bars:
No matter what we do, he stares at it!
What pity then deny? what debt defer?
We know he looks at us like all the stars,
And we shall never be as once we were,
This life will never be what once it was!"

He Heard the Newsboys Shouting "Europe! Europe!"

Dear Citizens,
I heard the newsboys shouting "Europe! Europe!"
It was late afternoon, a winter's day
Long as a prairie, wool and ashen gray,
And then I heard the silence, drop by drop,
And knew I must again confront myself:
"What shall I cry from my window?" I asked myself,
"What shall I say to the citizens below?
Since I have been a *privileged character*
These four years past. Since I have been excused
From the war for the lesser evil, merciless
As the years to girls who once were beautiful.
What have I done which is a little good?
What apples have I grasped, for all my years?
What starlight have I glimpsed for all my guilt?"

Then to the dead silence I said, in hope:
"I am a student of the morning light,
And of the evil native to the heart.
I am a pupil of emotion's wrongs
Performed upon the glory of this world.
Myself I dedicated long ago
—Or prostituted, shall I say?—to poetry,
The true, the good, and the beautiful,
Infinite fountains inexhaustible,
Full as the sea, old as the rocks,
                    new as the breaking surf—"

Such Answers Are Cold Comfort to The Dead

"What empty rhetoric," the silence said,
"You teach the boys and girls that you may gain
The bread and wine which sensuality
Sues like a premier or a president.
These are illusions of your sense of guilt
Which shames you like a vain lie when revealed.
The other boys slumped like sacks on desperate shores."

"But well you know the life which I have lived,
Cut off in truth by all that I have been
From the normal pleasures of the citizen.
How often in the midnight street I passed
The party where the tin horns blew contempt
And the rich laughter rose as midnight struck,
The party where the New Year popped and foamed,
Opening like champagne or love's wet crush,
The while I studied long the art which in
America wins silence like a wall.
—I am a student of the kinds of light,
I am a poet of the wakeful night,
In new and yet unknown America.
I am a student of love's long defeat.
I gave the boys and girls my mind and art,
I taught them of early morning light:
May I not cite this as a little good?"

from SUMMER KNOWLEDGE (1959)

Summer Knowledge

Summer knowledge is not the winter's truth, the truth of fall,
    the autumn's fruition, vision, and recognition:
It is not May knowledge, little and leafing and growing green,
    blooming out and blossoming white,
It is not the knowing and the knowledge of the gold fall and the
    ripened darkening vineyard,
Nor the black tormented, drenched and rainy knowledge of
    birth, April, and travail,
The knowledge of the womb's convulsions, and the coiled
    cord's ravelled artery, severed and cut open,
    as the root forces its way up from the dark loam:
The agony of the first knowledge of pain is worse than death, or
    worse than the thought of death:
No poppy, no preparation, no initiation, no illusion, only the
    beginning, so distant from all knowledge
    and all conclusion, all indecision and all illusion.

Summer knowledge is green knowledge, country knowledge,
    the knowledge of growing and the supple recognition
    of the fullness and the fatness and the roundness of ripeness.
It is bird knowledge and the knowing that trees possess when
The sap ascends to the leaf and the flower and the fruit,
Which the root never sees and the root believes in the darkness
    and the ignorance of winter knowledge
—The knowledge of the fruit is not the knowledge possessed by
    the root in its indomitable darkness of ambition
Which is the condition of belief beyond conception of
    experience or the gratification of fruition.
Summer knowledge is not picture knowledge, nor is it the
    knowledge of lore and learning.
It is not the knowledge known from the mountain's height, it is
    not the garden's view of the distant mountains of hidden
        fountains;
It is not the still vision in a gold frame, it is not the
    measured and treasured sentences of sentiments;
It is cat knowledge, deer knowledge, the knowledge of the full-
    grown foliage, of the snowy blossom and the rounding fruit.
It is the phoenix knowledge of the vine and the grape near
    summer's end, when the grape swells and the apple reddens:
It is the knowledge of the ripening apple when it moves to the
    fullness of the time of falling to rottenness and death.
For summer knowledge is the knowledge of death as birth,
Of death as the soil of all abounding flowering flaring rebirth.
It is the knowledge of the truth of love and the truth of growing:
    it is the knowledge before and after knowledge:
For, in a way, summer knowledge is not knowledge at all: it is
    second nature, first nature fulfilled, a new birth
    and a new death for rebirth, soaring and rising out
    of the flames of turning October, burning November,
    the towering and falling fires, growing more and
    more vivid and tall
In the consummation and the annihilation of the blaze of fall.

"I Am Cherry Alive," the Little Girl Sang

For Miss Kathleen Hanlon

"I am cherry alive," the little girl sang,
"Each morning I am something new:
I am apple, I am plum, I am just as excited
As the boys who made the Hallowe'en bang:
I am tree, I am cat, I am blossom too:
When I like, if I like, I can be someone new,
Someone very old, a witch in a zoo:
I can be someone else whenever I think who,
And I want to be everything sometimes too:
And the peach has a pit and I know that too,
And I put it in along with everything
To make the grown-ups laugh whenever I sing:
And I sing: *It is true; It is untrue*;
I know, I know, the true is untrue,
The peach has a pit, the pit has a peach:
And both may be wrong when I sing my song,
But I don't tell the grown-ups: because it is sad,
And I want them to laugh just like I do
Because they grew up and forgot what they knew
And they are sure I will forget it some day too.
They are wrong. They are wrong. When I sang my song, I
    knew, I knew!
I am red, I am gold, I am green, I am blue,
I will always be me, I will always be new!"

Baudelaire

When I fall asleep, and even during sleep,
I hear, quite distinctly, voices speaking
Whole phrases, commonplace and trivial,
Having no relation to my affairs.

Dear Mother, is any time left to us
In which to be happy? My debts are immense.
My bank account is subject to the court's judgment.
I know nothing. I cannot know anything.
I have lost the ability to make an effort.
But now as before my love for you increases.
You are always armed to stone me, always:
It is true. It dates from childhood.

For the first time in my long life
I am almost happy. The book, almost finished,
Almost seems good. It will endure, a monument
To my obsessions, my hatred, my disgust.

Debts and inquietude persist and weaken me.
Satan glides before me, saying sweetly:
"Rest for a day! You can rest and play today.
Tonight you will work." When night comes,
My mind, terrified by the arrears,
Bored by sadness, paralyzed by impotence,
Promises: "Tomorrow: I will tomorrow."
Tomorrow the same comedy enacts itself
With the same resolution, the same weakness.

I am sick of this life of furnished rooms.
I am sick of having colds and headaches:

You know my strange life. Every day brings
Its quota of wrath. You little know
A poet's life, dear Mother: I must write poems,
The most fatiguing of occupations.

I am sad this morning. Do not reproach me.
I write from a café near the post office,
Amid the click of billiard balls, the clatter of dishes,
The pounding of my heart. I have been asked to write
"A History of Caricature." I have been asked to write
"A History of Sculpture." Shall I write a history
Of the caricatures of the sculptures of you in my heart?

Although it costs you countless agony,
Although you cannot believe it necessary,
And doubt that the sum is accurate,
Please send me money enough for at least three weeks.

Seurat's Sunday Afternoon along the Seine

To Meyer and Lillian Schapiro

What are they looking at? Is it the river?
The sunlight on the river, the summer, leisure,
Or the luxury and nothingness of consciousness?
A little girl skips, a ring-tailed monkey hops
Like a kangaroo, held by a lady's lead
(Does the husband tax the Congo for the monkey's keep?)
The hopping monkey cannot follow the poodle dashing ahead.

Everyone holds his heart within his hands:

A prayer, a pledge of grace or gratitude
A devout offering to the god of summer, Sunday and plenitude.

The Sunday people are looking at hope itself.

They are looking at hope itself, under the sun, free from the teeth-
      ing anxiety, the gnawing nervousness
Which wastes so many days and years of consciousness.

The one who beholds them, beholding the gold and green
Of summer's Sunday is himself unseen. This is because he is
Dedicated radiance, supreme concentration, fanatically threading
The beads, needles and eyes—at once!—of vividness and
      permanence.
He is a saint of Sunday in the open air, a fanatic disciplined
By passion, courage, passion, skill, compassion, love: the love of life
      and the love of light as one, under the sun, with the love of life.

Everywhere radiance glows like a garden in stillness blossoming.

Many are looking, many are holding something or someone
Little or big: some hold several kinds of parasols:
Each one who holds an umbrella holds it differently
One hunches under his red umbrella as if he hid
And looked forth at the river secretly, or sought to be
Free of all of the others' judgement and proximity.
Next to him sits a lady who has turned to stone, or become a
    boulder,
Although her bell-and-sash hat is red.
A little girl holds to her mother's arm
As if it were a permanent genuine certainty:
Her broad-brimmed hat is blue and white, blue like the river, like
    the sailboats white,
And her face and her look have all the bland innocence,
Open and far from fear as cherubims playing harpsichords.
An adolescent girl holds a bouquet of flowers
As if she gazed and sought her unknown, hoped-for, dreaded
    destiny.
No hold is as strong as the strength with which the trees,
Grip the ground, curve up to the light, abide in the warm kind air:
Rooted and rising with a perfected tenacity
Beyond the distracted erratic case of mankind there.
Every umbrella curves and becomes a tree,
And the trees curving, arise to become and be
Like the umbrella, the bells of Sunday, summer, and Sunday's
    luxury.
Assured as the trees is the strolling dignity
Of the bourgeois wife who holds her husband's arm
With the easy confidence and pride of one who is
—She is sure—a sovereign Victorian empress and queen.
Her husband's dignity is as solid as his *embonpoint:*
He holds a good cigar, and a dainty cane, quite carelessly.

He is held by his wife, they are each other's property,
Dressed quietly and impeccably, they are suave and grave
As if they were unaware or free of time, and the grave,
Master and mistress of Sunday's promenade—of everything!
—As they are absolute monarchs of the ring-tailed monkey.
If you look long enough at anything
It will become extremely interesting;
If you look very long at anything
It will become rich, manifold, fascinating:

If you can look at any thing for long enough,
You will rejoice in the miracle of love,
You will possess and be blessed by the marvellous blinding radi-
    ance of love, you will be radiance.
Selfhood will possess and be possessed, as in the consecration of
    marriage, the mastery of vocation, the mystery of gift's mastery,
    the deathless relation of parenthood and progeny.
All things are fixed in one direction:
    We move with the Sunday people from right to left.

The sun shines
In soft glory
Mankind finds
The famous story
Of peace and rest, released for a little while from the tides of
    weekday tiredness, the grinding anxiousness
Of daily weeklong lifelong fear and insecurity,
The profound nervousness which in the depths of consciousness
Gnaws at the roots of the teeth of being so continually, whether
    in sleep or wakefulness,
We are hardly aware that it is there or that we might ever be free
Of its ache and torment, free and open to all experience.

The Sunday summer sun shines equally and voluptuously
Upon the rich and the free, the comfortable, the *rentier,* the poor,
    and those who are paralyzed by poverty.

Seurat is at once painter, poet, architect, and alchemist:
The alchemist points his magical wand to describe and hold the
     Sunday's gold,
Mixing his small alloys for long and long
Because he wants to hold the warm leisure and pleasure of the
     holiday
Within the fiery blaze and passionate patience of his gaze and mind
Now and forever: O happy, happy throng,
It is forever Sunday, summer, free: you are forever warm
Within his little seeds, his small black grains,
He builds and holds the power and the luxury
With which the summer Sunday serenely reigns.

—Is it possible? It is possible!—
Although it requires the labors of Hercules, Sisyphus, Flaubert,
     Roebling:
The brilliance and spontaneity of Mozart, the patience of a
     pyramid,
And requires all these of the painter who at twenty-five
Hardly suspects that in six years he will no longer be alive!
—His marvellous little marbles, beads, or molecules
Begin as points which the alchemy's magic transforms
Into diamonds of blossoming radiance, possessing and blessing
     the visual:
For look how the sun shines anew and newly, transfixed
By his passionate obsession with serenity
As he transforms the sunlight into the substance of pewter, glit-
     tering, poised and grave, vivid as butter,
In glowing solidity, changeless, a gift, lifted to immortality.

The sunlight, the soaring trees and the Seine
Are as a great net in which Seurat seeks to seize and hold
All living being in a parade and promenade of mild, calm
     happiness:
The river, quivering, silver blue under the light's variety,
Is almost motionless. Most of the Sunday people

Are like flowers, walking, moving toward the river, the sun, and
　　the river of the sun.
Each one holds some thing or some one, some instrument
Holds, grasps, grips, clutches or somehow touches
Some form of being as if the hand and fist of holding and
　　possessing,
Alone and privately and intimately, were the only genuine lock or
　　bond of blessing.

A young man blows his flute, curved by pleasure's musical activity,
His back turned upon the Seine, the sunlight, and the sunflower
　　day.
A dapper dandy in a top hat gazes idly at the Seine:
The casual delicacy with which he holds his cane
Resembles his tailored elegance.
He sits with well-bred posture, sleek and pressed,
Fixed in his niche: he is his own mustache.
A working man slouches parallel to him, quite comfortable,
Lounging or lolling, leaning on his elbow, smoking a meerschaum,
Gazing in solitude, at ease and oblivious or contemptuous
Although he is very near the elegant young gentleman.
Behind him a black hound snuffles the green, blue ground.
Between them, a wife looks down upon
The knitting in her lap, as in profound
Scrutiny of a difficult book. For her constricted look
Is not in her almost hidden face, but in her holding hands
Which hold the knitted thing as no one holds
Umbrella, kite, sail, flute or parasol.

This is the nervous reality of time and time's fire which turns
Whatever is into another thing, continually altering and changing
　　all identity, as time's great fire burns (aspiring, flying and dying),
So that all things arise and fall, living, leaping and fading, falling,
　　like flames aspiring, flowering, flying and dying—
Within the uncontrollable blaze of time and of history:
Hence Seurat seeks within the cave of his gaze and mind to find

A permanent monument to Sunday's simple delight; seeks death-
    less joy through the eye's immortality:
Strives patiently and passionately to surpass the fickle erratic
    quality of living reality.

Within the Sunday afternoon upon the Seine
Many pictures exist inside the Sunday scene:
Each of them is a world itself, a world in itself (and as a living
    child links generations, reconciles the estranged and aged so
    that a grandchild is a second birth, and the rebirth of the irra-
    tional, of those who are forlorn, resigned or implacable),
Each little picture links the large and small, grouping the big
Objects, connecting them with each little dot, seed or black grain
Which are as patterns, a marvellous network and tapestry,
Yet have, as well, the random freshness and radiance
Of the rippling river's sparkle, the frost's astonishing systems,
As they appear to morning's waking, a pure, white delicate still-
    ness and minuet,
In December, in the morning, white pennants streaked upon the
    windowpane.

He is fanatical: he is at once poet and architect,
Seeking complete evocation in forms as strong as the Eiffel Tower,
Subtle and delicate too as one who played a Mozart sonata, alone,
    under the spires of Notre-Dame.
Quick and utterly sensitive, purely real and practical,
Making a mosaic of the little dots into a mural of the splendor of
    order:
Each micro pattern is the dreamed of or imagined macrocosmos
In which all things, big and small, in willingness and love surrender
To the peace and elation of Sunday light and sunlight's pleasure,
    to the profound measure and order of proportion and relation.

He reaches beyond the glistening spontaneity
Of the dazzled Impressionists who follow

The changing light as it ranges, changing, moment by moment,
　　arranging and charming and freely bestowing
All freshness and all renewal continually on all that shows and
　　flows.

Although he is very careful, he is entirely candid.
Although he is wholly impersonal, he has youth's frankness and,
　　such is his candor,
His gaze is unique and thus it is intensely personal:
It is never facile, glib, or mechanical,
His vision is simple: yet it is also ample, complex, vexed, and
　　profound
In emulation of the fullness of Nature maturing and enduring and
　　toiling with the chaos of actuality.

An infinite variety within a simple frame:
Countless variations upon a single theme!
Vibrant with what soft soft luster, what calm joy!
This is the celebration of contemplation,
This is the conversion of experience to pure attention,
Here is the holiness of all the little things
Offered to us, discovered for us, transformed into the vividest
　　consciousness,
After the shallowness or blindness of experience,
After the blurring, dirtying sooted surfaces which, since Eden
　　and since birth,
Make all the little things trivial or unseen,
Or tickets quickly torn and thrown away
En route by rail to an ever-receding holiday:
—Here we have stopped, here we have given our hearts
To the real city, the vivid city, the city in which we dwell
And which we ignore or disregard most of the luminous day!

... Time passes: nothing changes, everything stays the same.
　　Nothing is new

Under the sun. It is also true
That time passes and everything changes, year by year, day by day,
Hour by hour. Seurat's *Sunday Afternoon along the Seine* has gone
    away,
Has gone to Chicago: near Lake Michigan,
All of his flowers shine in monumental stillness fulfilled.
And yet it abides elsewhere and everywhere where images
Delight the eye and heart, and become the desirable, the admira-
    ble, the willed
Icons of purified consciousness. Far and near, close and far away
Can we not hear, if we but listen to what Flaubert tried to say,
Beholding a husband, wife and child on just such a day:
Ils sont dans le vrai! They are with the truth, they have found the
    way
The kingdom of heaven on earth on Sunday summer day.
Is it not clear and clearer? Can we not also hear
The voice of Kafka, forever sad, in despair's sickness trying to say:
"Flaubert was right: *Ils sont dans le vrai!*
Without forbears, without marriage, without heirs,
Yet with a wild longing for forbears, marriage, and heirs:
They all stretch out their hands to me: but they are too far away!"

Once and for All

Once, when I was a boy,
Apollo summoned me
To be apprenticed to the endless summer of light and
   consciousness,
And thus to become and be what poets often have been,
A shepherd of being, a riding master of being, holding the
   sun-god's horses, leading his sheep, training his eagles,
Directing the constellations to their stations, and to each grace
   of place.
But the goat-god, piping and dancing, speaking an unknown
   tongue or the language of the magician,
Sang from the darkness or rose from the underground, whence
   arise
Love and love's drunkenness, love and birth, love and death,
   death and rebirth
Which are the beginning of the phoenix festivals, the tragic
   plays in celebration of Dionysus,
And in mourning for his drunken and fallen princes, the singers
   and sinners, fallen because they are, in the end,
Drunken with pride, blinded by joy.

And I followed Dionysus, forgetting Apollo. I followed him far
   too long until I was wrong and chanted:
"One cannot serve both gods. One must choose to win and
   lose."
But I was wrong and when I knew how I was wrong I knew
What, in a way, I had known all along:
This was the new world, here I belonged, here I was wrong because
Here every tragedy has a happy ending, and any error may be
A fabulous discovery of America, of the opulence hidden in the
   dark depths and glittering heights of reality.

from *Narcissus*

The mind is a city like London,
Smoky and populous: it is a capital
Like Rome, ruined and eternal,
Marked by the monuments which no one
Now remembers. For the mind, like Rome, contains
Catacombs, aqueducts, amphitheatres, palaces,
Churches and equestrian statues, fallen, broken or soiled.
The mind possesses and is possessed by all the ruins
Of every haunted, hunted generation's celebration.

"Call us what you will: we are made such by love."
We are such studs as dreams are made on, and
Our little lives are ruled by the gods, by Pan,
Piping of all, seeking to grasp or grasping
All of the grapes; and by the bow-and-arrow god,
Cupid, piercing the heart through, suddenly and forever.

Dusk we are, to dusk returning, after the burbing,
After the gold fall, the fallen ash, the bronze,
Scattered and rotten, after the white null statutes which
Are winter, sleep, and nothingness: when
Will the houselights of the universe
Light up and blaze?
               For it is not the sea
Which murmurs in a shell,
And it is not only heart, at harp o'clock,
Is is the dread terror of the uncontrollable
Horses of the apocalypse, running in wild dread
Toward Arcturus—and returning as suddenly ...

from LAST & LOST POEMS (1989)

This Is a Poem I Wrote at Night, before the Dawn

This is a poem I wrote before I died and was reborn:
— After the years of the apples ripening and the eagles soaring,
After the festival here the small flowers gleamed like the first stars,
And the horses cantered and romped away like the experience of
    skill; mastered and serene
Power, grasped and governed by reins, lightly held by knowing
    hands.

The horses had cantered away, far enough away
So that I saw the horses' heads farther and farther away
And saw that they had reached the black horizon on the dusk of day
And were or seemed black thunderheads, massy and ominous
    waves in the doomed sky:
And it was then, for the first time, then that I said as I must
    always say
All through living death of night:
It is always darkness before delight!
The long night is always the beginning of the vivid blossom of day.

America, America!

I am a poet of the Hudson River and the heights above it,
        the lights, the stars, and the bridges
I am also by self-appointment the laureate of the Atlantic
        —of the peoples' hearts, crossing it
                to new America.

I am burdened with the truck and chimera, hope,
        acquired in the sweating sick-excited passage
                in steerage, strange and estranged
Hence I must descry and describe the kingdom of emotion.

For I am a poet of the kindergarten (in the city)
        and the cemetery (in the city)
And rapture and ragtime and also the secret city in the heart and
    mind
This is the song of the natural city self in the 20th century.

It is true but only partly true that a city is a "tyranny of numbers"
(This is the chant of the urban metropolitan and metaphysical self
After the first two World Wars of the 20th century)

— This is the city self, looking from window to lighted window
When the squares and checks of faintly yellow light
Shine at night, upon a huge dim board and slab-like tombs,
Hiding many lives. It is the city consciousness
Which sees and says: more: more and more: always more.

Metro-Goldwyn-Mayer

I looked toward the movie, the common dream,
The he and she in close-ups, nearer than life,
And I accepted such things as they seem,

The easy poise, the absence of the knife,
The near summer happily ever after,
The understood question, the immediate strife,

Not dangerous, nor mortal, but the fadeout
Enormously kissing amid warm laughter,
As if such things were not always played out

By an ignorant arm, which crosses the dark
And lights up a thin sheet with a shadow's mark.

Poem

You, my photographer, you, most aware,
Who climbed to the bridge when the iceberg struck,
Climbed with your camera when the ship's hull broke,
And lighted your flashes and, standing passionate there,
Wound the camera in the sudden burst's flare,
Shot the screaming women, and turned and took
Pictures of the iceberg (as the ship's deck shook)
Dreaming like the moon in the night's black air!

You, tiptoe on the rail to film a child!
The nude old woman swimming in the sea
Looked up from the dark water to watch you there;
Below, near the ballroom where the band still toiled,
The frightened, in their lifebelts, watched you bitterly—
You hypocrite! My brother! We are a pair!

Philology Recapitulates Ontology, Poetry Is Ontology

Faithful to your commandments, o consciousness, o

Holy bird of words soaring ever whether to nothingness or to inconceivable fulfillment slowly:

And still I follow you, awkward as that dandy of ontology and as
awkward as his albatross and as

another dandy of ontology before him, another shepherd and
watchdog of being, the one who

Talked forever of forever as if forever of having been and being
an ancient mariner,

Hesitant forever as if forever were the albatross

Hung round his neck by the seven seas of the seven muses,

and with as little conclusion, since being never concludes,

Studying the sibilance and the splashing of the seas and of seeing
and of being's infinite seas,

Staring at the ever-blue and the far small stars and the faint white
endless curtain of the twinkling play's endless seasons.

What Curious Dresses All Men Wear

What curious dresses all men wear!
The walker you met in a brown study,
The President smug in rotogravure,
The mannequin, the bathing beauty.

The bubble-dancer, the deep-sea diver,
The bureaucrat, the adulterer,
Hide privates parts which I disclose
To those who know what a poem knows.

The Poet

The riches of the poet are equal to his poetry
His power is his left hand
      It is idle weak and precious
His poverty is his wealth, a wealth which may destroy him like
    Midas
Because it is that laziness which is a form of impatience
And this he may be destroyed by the gold of the light which
    never was
On land or sea.
He may be drunken to death, draining the casks of excess
That extreme form of success.
He may suffer Narcissus' destiny
Unable to live except with the image which is infatuation
Love, blind, adoring, overflowing
Unable to respond to anything which does not bring love
    quickly or immediately.

… The poet must be innocent and ignorant
But he cannot be innocent since stupidity is not his strong
    point
Therefore Cocteau said, "What would I not give
To have the poems of my youth withdrawn from existence?
I would give to Satan my immortal soul."
This metaphor is wrong, for it is his immortal soul which he
    wished to redeem,
Lifting it and sifting it, free and white, from the actuality of
        youth's banality, vulgarity,
        pomp and affectation of his early
        works of poetry.

So too in the same way a Famous American Poet
When fame at last had come to him sought out the fifty copies
of his first book of poems which had been privately printed
by himself at his own expense.
He succeeded in securing 48 of the 50 copies, burned them
And learned then how the last copies were extant,
As the law of the land required, stashed away in the national
     capital,
at the Library of Congress.
Therefore he went to Washington, therefore he took out the last
     two copies
Placed them in his pocket, planned to depart
Only to be halted and apprehended. Since he was the author,
Since they were his books and his property he was reproached
But forgiven. But the two copies were taken away from him
Thus setting a national precedent.

For neither amnesty nor forgiveness is bestowed upon poets,
     poetry and poems,
For William James, the lovable genius of Harvard
spoke the terrifying truth: *"Your friends may forget, God*
          may forgive you, But the brain cells record
          your acts for the rest of eternity."
What a terrifying thing to say!
This is the endless doom, without remedy, of poetry.
This is also the joy everlasting of poetry.

Unpublished Poems

Editor's note

Robert Phillips, in editing *Last & Lost Poems,* thoroughly combed Schwartz's papers, which are held in the Beinecke Rare Book and Manuscript Library at Yale. That volume represents the poems Schwartz brought near to complete or publishable form. I found the two pieces that follow through my own research in the Schwartz archive; the pages I found were typescripts with handwritten changes and subsequent drafts written on the same sheet. These were not poems Schwartz intended to publish, at least not in this form; there may have been subsequent drafts that I did not find or that no longer exist.

Nonetheless, I think they will be of interest to the reader. The first is a birthday poem to Schwartz's first wife, Gertrude Buckman. The second is a longer draft of a poem written as Schwartz's marriage to Buckman was ending; a short version appears in James Atlas's biography, *Delmore Schwartz: The Life of An American Poet*.

In both cases, I did my best to interpret Schwartz's handwriting and draft sequences to assemble as finished versions as possible of the poems. To my knowledge, they haven't been published before in these versions.

A Poem For Gertrude's Birthday (1937)

Where the will moves, time is
And it's your will I wish
Which is the truth of every kiss,
Beneath its butter-like touch:
For you are beautiful
For death is in your look,
Yet your joy is every joy
Which is remarkable.
But by no machine is luck
Only by the temporal clock
Can I grasp and wholly take
That new will of twenty-five
(Original, day by day
As every moment has its play
And the kings and ghosts arrive,
Only in time, the orange West,
O sister, doll, and animal,
Can I arrive at your rich breast
And taste the gift of your sweet will

Doggerel Beneath the Skin [fragment]

Poor Schwartz! Poor Schwartz!
Love anyway to all of them!
And may they live to see the peace
When no one has to drink to live
And work without hysteria,
Self-pity and insomnia,
Poor Schwartz! Poor Schwartz!
Self-doubt and sun deliria!
Poor Blackmur and poor Schwartz!
Poor Schwartz, he meant well anyway?
But all for parents loves must pay!
Poor Berryman! Poor Schwartz,
All poet's wives have rotten lives,
Their husbands look at them like knives,
Exactitude their livelihood
The audience would have them miss
Poor Gertrude, poor Eileen
(No longer seventeen)
But back to children, not yet done,
(The infamy has just begun!)
When Sage bathed in the Swishe's house,
with joy came in and looked,
—And all looked on
Sage stared right back, cold, bored, polite
(This was an act Keith would have booked!),
While Susie glittered in the light!
And now with sudden happiness,
I think of last year's New Year's Eve,
(When Nela falls on Hortin's stairs,
Strange God is kind or he is luck),
And if God is, or is good luck
Some of us may enjoy a duck!

Verse Drama

DR. BERGEN'S BELIEF

PERSONS OF THE PLAY

Anthony Norman	Mrs. Bergen
Dr. Newman	Martha Bergen
Dr. Bergen	Dr. Bergen's Disciples

INTRODUCTION

[*A room bare of all but an oval mirror and a table before which* Dr. Bergen *stands, regarding himself as he rehearses his speech, as if assuming an audience in an auditorium.*]

Dr. Bergen:
There seems to be no Santa Claus. The air
Is free, the park's nature open until
Ten o'clock comes once more, the starlight admirable,
The unemployed unobtrusive, the traffic's hum
Subdued as one's attention shifts,

                                but otherwise
A final emptiness confronts your eyes.

For otherwise, there is no Santa Claus,
Though the scene shifts to the seashore at dusk
—The summer over, the carousel rusts,
The twilight is cold, it is October—
Where he who walks in solitude, who pauses
At last upon the verge of rocks, dim, dim,
Gazing upon the curled and curling waters,
Does not look up unto the curving sky
Sure that his fate must be coherent there.
The sky is merely dim and vacancy
Through which the airman may ascend for years
And not hear any word, not one, nor see
A face intelligent amid the clouds
Unless the bulged face of the clouds' heaped-up
And foaming coma.
                                If he lifted his arms
And bent his knee and bowed his head, what would
He to his own self seem? Grotesque, grotesque,
The sad comedian of cane and derby
Collapsed upon the pavement.
                                Prayer is now
Ridiculous. Appeal, apostrophe,
And invocation are but mutterings,
Turning from side to side in ignorant sleep.

No one regards you, no one cares for you, none
Shall find cake on the pavement, none
Shall have the past forgiven, and no one
Hears the benevolent white-bearded one
Descend the chimney, rise in the elevator,
Arrive to dispense gratis and for no toil
All justice, loving-kindness, and good will.

But every side is wrong, but every man
Is guilty, every child is used, and now
Effort is useful as spitting in the sea,
Good and evil are merely expressions of pain
In the perpetual return of the blind night
And the bit by bit disorder of the rain.

When music makes the whole room radiant,
Spreading the dream of sweet societies
Where all dance out their gifts, their needs, their choices,
One knows that heaven is epiphenomenal,
Rising from peaked musicians with bad complexions.
Breakfast is good. An income is good.
It is good to be sunburnt, warm, and clean.
Besides this, what can you say with certainty?
In fact, what can you mean but this,
The sunlight where you are in turning time?

Who will rise up, speak out, convinced, convinced,
Affirm once more that nothing can be done
Without the help of that great Santa Claus
Promised to children in the middle ages
—Not now! But with cigar-store Indians
Remembered only in old vaudeville.
—I will speak out! I will show you a wonder,
The secret satisfaction of every wish!

Ladies and Gentlemen, I know you all,
I know you all, I know all that you want.
Which is, though vaguely, all. O you require
A big black piano
And skates for poise
A safe for memory, a giant glass
To drink each dear,
Wit, learning, and a deck of cards

Stacked by the will,
The genuine she to whom your shameless he
Is me and me,
Double-delighting in a box which is
A tender sea—

None of these things are given. But you get
What you do not want, what you do not need,
Do not expect, or do not recognize—
Strength to be patient, naiveté to hope,
Perplexed affection, inexhaustible will,
Brief visits from the dead, and love unwanted,
Too much, too little, overwhelming all.

Ladies and Gentlemen, this is the emptiness
Which you know well, which is unbearable,
A boredom which no man escapes unless
An animal need preempts and but defers
The question all must face, which I have faced:
What is this life? What can man ask to have?

I know the answer, I have known enough
To leap, jump, jig, and somersault until
Absurdity itself is searched
For Who Knows Him, the dream behind the dream.
I come, I say, having understood in part
The formless vacancy between the stars,
The marvelous light in which all things move and seem,
And the Santa Claus of the obsessed, obscene heart.

[*The living room of the Bergen apartment in the year* 1920.
French windows at the back are half-open, showing the terrace,
which has a wide parapet. It is an afternoon in October. Enter
ANTHONY NORMAN, *fiancé of Eleanor Bergen, who killed herself*

three months before. He walks to the mantelpiece, gazes at the
photograph of Eleanor which stands there.]

ANTHONY:
This is the house of the dead, this is the house
Perplexed by a girl who killed herself.
In the morning when they came to wake her
The time to dress herself, prepare her face,
Eat breakfast, and seek the day's interests,
Had been evaded utterly by her;
Also my will, which I had given her.
—Here they construct a system to make their lives
Self-regarding, self-gratifying, self-conscious,
Indulging their minds in the old foolishness,
The vain vanity: to correct the heart of man,
A mission, a justification, a declaration.
—The true motive is private unhappiness.
But they cannot forget the girl who killed herself,
Though they seek to see in her death a deliberate witness,
As I seek to see in her death my own grave fault,
My weakness, my failure, having offered explicitly
My face, my heart, my will. The I beneath
My quivering eyes cannot support
Her utter rejection of my life, my face, my heart;
I cannot endure myself until I know
Why she turned from me, seeking nothingness.
I must come here again and again to stare
At her parents, her bedroom, her photograph,
While they make of her death their myth and mystery.
The love whose answer was the wish to die
Gasps in a vacuum, seeks the fading face,
Fading and flickering in memory's cinema.
One million times a single question drags
Its incompleteness, its unfinishedness

Through the unending corridors of unconsciousness.
Why did she kill herself? The photograph
Shows only the look for the photographer.

[*Exit* ANTHONY, *as* MRS. BERGEN *and* DR. NEWMAN *enter,*
MRS. BERGEN *nodding to* ANTHONY.]

MRS. BERGEN: Please smoke if you care to do so, Dr. Newman.
There are cigarettes next to you.

DR. NEWMAN: Thank you, Mrs. Bergen. Suppose you tell me all
that concerns you and exactly what you think I can do.

MRS. BERGEN: Dr. Newman, it was only after I had tried every
other alternative that I decided to speak to you. If I were not
desperate, I would not discuss these matters with anyone not
of the family; but God only knows what will happen to us next,
and my sister Emma has been urging me to speak to you for
a long time.

DR. NEWMAN: I understand perfectly, Mrs. Bergen. You can be
sure that no one else will hear of your family troubles. But on
the other hand, I should remind you that complete frankness
is necessary from you, even though you are not the patient.
Only the full truth can enable me to do any good, and yet I have
never had a patient who from the start hid nothing.

MRS. BERGEN: I will try to be the exception. As you know, my
eldest child, Eleanor, killed herself, or seemed to do so, three
months ago. She had taken too many sleeping powders. That
is why we are not sure that it was a deliberate act. No one
knows her reason for killing herself, although my husband,
for reasons of his own, says that he does know. She seemed
to be happy enough, although always an over-emotional girl.
But we knew little of what she did during the past few years.
She insisted, as she would say, on leading her own life. She
wrote verse, she studied dancing, she studied for the theatre,
she had many friends whom we did not know, she went from
one interest to another, and although we were anxious about

her moods and her unrest, her habits seemed typical of the girls of today. When she became engaged, I thought all my anxiety was over. And then, a few weeks before her marriage, she killed herself—

DR. NEWMAN: Perhaps before you go on to speak of your husband, I had better say now that I knew your daughter well, and intended to visit you, after she died, but hesitated for various reasons.

MRS. BERGEN [*surprised*]: You knew Eleanor? Was she a patient of yours?

DR. NEWMAN: Yes, she was. But I think we had better speak of that later. Now tell me about your husband.

MRS. BERGEN: A year ago, after a year of despondency, Dr. Bergen began his religious society, which has brought us so much trouble, and now I am afraid, Dr. Newman, that everything is becoming worse. My son Titus and I refuse to accept Dr. Bergen's ideas and practices, and he considers that we are betraying him. We interfere only when he tries to do such things as giving away immense sums of money to his disciples, who are in the house night and day, and whom he supports. There are eight and my youngest child, Martha, and at least two of them are obviously after my husband's money, which is to be used for various projects having to do with my husband's religion. I am sure, however, that some of the others are quite sincere. [*A short pause.*]

Dr. Newman, I love my husband dearly. He is a kind and good man, and in the past we were very content. I am horrified when I think of attempting to have him declared legally insane and shut up in an asylum, but I will have no other recourse, there is so much conflict, so much money is being thrown away. Worst of all, my daughter's death is taken as a great example by my husband who says that she killed herself in obedience to his doctrines, his imperatives, as he calls them, so that I am afraid that another one will kill himself.

DR. NEWMAN: What are these doctrines of your husband?

MRS. BERGEN: Perhaps it would be best if you found out from him. However, the main belief is that God's blue eye is the sky. It is God's organ of perception, he says, and he thinks that when the whole world can be brought to an awareness of this fact, then human life will be transformed and such horrors as wars and the oppression of the poor will cease.

DR. NEWMAN: I do not understand. Why will a belief that God regards human life do away with evil? Most religions have said that the deity knows all things at all times.

MRS. BERGEN: My husband thinks that he has found the true medium by which the deity acts and moves nature and human life. He thinks that other previous religions had only an abstract idea of the divine will, but he has found the direct experience. You must look at God's blue eye, he says, then you will know what is good and what is evil. He calls this the intuitive understanding or inspiration. But it is all very complex. Perhaps I do not understand him. He says I do not, and that it is the evil of my nature which prevents me from understanding and believing.

DR. NEWMAN: You know, in America during the 19th century there were hundreds of such cults and societies, though few as original, and even today there is a man in Harlem believed to be God by thousands.[1]

MRS. BERGEN: Yes, I know. My husband is not at all disturbed by such comparisons. He says that no other religion showed how to get a direct experience of the divine will. And he has a whole schedule of rituals, which his disciples perform, and which is supposed to bring this experience to all who will believe. No one of the disciples, no one but my husband, has had this intuitive experience as yet.

DR. NEWMAN: The whole matter is probably beyond my sphere. As you probably know, the psychiatrist deals with difficulties

---

1. *believed to be God by thousands*: Allusion to Marcus Garvey (1887–1940), leader of the first important U.S. black nationalist movement, based in New York City's Harlem.

which are relatively contained in the individual—fixations, compulsions, fetiches which usually have their origin in some childhood event or misunderstanding, or some kind of deep-seated frustration. But your husband's fantasy may not be pathological in this sense at all. The fact that he has won disciples suggests that it is not.

MRS. BERGEN: His disciples have good practical reasons for listening to him. He helps them financially and otherwise.

DR. NEWMAN: Still, your husband's belief may be a response to the kind of world in which we now exist, not a personal fantasy. Our society is breaking up, tearing itself to pieces, being transformed, and that is why many curious schemes are invented by individuals who have a blind but intense awareness that their world, their way of life, everything dear to them, is turning into something else, slipping from them, becoming strange, repugnant, too difficult for them.

MRS. BERGEN [*sighing*]: I feel that way myself, Dr. Newman.

DR. NEWMAN: If such is the case, I cannot help your husband, and I assure you that he is not insane in the legal sense. Of course, I can as a reasonable person try to persuade him that he mistakes the source of his belief, but I would surely fail.

MRS. BERGEN: Speak to him, Dr. Newman, do what you can. I am afraid another person will kill himself now that they believe that Eleanor's death was the most wonderful act possible.

DR. NEWMAN: I should have come here before this, knowing your daughter as I did. But I hesitated.

MRS. BERGEN: Please stay for their daily ceremony, which will begin on the terrace shortly, and you will see that something is wrong with them and that my husband's doctrines are dangerous. Eleanor is dead, I am not concerned about her now, but perhaps you can speak to the others, especially my daughter Martha, who mistakes a devotion to her father for a belief in what he says.

DR. NEWMAN: Very well, if you wish me to do so. But I am afraid I can do nothing to help you. [*Rising, he goes to the mantelpiece, and takes Eleanor's photograph in his hand.*] I should have come to you before this, but I did not want to intrude in a home of mourning, I did not know how your daughter's death was understood, I was sure that my news would be unwelcome.

MRS. BERGEN: What did you know about my daughter?

[*Before* DR. NEWMAN *can answer,* DR. BERGEN *enters with his nine disciples—*HERRIOT, SCHMIDT, RAKOVSKY, FRIETSCH, ROSENBERG, PERRY, PORTER, MONTEZ—*and his daughter* MARTHA, *who is by his side and holds his hand. The other disciples follow in twos, conversing quietly, and with looks of concentration and seriousness.*]

DR. BERGEN: How do you do, sir?

MRS. BERGEN: Felix, this is Dr. Newman, a friend of Emma's.

DR. BERGEN: O I see! You are that psychiatrist who is going to persuade me that I am merely a deluded old man. We shall see. We are glad to have you here and glad to have you present at our ceremony. Perhaps that persuasion will be other than you expect, although the cynicism I see on your face is a distinct handicap. [*To the disciples:*] Let us proceed.

[*They mount to the terrace, and seat themselves at the long table which stands there,* DR. BERGEN *at the head and* MARTHA *at the other end. They are at an obvious distance from the audience and all that they speak and do has a formalized character, which is partly created by the fact that the living room is intermediate between them and the audience, so that* MRS. BERGEN *and* DR. NEWMAN, *who remain in the living room and watch them, are as if a prior audience.*]

DR. BERGEN: We will begin as we usually do, by reading this week's version of our first imperative. [*He reads.*]

Be conscious of what happens to you from minute to minute, be conscious of what you have done and what is done to you, the event active or passive, multitudinous, misunderstood at the moment of being.

Be self-conscious of the complexities of the personal event by a certain effort. Write before sleep, at night, in a book which can be taken with you as the past is taken with you, as the past takes you, which you will read with shame, remorse, and astonishment long after, in other circumstances.

To keep a diary is an act of prayer, duplicating in your own meager power the gaze of the deity's blue eye upon you. Pray then, by seeking the full awareness of what is written, which is not soon removed, which you must read once more when you are different, when you are disinterested.

Write before sleep, when, in the silence, the night sounds become distinct, and a car starts downstairs, and the typical

Ticking of the clock repeats its dry sound, while outside the bedroom window the great city squats,

Silent and black beneath the ignorance of night. Be conscious thus. Be troubled by the shortcoming of all through which justification is assured.

Write exactly what you have felt, your motives, your intention in appearance and after examination, your hope and desire, all that has happened

During the long day which has slipped past without being counted, which will never be renewed, which must be known.

Do not be concerned with the false tone, the affected phrasing, the necessary pretentiousness of all self-consciousness,

But deny the desire to invent, distort, defend, omit, forget, when confronted with your own foolishness.

Because this examination of consciousness is your duty and your consolation. Thus is the past carried forward, thus do you take hold of your life,

Otherwise it slips from you. Thus this nightly act will be your correction, your memory,

Your freely-given offering to the deity whose blue eye shines overhead, to whom

Our hearts are in debt forever.

[*He pauses for a moment.*]

And now before we go ahead to this week's version of the second imperative, we will discuss "Problems." Who will propose the problem?

RAKOVSKY: I will, Dr. Bergen. Last night as I wrote the day's entries in my diary, the following predicament occurred to me. Suppose I were on an ocean liner which struck an iceberg and began to sink, and suppose that subsequently I was in the water, holding a spar, unable to swim (although I am able to swim) and another man came towards me and told me that he could not keep afloat much longer unless I let him hold the spar also, but it was obvious that the spar could not support the weight of two men. Furthermore, both myself and my suppliant were adult men, there was no question of a woman or a child. What ought one to do? Ought one to save one's own life or that of one's neighbor? How is one to decide, by what measure?

Dr. Bergen: The problem is of no slight interest. Will you attempt an answer, Rosenberg?

Rosenberg: May I observe parenthetically that the problem is artificial in the sense that most moral questions are not so sharply a choice between the self's good or another's, but most ends turn out to be commonly held by the community.

Rakovsky [*angered*]: The problem is not artificial. On the contrary, it is just such an acute predicament that bares the moral and cuts away all other considerations.

Dr. Bergen: What is your answer, Rosenberg?

Rosenberg: As an answer, I can suggest only the questionable one of an effort to decide which man is of greater value, professionally let us say, to humanity. A lawyer ought to sacrifice his life for a doctor. [*Laughter*] A good doctor, I mean. But I admit that one could hardly make a thorough inquiry into a man's professional capacities while in the water. [*Laughter*]

Dr. Bergen: Your answer is weak and perhaps begs the question again. The good of humanity may be divided and contradictory. I will consider this matter myself and afford you the intuitive reply next week.

Mrs. Bergen [*to* Dr. Newman, *sotto voce*]: He stares at the sky until an answer comes to him. That is what he means by an intuitive reply.

Dr. Bergen: Let us continue with the second imperative. You will observe that a number of modifications have been made since last week. These changes flow from a greater grasp of the inspiration which the deity's blue eye affords me.

You are with each other, you are not alone, you depend on each other, and you speak to each other.

To further a desire, or to make an hour interesting, or in order to have a friend and engage his affection,

Or to increase the aura and warmth of company, while eating or in the theatre or while two are alone and with their hands seek each other,

So that, in this ineluctable mixture of lives, the necessity of speech requires the perfect effort to speak

The word which occurs to you, the thought which oppresses you, the anger or love

Which rises to the fluent or hesitant tongue, which rises and is suppressed because of fear or tact or in order to avoid laughter.

Suppress nothing. Speak your whole mind fully and lucidly and without omission,

Do not exclude the least childlike pun, the sudden nonsense syllable, the comment which will surely be nursed in resentment.

For frankness, sincerity, articulation, explicitness are the attributes of the man aware that God's blue eye regards him.

Permit yourself to be ridiculous as a man weeping, an actor hissed, a girl deliberately tripped.

Adopt with voluntary act the naive, the ingenuous, the stupid.

Accept harm

Until you are certain that you know what you do, and why your act is enacted, and that your whole heart and mind have consented.

Let every emotion be large, black and white, scrawled upon your countenance as a cartoon,

Gross, clumsy, foolish.

Pride, dignity, assurance

Are nothing without the power of righteousness, but once righteous.

They are garments, sweet fruits, the best pleasures of man.

[*There is a pause. The* Disciples *are obviously moved, and they display their emotions differently.*]

Dr. Bergen: Let us continue with the third imperative in this week's formulation, omitting today your proposal of "Questions of Exact Communication." I will answer tomorrow, Herriot, your question as to how to communicate exactly the feeling of respect in the midst of desire, and the emotion of wishing to teach and yet not presume complete superiority.

Think of the objects for which you care. Discover why you care for them. Be conscious of the different worth you confer upon them, which would be surrendered, exchanged or passed over, which things are equivalent to life itself for you.

Because man's desires govern his acts, if he governs them; because his desires are himself as an acting being and because by his desires and his choices man must be judged and understood,

Resort to a painstaking examination in the fullness of consciousness, examine your desires in the detail of a moment, seize the moment of feeling, grasp the care involved in such statements as "salt," "sugar," "a gleaming automobile,"

"The pungency of tobacco," "the crinkling of her cheeks when she smiles," "the pleasant sense of health which flows from a dinner well-digested,"

"The continuous exercise of the much-used body," "the complexities of sleep when at times the mind confronts itself," "the look of the white pitcher upon the brown dresser," "the distortion of tiredness, weakness, and pain."

Examine the times and conditions of these cares, the circumstances upon which they depend, the hours and the places when they become without meaning for you,

As well as the environment of their full meaning. Decide once and for all which sentiments, which cares, which desires are most permanent, justifiable, and necessary.

Your decision decides your fate, your decision can be true only if you open your heart and give your mind to that being whose blue eye is actual in the arching, domed, and ineluctable scene which is infinite overhead, your decision before that being's blue eye,

In whom "Justice," "Truth," "Beauty," are genuine and absolute.

[*There is a pause.* DR. BERGEN *appears to be exhausted. Then, raising his voice, he addresses* DR. NEWMAN.]

I hope that you do not find our ritual too oppressive, Dr. Newman. [*Several* DISCIPLES *turn to look at* DR. NEWMAN.]

DR. NEWMAN: On the contrary, I have been completely absorbed. Please go ahead. I am very much impressed by the somewhat intellectual character of your doctrines, which is so different from the emphasis upon emotion in most latter-day religious societies.

DR. BERGEN: Thank you. I regard that as praise. [*To the* DISCI-
PLES.] Let us continue. I now ask each of you to render "Witness and Testimony" to your inmost cares, thoughts, and ob-
servations. Each one in turn. And let me quote from the second
imperative: "Speaking your whole mind fully and lucidly and
without omission, nothing excluded because of fear or tact or
in order to avoid laughter." In your usual order, beginning with
Herriot.

HERRIOT: Last summer by means of playing tennis for five hours
every day, I gained poise, dignity, bearing, rid myself of shyness, spoke with complete assurance. This effect has made me
meditate on the relationship of the body to the mind. They
seem to be one. And yet they seem to be two. Is consciousness the inside of what is seen from the outside as the nervous
system? Is the spirit of man merely his nervous system? I do
not think so.

DR. BERGEN: Thank you Herriot. I would remind you that we
are not engaged in "Problems." But your problem is very important and I will seek the intuitive answer. Schmidt!

SCHMIDT: I have been troubled by sexual desire. I reflected on
the mot of a few years back: "Sexual intercourse is the lyricism
of the people." I remembered with a kind of sad glee my previous habit of asking all adults whom I encountered: "Have you
had your orgasm today?" [*Laughter.*]

MRS. BERGEN [*interrupts, in an anguished voice*]: Felix, is it
necessary that Martha hear all these things? Is it absolutely
necessary?

DR. BERGEN: It is necessary, absolutely [*ironically mimick-
ing her*]. Nothing may be secret or undisclosed. The secret
corrupts. Thank you for being frank, sincere and explicit,
Schmidt. Rakovsky!

RAKOVSKY: I summed up all the acts for which I have been unable to forgive myself. How, meeting S. last week, I fell into an
attitude immediately, an attitude full of lies, though I wished
merely to tell him of how radically my life had been altered. I

had to compose, invent. I could not tell the truth without improving it, because the truth does not satisfy me. When shall I be truthful, utterly candid?

DR. BERGEN: Thank you. You have been candid today. Frietsch.

FRIETSCH: Last night I said to myself: what is there left of the day's activity? Can anything be said of it but this, that it consisted of waiting for the moment of lucidity and prayer? We know not what we do from day to day until some external demand compels us, creates a great unrest and we work with immense nervousness until a whole is completed, so that we will be able to return to the other unrest of waiting. If it were true that our lives were created by our own wills . . . but the will is said to be a myth, hypostatized. This is the most modern belief, that what we call the will is muscular tension.

DR. BERGEN: Thank you, Frietsch. Your testimony is completely adequate. You too raise a problem demanding intuitive consideration. Rosenberg!

ROSENBERG: I considered the poor, how their lives are sucked from them in a thousand unseen ways. In work is happiness. Such is the old thought, I said to myself, old and no longer true for the work of the poor is the degradation of the automaton, the acquisition of perfectly behaving nervous reflexes until all sensitivity and imagination have been destroyed. Yet who would be happy? Children give no thought to happiness. Only brides embarking upon marriage think in such terms. The word "embark" betrays the inexactitude of the thought. Yet happiness may be the only term for the possession of all intrinsic goods.

DR. BERGEN: Thank you, Rosenberg. You are still concerned, quite rightly, with the injustices of society. Perry!

PERRY: I was concerned with understanding my adolescent passions—professional baseball and playing cards. I saw that the essence of baseball was constituted by the element of contingency. The game was a framework for spontaneous drama, quickly-rising. I remembered my greatest excitement: the

World Series in which the conclusion was this—a base runner attempting to score from second base on a sharp and hard-hit single to right field. If he was safe, the score would be tied. The right fielder threw perfectly to the catcher on one bounce, a long and fatal arc, and the base runner was tagged out sliding into the catcher in a burst of dust, and the team for which I rooted had been defeated in the contest for the world's championship. Reflecting upon this and gazing upon the sky, I understood that contingency is the most intoxicating of liquors, and I saw that this obsession also created the love of gambling. It was an interest in the processes of chance, which in turn depended upon our hope and poverty and wish to get rich quick, a sudden vast acquisition, which was in turn our enormous interest in the grace of God.

DR. BERGEN: Thank you. That is very interesting and useful. Porter!

PORTER: Dr. Bergen, I too considered games and remembered how in playing tennis, the racquet with which I swung toward my opponent seemed to me to be my will, and his racquet, his will—both adolescent swords.

DR. BERGEN: You are permitting your fellows to suggest the terms and the character of your thought to you. You ought to look into your own mind with greater care and freshness, Porter. Montez!

MONTEZ: I looked at the heaven at night, and it seemed to me, Dr. Bergen, that the stars might be compared to diamonds, and diamonds might in turn be compared to the values which surround the heart of man, so that there was this triple analogy—stars, diamonds, values, and the heart of man in the midst of them.

DR. BERGEN: I would say the same to you as to Porter. You are not using your own experience sufficiently, but merely my terms. Martha!

MARTHA: In my dream at night I wished with all my heart to participate in the minds of the people I like very much, I mean directly, not indirectly: to feel their consciousness as they do.

And in my dream I was trying to open Eleanor's forehead and look inside. And I told her how noble she had been to kill herself and how it had helped all of us. [MRS. BERGEN *suppresses an outcry.*]

DR. BERGEN: Thank you, Martha. You have done well. My own thoughts, which I must now testify, concern Eleanor also. She died in her enactment of the method of our belief. By gazing at the sky until the self-evident intuition was given to me, I have again confirmed my previous announcement of the reason for her death. She killed herself because she had come to the impasse where she could not understand her own heart and could not decide once for all what she wanted, except by examining her heart in the perspective of death. It is a method which we must use only as a last resort; but it was her last resort and she recognized it, and accepting our belief she killed herself and thus became our first witness. Let us hear once more the poem she wrote and made a recording of when she still hoped to find in poetry a way of life for herself.

[*There is a victrola on the terrace, unseen by the audience.* POR-TER *gets up and starts the victrola. The voice which issues from it is distant, low, husky yet feminine, and in a way, oracular and dramatic. It actually comes from a victrola record, and is not an off-stage voice.*]

ELEANOR'S SONG:
  I said, as by the river, we
  Gazed at the sliding water's gray,
  "This life's a dream, as others say,
  A dream confirmed when memory
  Holds up the past and dims the day,
  As in the future we shall see
  The present quickly passed away,
  Irrelevant to our belief,

Misunderstood as every play,
Full of a secret actuality
Which worked its wish consummately
And held the conscious will at bay."

[*Enter* ANTHONY, *at right of living room. He walks toward the terrace and mounts the steps.*]

ANTHONY:
Was that her voice? That was her voice indeed.
Who can distinguish now between the ghost
And the actual, the living and the immortal?
One hundred times the globe has whirled about,
Carrying her small grave in its turning ground.
One thousand times the I beneath my face
Has winced to think that she surpassed my love.
One million times a single question raises
Its expectation, its unfinishedness,
In the unending corridors of unconsciousness.
Why did she kill herself? The phonograph
Speaks only what's plausible to the small ear.
But death in Gothic letters confronts my face,
Cannot be read, too near, cannot be known.

DR. BERGEN [*obviously annoyed*]: We are glad to have you here, Anthony, you are always welcome. But it is unnecessary for you to affirm continually your refusal to accept our reason for Eleanor's death. [*Turning to his* DISCIPLES.] To conclude today's ceremony we will have a second antiphony devoted to each one's thoughts of Eleanor, our witness. Martha! And then all of you in that order.

MARTHA: I remember the day we went shopping together. Eleanor bought some things at Wanamaker's, I do not remember what. We both had ice-cream sodas at their fountain, and then drove to Long Beach and went swimming.

She was very excited. She swam as if she were hysterical or drowning.

MONTEZ: I remember how charming and vivacious she was last summer.

PORTER: I remember how devoted and loyal she was to her father.

PERRY: I remember with what poise and grace she tidied her hair before the looking-glass. She was very beautiful.

ROSENBERG: I remember her coming from the telephone one day and looking like one who has just taken off her glasses and has a dazed look and a welt on the bridge of the nose between the eyes.

FRIETSCH: I remember her coming from the telephone another day and when she saw me, looking as if I had seen her unexpectedly with her clothes off.

SCHMIDT: I had reason to believe that she was fond of me. I was in love with her. She was very beautiful.

RAKOVSKY: She was excited and high-strung and this gave her a theatrical quality which was very attractive.

HERRIOT: We dined together once at the Commodore when I returned from a trip to Chicago. I was amazed at the variety of her emotions during the course of one evening. She retired several times in order to make phone calls. Her life and death seem to me to be models for imitation.

DR. BERGEN: I agree with you, Herriot.

[*A pause. Several* DISCIPLES *are weeping.* DR. NEWMAN *gets up and goes toward the terrace.*]

DR. NEWMAN: [*To* MRS. BERGEN] An opportunity has come much sooner than I expected. [*To* DR. BERGEN] Dr. Bergen, in all sincerity and sympathy, I would like to suggest to you certain difficulties in your scheme of things. I would not intrude except for the fact that your wife has asked me to speak to you, and in addition, the fact that your doctrines have an aspect which would be impossibly dangerous and foolish, unless they are, in fact, true doctrines. I mean that your final test, that of dying to find one's true self is indefensible unless you are sure that you are right. But perhaps you prefer to discuss these matters with me in private.

DR. BERGEN [*impatiently*]: Go right ahead, sir. I hide nothing from my students and we believe, as you heard, that to hide anything is to multiply ignorance and blindness.

DR. NEWMAN: How, then, do you know that your belief in the sky as God's great eye is true? What possible proof have you?

DR. BERGEN: I know by intuition—by gazing upon the inevitable blue until it becomes self-evident that it is so.

DR. NEWMAN: Intuition is not proof. Proof is afforded when an hypothesis is framed—forgive me for using the jargon of science—making certain predictions about future events. If these events occur, the statement or hypothesis is true. If not, they are false. But intuition is something else again. The drunkard and the lunatic also have their indubitable intuitions—although I am not, I humbly assure you, suggesting that you are like one or the other. Many people have different and contradicting intuitions. Suppose another person had an intuition of the sky as God's round wall to hide the realm of heaven. How would you show him that he was wrong and you, on the contrary, correct?

DR. BERGEN [*becoming heated, but still full of assurance*]: How do you know that the grass is green? By looking at the grass. But some are color-blind. How can you prove the greenness of the grass to them? You cannot because of their incapacity to see color. Thus to some the sky is merely blueness and nothingness. Only by looking at the sky, grasping its nature by means of pure attention, can you be convinced that the sky is God's sensorium, God's blue eye. [*There is a murmur of pleasure among the* DISCIPLES.]

DR. NEWMAN: What you are saying amounts to this, that your belief can neither be proven nor disproven, for you provide no specific test of your assertion. The sky remains what it is for perception, no matter what is said about it, and almost anything can be said. If one does not see the sky in your fashion, one is blind.

DR. BERGEN [*sharply*]: Yes, one is blind. You are blinded by scientific method which looks past and beneath the facts of direct experience and forgets them. Consider, for example, the difference between the physicist's time—readings on a clock, a machine's abstract numbers—and felt time, time as we experience it from moment to moment. Surely you cannot deny that the latter is prior and ultimate, for without that actual experience how could the physicist get his kind of time? How could he have any experience whatever?

DR. NEWMAN [*as if concerned with other thoughts*]: There are a hundred other religions, a thousand more systems of belief, all of them asserting that they have the true path to the divine.

DR. BERGEN [*smiling with assurance*]: All of them fail in one thing, they have not attained knowledge of what mediates between the divine and the human, the infinite and the finite, which is the chief religious problem. Some have had direct experience of that mediator, which accounts for their frequent truths. But none have recognized fully nor correctly named the actual fact which mediates between God and man. I know I am right because I have direct experiences of what I assert, the only means of arriving at certainty.

DR. NEWMAN: Dr. Bergen, I am full of misgivings about what I now must do. I have delayed this interview with you for weeks, fearing the consequences of what I am about to tell you. But worse may come if I do not speak.

You believe that your daughter Eleanor killed herself because of one of your doctrines. You think that she believed as you do, and you say that intuition has made you certain that she killed herself, accepting your doctrine. You are wrong. She killed herself for a wholly different reason. She was in love with a man who would not marry her, partly because he was already married. Though he loved your daughter, he would not divorce his wife for her. He brought her to me, hoping that an analysis might free her from her obsessive passion for him. It did not, unfortunately, although we tried for more than a year. She became desperate because he had refused to see her for almost three months, and she killed herself when she was convinced that he would never marry her. Her predicament was almost commonplace in modern life. Only her means of adjusting herself was extraordinary, and that is accounted for by her inability to control her emotions, such an emotion of despondency as is clear in the victrola record you played. She killed herself because she was in love with a married man.

DR. BERGEN [*shocked and at a loss*]: You are lying! How can you prove what you say? It is what you wish to believe, not the truth. Whether consciously or not, you lie.

DR. NEWMAN: I have conclusive proof, the kind which you do not possess for your fantastic belief. It is a letter from your daughter written and posted an hour before she killed herself. You will see why I hesitated so long before coming to you, though I knew that her death was a mystery. By the time this letter was written, I was the only one in whom she would or could confide. The point is that despite your intimacy with God's blue eye, you wholly misconstrued her act. [*He reads the letter.*]

"Dear Dr. Newman:

You have been so kind to me that I don't like to use you for an unpleasant task, but M. (her lover's name) destroys all letters from me. I am killing myself because I cannot live without him. I want him to know that in his heart, but without any scandal which will hurt his wife and children, and he will not know this unless you tell him because I am trying to be good and useful for something for once by letting my poor father suppose that I am killing myself in obedience to his religious belief, of which you will hear more from others. Please forgive me and do this for me—tell M. that he was wrong to let anything stand in the way of love.

Your poor friend,
Eleanor."

DR. BERGEN [*desperately*]: Is that your sister's handwriting, Martha? [DR. NEWMAN *gives* MARTHA *the letter. She looks at it and reads it.*]

MARTHA [*after a moment, in a strange tone*]: O Father! Yes—it is her handwriting. He read the letter correctly.

DR. BERGEN [*as if completely humbled*]: Agh! I have shown myself a deluded fool, I suppose. I have been taken in by my own fraud, it seems. It seems that I deceived myself and I deceived all of you. No! It is inconceivable to me.

DR. NEWMAN: The whole thing will pass from your mind quickly. In a few months it will be merely a bad dream, or something about which you smile. Perhaps I should have broken the true story to you differently, in gradual stages.

MRS. BERGEN [*going over to her husband, who holds his face in his hands*]: This has separated us for a long time. It is probably for the best that this should have happened. It may be that her death has saved us from unending hatred for one another.

DR. BERGEN: No, I was sure. It was no illusion.

ANTHONY:

What of myself and my illusion,
Who loved her very much in perfect blindness?
I loved a phantom which my infatuation
Engendered. She was, it seems, a dream
Foisted upon me by my fatuous mind,
While in my sleep I walked near an abyss
Upon the 57th story window ledge,
Teetering on tiptoe.
               Belief contrives
A curious house, peculiar pyramid
Which narrows as it must to nothingness.
And on that tiny top we stand until
The actual sand shifts as it must, betrays
The desert of our lives, our broken sleep.
All right, let it be so. The worst has come.
I to the common world must pass

Who lived long privately. O worst of all,
I was not insufficient, but I was
Merely irrelevant to her being and her pain.

DR. BERGEN [*as if decided*]: That does not apply to me. I did
not deceive, I was not deceived, except by one poor miserable
distraught girl. One example proves nothing. She deceived me.
But I was not deceived in all, only in her.

[*He steps quickly from the long table on the terrace to the parapet, lifting himself upon it clumsily and standing up to full height before them,
as all move toward him in a ring, uttering their dismay variously.*]

Now I am going to kill myself! If you come closer, it will serve
no purpose, except to make me jump sooner. I wish to make
several idle remarks before I depart. If you wish to hear them,
you will keep your distance. I am decided. There is nothing
you can do to prevent me.

MARTHA: Father! Father!

MRS. BERGEN [*hysterical*]: For God's sake, for our sake, don't
kill yourself. Wait! Wait! You said that one example proves
nothing. You said so. You have no reason for killing yourself.

DR. BERGEN: Every reason. I wish to be sure once and for all. I
cannot endure the long experience of doubt once more. Will
you listen to me and hear what I have to say?

DR. NEWMAN: Wait! Do not increase the tragedy in this house.
Time takes away both good and bad. In three months all
will seem different to you. It will always be possible for you
to die.

VARIOUS DISCIPLES [*successively*]: We need you! We depend on
you! We are lost without you! We believe in you! You taught us!

DR. BERGEN: It is too late, there is only one act left for me. The
horror of doubt crowds my mind and I cannot endure it.
[*Turning and looking down.*] Will you listen to me? On the
tiny street fifteen stories below the tiny figures of human beings
and of cars move with sharp, short motions, quickly, neatly, and

wholly without meaning. I am going the shortest distance past them, which will at least convince you of my sincerity.

MARTHA: Father, wait!

DR. BERGEN: This is what terrorizes you, a human being about to die of his own will.

DR. NEWMAN: If you kill yourself now, they will say that you are insane.

DR. BERGEN: I am not concerned about what will be said any longer. I am going to perfect certainty. I am going to find out for myself. Let me say what I have to say. [*To* MRS. BERGEN] Elsa, I am sorry. You do not understand, but I do not blame you. You were good to me for a long time, not lately; but my gratitude remains. [*To* MARTHA] Martha, be a good girl, be satisfied with what life itself provides, although it is insufficient. Do not imitate your father. [*To the* DISCIPLES] I can no longer help you, but you will know that I am sincere, and you will surely know once and for all at some time if I was right. I can not tolerate the mere possibility that I have suffered from some dream or hallucination.

I knew long ago that I would come to this pass, when death alone would be left for me, as a means of satisfying my mind and my heart. For a long time, I lived from one satisfaction to another—my profession, my wife, my family, my increasing success as a doctor. Then one day I became wholly aware of what all deliberately forget—that life is not a self-contained sphere, which exists unendingly. I knew to my fingertips that I must die, as I had seen so many die. This me must die, this body must rot; I would see, hear, feel, taste, touch, think, no more. For a year I was a prey to the worst despondency. Nothing had meaning for me. Then I was visited by the first of repeated special experiences and all was changed until now. Do you understand me? I cannot return to my old unrest and uncertainty. What does one have, having lived long? What is the virtue and fruit of old age? A bedpan, a failing memory, a drooling mouth, the sense of one's own inadequacy at last. But I am going to find out for myself once and for all. There is only one means of knowing.

DR. NEWMAN: I believe that you were right! I accept your belief! One example proves nothing.

DR. BERGEN: No! You are insincere! I hear the duplicity in your voice. I am faced by my own doubt. I have the will to know and nothing else. Death is the only satisfaction left to me. The stench of this life offends me too much at last. I am done. Whereas the consequence is final and the exodus is irreparable; whereas the notion is unanalyzed, the dream unexhausted, the procedure without rationale, the belief a verbalism, there remains the complete conclusion of utter light or at least a little unnervous peace. I will feel the parts of my body one last time, for my own patience is intolerable to me; I can no longer endure my own thoughts, I have much to say, but my own speech appalls me. There is a fine abyss which waits to receive me and please me and satisfy me as never before.

MARTHA [*moving towards him*]: Father! Father!

DR. BERGEN: Stand back, Martha. I am faced with my own ignorance. But I am going to find out for myself once and for all!

[*He jumps to his death as several scream.* MARTHA, *running from among them, jumps up and also leaps from the parapet.*]

DR. NEWMAN: Nothing is left to say, everything to do, question my own heart, justify myself, if I can. Belief and knowledge consume the heart of man.

RAKOVSKY [*as if in echo*]: Knowledge and belief devour the mind of man.

ANTHONY: Belief, knowledge, and desire—desire most of all.

DR. NEWMAN: Man destroys his own heart.

CURTAIN

SHENANDOAH

Delmore Schwartz

The Poet of the Month

NEW DIRECTIONS,   NORFOLK, CONN.

TITLE PAGE OF THE ORIGINAL
NEW DIRECTIONS EDITION, 1941.

SHENDANDOAH

(To Francis Ferguson)

It is the historic nature of all particulars to try to prove that they are universal by nature—

ENCYCLOPEDIA BRITTANICA

Wer sass nicht bang vor seines Herzens vorhang?
Der schlug sich auf: die Szenerie war Abschied....

RILKE

PERSONS OF THE PLAY

Shenandoah Fish
Elsie Fish
Mrs. Goldmark
Jacob Fish
Walter Fish and wife
Joseph Fish and wife
Leonard Fish
Dolly Fish

Sarah Harris
Edna Harris
Jack Strauss
Harry Lasky
Edith Strauss
Bertha Lasky
The baby Shenandoah
Dr. Adamson

[Enter SHENANDOAH, *to the right. A spotlight shines on him as the theater is darkened and the curtain rises on a darkened stage.*]

SHENANDOAH:
　　This was the greatest day of my whole life!
　　I was eight days of age:
　　　　　　　　　　　　Twenty-five years
　　Consume my being as I speak (for we
　　Are made of years and days, not flesh and blood),
　　And no event since then is as important!
　　In January 1914 a choice was made
　　Which in my life has played a part as endless
　　As the world-famous apple, eaten in Eden,
　　Which made original sin and the life of man
　　—Or as the trigger finger with a bitten nail
　　Which Prinzip's mind was soon to press
　　In Sarajevo, firing at Verdun,
　　St. Petersburg, Vienna, and Berlin—
　　And like the length of Cleopatra's nose,
　　And like the grain of sand in Cromwell's kidney,
　　As Pascal said, who knew a thing or two,
　　Or like the pinpoint prick which gave the great
　　Eloquent statesman lockjaw in the prime of life
　　(O Death is eminent, beyond belief!)
　　—Return with me, stand at my point of view,
　　Regard with my emotion the small event
　　Which gave my mind and gave my character,
　　Amid the hundred thousand possibilities
　　Heredity and community avail,
　　Bound and engender,
　　　　　　　　　　　the very life I know!

[*The stage lights up and the curtain rises.*]

The curtain rises on a dining room
In the lower middle class in 1914:
Gaze briefly at the period quality,
Not at the quaintness, but at the pathos
Of any moment of time, seen in its pastness,
The ignorance which prophet, astrologist,
And palmist use as capital and need
—The dining room contains in vivid signs
Certain clear generals of time and place:
Look at the cut glass bowls on the buffet,
They are the works of art of these rising Jews,
—The shadow of Israel and the shadows of Europe
Darken their minds and hearts in the new world.
They prosper in America. They win the jewels
(My mind intends no pun, but falls on one:
Jews are no jewels, as Angles are no angels.)
Of cut glass bowls to place upon their tables,
Moved by the taste and trend of the middle class—

[*Enter* ELSIE FISH *with her child in a bassinet and* EDNA GOLD-
MARK, *her next door neighbor. Both are young married women, but*
MRS. GOLDMARK *is plainly the older of the two. As* SHENANDOAH
speaks, ELSIE *is engaged in tending the baby, while* MRS. GOLD-
MARK *regards her.*]

Explain the other furniture yourself,
But lift your mind from the local color,
For the particular as particular
Is not itself, as a house is not its front,
And as a man is not his flesh:
                              Come now,
See the particular as universal,
Significance like sunlight, the symbol's glory,
As two crossed sticks of wood shine with the story
Of Jesus Christ and several institutions,

—The union of particular and universal,
That's what one ought to see, as Aristotle
Has said for years:

                    he knew a thing or two—

[*During the speeches of all the characters except* SHENANDOAH, *there is a systematic shift back and forth from formal speech to colloquial speech, a shift which is reflected in their actions, and echoed, so to speak, in the shift from verse to prose.*]

ELSIE FISH: My father-in-law is coming to see me before the ceremony. I wonder what he wants. When he called, he was very disturbed and upset.

MRS. GOLDMARK: Maybe he wants to spend some time with his new grandson before the ceremony. We do not know what it is to be a grandparent, we are too young. Just think, a grandparent has all the pleasure, none of the pain and expense.

ELSIE FISH: I do not think he is so pleased. This is no novelty to him. He has been made a grandparent five times already by his other sons and daughters. Do you know, he said it was a question of life and death that he wanted to speak to me about. What can it be? But he is always like that, always nervous, always disturbed.

MRS. GOLDMARK: Maybe he wants to speak to your husband too. Where is your husband now?

ELSIE FISH: How should I know where my husband is? Who am I to know such a thing?

SHENANDOAH [*standing at an angle to the scene, unseen and unheard*]:
This marriage is a stupid endless mistake,
Unhappiness flares from it, day and night,
The child has been desired four long years,
For friends have told the young married woman
The child will change his father, alter her image
Both in his mind and heart. For he is cruel.

How can two egos live near by all their days,
If Love and Love's unnatural forgiveness
Do not give to the body's selfishness
And the will's cruelty lifelong *carte blanche*?

[*A doorbell rings. The negro* SERVANT GIRL *passes from the kitchen at the left through doorway in back of dining room which leads to the hall.*]

ELSIE FISH: That must be my father-in-law now. Since he has come about something very important, would you go now, Mrs. Goldmark, and come back when he has gone? You have been a wonderful neighbor.

MRS. GOLDMARK [*departing*]: I have had two children myself. I know what it is to be a mother for the first time.

[*Enter* JACOB FISH, *a man of sixty.*]

JACOB FISH [*plainly preoccupied*]: Dear Elsie, I was very anxious to see you before the ceremony. So this is my new grandson: what a fine boy! May he live to a hundred and ten!

SHENANDOAH:
God save me from such wishes, though well meant:
This old man has not read Ecclesiastes
Or Sophocles. Yet he has lived for sixty years,
He should know better what long life avails,
The best seats at the funerals of friends.

JACOB FISH: My dear girl, last night I heard that you were going to name the boy Jacob, after your dead father. Have you forgotten that Jacob is my name also? Have you forgotten what it means to have a child named after you, when you are still living?

ELSIE FISH: What is it, except an honor? An honor to you, father-in-law, as well as to my dear dead father, although I admit I had him in mind first of all.

JACOB FISH: Elsie, I do not blame you for not knowing the beliefs
of your religion and your people. You are only a woman, and
in this great new America, anyone might forget everything but
such wonderful things like tall buildings, subways, automobiles, and iceboxes. But if the child is named Jacob, it will be
my death warrant! Thus all the learned ministers have said. It is
written again and again in various commentaries and interpretations of the Law. It has been believed for thousands of years.

SHENANDOAH:

How powerful the past! O king of kings,
King of the elements,
                    king of all thinking things!

ELSIE FISH: I am surprised that you accept such beliefs, father-
in-law. I never thought that you were especially religious.

JACOB FISH: Wisdom comes with the years, my dear girl. When
you are my age, you will feel as I do about these matters.

SHENANDOAH:

This old man is afraid of death, though life
Has long been cruel as jealousy to him.
How often death presides when birth occurs:
Yet to disturb the naming of a child
Is wrong,
            though many would behave like this—
O to what difficult and painful feat
Shall I compare the birth of any child
And all related problems? To the descent
Of a small grand piano from a window
On the fifth-floor: O what a *tour de force*,
Clumsy as hippos or rich men *en route*
To Heaven through the famous needle's eye!
Such is our *début* in the turning world....

ELSIE FISH: How can I change the child's name now? Some of
the presents already have his initials and his name has been
announced on very expensive engraved cards. What will I say

to my mother, my father's widow? This is her first grandchild. Do you really think a name will make you die?

JACOB FISH: Elsie, look at the problem from this point of view: why take a chance? If I die, think of how you will feel. There are hundreds of names which are very handsome.

ELSIE FISH: Father-in-law, you know I would like to please you.

JACOB FISH: You are a good woman, Elsie. You are too good for my son. He does not deserve such a fine wife.

ELSIE FISH: You do not know how he behaves to me. You would not believe me, if I told you. I have not had a happy day in the four years of my marriage.

JACOB FISH: I know, I know! He ran away from home as a boy and has never listened to anyone. I tell him every time I see him that he does not deserve such a wife, so intelligent, so good-looking, so kind and refined!

ELSIE FISH: I will do what you ask me to do. I will change the child's name. Jacob is not a fine name, anyhow. I want the boy to have an unusual name because he is going to be an unusual boy.

[*The* BABY *begins to howl, in a formalized way which does not get in the way of the dialogue, but seems a comment on it.*]

You understand, I would not do this for anyone but you.

JACOB FISH: I will be grateful to you to my dying day!

ELSIE FISH: You have many years of life ahead of you!

JACOB FISH: You are a wonderful woman!

[*In this dialogue, the shift back and forth between formalized and colloquial speech becomes especially pronounced.* ELSIE FISH *hands the child to* SHENANDOAH, *as if absentmindedly, and leaves the dining room to go to the door with her father-in-law.*]

SHENANDOAH:
She thinks to please her husband through his father.

Do not suppose this flattery too gross:
If it were smiled at any one of you
You would not mind! You might not recognize
The flattery as such. And if you did,
You would not mind! Such falseness is too pleasant:
Each ego hides a half-belief the best is true,
Good luck and sympathy are all it lacks
To make the bright lights shine upon its goodness,
Its kindness, shyness, talent, wit, and charm!
—In any case, what can she do? Fight Death,
The great opponent ever undefeated
Except perhaps by Mozart?
                                    As for belief,
To make a man give up but one belief
Is just like pulling teeth from a lion's mouth—

[SHENANDOAH *turns his attention to the child in his arms, re-*
gards the child with lifted eyebrows and a doubtful smile. As he does
so, the spotlight falls on him, while the scene is left in a half-light.]

Poor child, the center of this sinful earth,
How many world-wide powers surround you now,
Making your tears appropriate to more
Than the un-understood need and disorder
Your body feels. True and appropriate
Your sobs and tears, because you hardly know
How many world-wide powers surround you now,
And what a vicious fate prepares itself
To make of you an alien and a freak!
—I too am right to sympathize with you,
If I do not, who will? for I am bound
By the sick pity and the faithful love
The ego bears itself, as if Narcissus
And Romeo were one: for I am you

By that identity which fights through time,
No matter what Kant and other skeptics say
—Is it not true that every first-born child
Is looked on by his relatives as if
They were the Magi, seeking Zion's promise?
At any rate, children for long have been
The prizes and angels of the West,
But what this signifies let us omit
—Now in the great city, mid-winter holds,
The dirty rags of snow freeze at the curb,
Pneumonia sucks at breath, the turning globe
Brings to the bitter air and the grey sky
The long illness of time and history,
And in the wide world Woodrow Wilson does
What he can do. In the wide world, alas!
The World War grows in nations and in hearts,
Bringing ten million souls an early death!
—Forgive my speech: I have nor youth nor age,
But as it were an after-dinner speech,
Speaking of both, with endless platitudes—

[*The spotlight goes out, the scene is once more fully lighted,* ELSIE FISH *returns to the dining room with* MRS. GOLDMARK, SHENANDOAH *gives the child back to his mother, who acts as if he were not there, and then* SHENANDOAH *returns to his position at the side, removed from the scene and at an angle to both audience and scene.*]

ELSIE FISH: I felt for the old man and you know how I am: I
  always give in to my sympathies. I know it is a weakness. But
  what a shame that he should let such beliefs make him afraid.
MRS. GOLDMARK: When one is old, one is like a child.
ELSIE FISH: And after all, I said to myself, he is a poor unhappy old man who came to America because his children
  had come. His wife abuses him because he does not work and

his grown-up children support him, but give the mother the money, so that he has to come to his wife for a dollar.

Mrs. Goldmark: That's the way it is, that's old age for you.

Elsie Fish: But now I must find a new name for my boy before the guests come. My husband's relatives are coming and some of the men who work for my husband, with their wives. Mrs. Goldmark, you gave your children such fine names, maybe you can think of a name for me.

Mrs. Goldmark: Thank you for the compliment. I like the names Herbert and Mortimer more all the time. They are so distinguished and new and American. Do you know how I came to think of them? I was reading the newspaper in bed after my first boy was born. I was reading the society page, which is always so interesting.

Elsie Fish: Let's get the morning paper and we will see what luck I have. I wish my husband were here, I must have his approval. He gets angry so quickly.

[Mrs. Goldmark *goes into the living room at the right and returns with the newspaper.*]

Elsie Fish [to herself]: I wonder where Walter is.

Mrs. Goldmark: Now let us see what names are mentioned today.

Shenandoah:
    While they gaze at their glamorous ruling class,
    I must stand here, regardant at an angle,
    I must lie there, quite helpless in my cradle,
    As passive as a man who takes a haircut—
    And yet how many minds believe a man
    Creates his life *ex nihilo*, and laugh
    At the far influence of deities,
                                and stars—

Mrs. Goldmark: "Mr. and Mrs. Frederick Somerville sailed yesterday for Havana—" What a life! to be able to enjoy sunshine and warmth in the middle of winter: one would never have colds—

ELSIE FISH: Maybe some day you too will be able to go south in the winter. Who would have believed we would all be as well as we are, ten years ago? Read some of the first names, one after another.

MRS. GOLDMARK: Russell, Julian, Christopher, Nicholas, Glenn, Llewellyn, Murray, Franklin, Alexander: do you like any of those?

ELSIE FISH: I like some of them, Mrs. Goldmark, but I might as well pick one from a whole many. Read some more.

MRS. GOLDMARK: Lincoln, Bertram, Francis, Willis, Kenneth—

ELSIE FISH: Kenneth: that's a fine name—

MRS. GOLDMARK: I don't like it: it sounds Scandinavian—[1]

ELSIE FISH: What's wrong with that?

MRS. GOLDMARK: You should hear some of the things my husband tells me about the Scandinavians! Marvin, Irving, Martin, James, Elmer, Oswald, Rupert, Delmore—

ELSIE FISH: Delmore! What a pretty name, Mrs. Goldmark—

MRS. GOLDMARK: Vernon, Allen, Lawrence, Archibald, Arthur, Clarence, Edgar, Randolph—

SHENANDOAH:
This shows how all things come to poetry,
As all things come to generation's crux:
Every particular must have a name,
Every uniqueness needs a special sound,
In the Beginning is the word
                    and in the End
Gabriel will call the blessèd by their nicknames,
And summon up the damned by the sweet petnames
They called each other in adulterous beds—

MRS. GOLDMARK: Elliott, Thomas, Maxwell, Harold, Melvin, Mitchell, Tracy, Norman, Ralph, Washington, Christopher—

---

1. "... *Scandinavian*": A private joke; Schwartz's brother Kenneth (1916–1990) was the object of ambivalent feelings. Schwartz persistently turned Kenneth into a girl in his autobiographical fiction, as noted by his biographer, James Atlas. See his *Delmore Schwartz: The Life of An American Poet* (Farrar, Straus & Giroux, 1977), p. 13.

ELSIE FISH: I like those names, but none of them really stands out. How do you think they would sound with Fish? Washington Fish? Christopher Fish? I would like an unusual sound.

SHENANDOAH:

She comes close to the problem's very heart,
She has a sense of connotation. But wrongly,
As if, somehow, she stood upon her head
And saw the room minutely,

upside down!

MRS. GOLDMARK: Do you know, I could read the society page for weeks at a time? If I am ever sick, I will. I feel as if I had known some of the members of the Four Hundred, the Vanderbilts and the Astors, for years. And I know about the less important families also. I know their friends and where they go in winter and summer. For instance, the Talbot Brewsters, who are mentioned today: every year they go to Florida in January. Mr. Brewster has an estate in the Shenandoah Valley ...

ELSIE FISH: Shenandoah! What a wonderful name: Shenandoah Fish!

[*The baby begins to howl.*]

MRS. GOLDMARK: It is not really the name of a person, but the name of a place. Yet I admit it is an interesting name.

ELSIE FISH: He will be the first one ever to be called Shenandoah! Shhhhh, baby, shhhhh: you have a beautiful name.

SHENANDOAH:

Now it is done! quickly! I am undone:
This is the crucial crime, the accident
Which is more than an accident because
It happens only to certain characters,
As only Isaac Newton underwent
The accidental apple's happy fall—

[As before, the spotlight shines on SHENANDOAH, *the scene itself is left in a half-light,* ELSIE FISH *gives* SHENANDOAH *the crying child and leaves the dining room with her neighbor.* SHENANDOAH *steps to the footlights, goes through motions intended to soothe the crying child, and speaks as if to the infant.]*

Cry, cry, poor psyche, eight days old:
Primitive peoples, sparkling with intuition,
Often refuse to give the child a name,
Or call him "Filth," "Worthless," "Nothingness,"
In order to outwit the evil powers.
Sometimes a child is named by the event
Which happened near his birth: how wise that is—
This poor child by that rule would thus be named
"The First World War"—
                Among the civilized,
A child is often named his father's son,
Second and fresh identity: the wish is clear,
All men would live forever—
                Some are named
After the places where they live, tacit
Admission of the part the *milieu* plays
And how it penetrates each living soul—
Some are called the professions, some are saints
As if to'express a hope of lives to come:
But everywhere on all sides everyone
Feels with intensity how many needs
Names manifest, resound, and satisfy—
The Jews were wise, when they called God
                    "The Nameless"
(He is the'anonymous Father of all hearts,
At least in *my* opinion). Legal codes
Are right too when they make most difficult
The change of names, flight from identity—

But let me now propose another use,
Custom, and rule: let each child choose his name
When he is old enough? Is this too great
An emphasis upon the private will?
Is not the problem very serious?

[*The dining room fills with relatives and guests. Among those present are the infant's father,* WALTER FISH; *Walter Fish's brothers,* JOSEPH *and* LEONARD, *and their wives;* JACOB *and* DOLLY
FISH, *Walter's father and mother; Elsie Fish's mother,* SARAH
HARRIS, *and her sister,* EDNA HARRIS; JACK STRAUSS *and*
HARRY LASKY, *two men who work for* WALTER FISH, *and their
wives,* EDITH STRAUSS *and* BERTHA LASKY. SHENANDOAH
*passes the infant in his arms to one of the relatives, and for a mo-
ment the infant is passed from person to person like a medicine
ball, while everyone wears a broad grin. Then the infant is placed
in his bassinet. Some are eating the sandwiches and fruits on the
buffet, and* WALTER FISH *gives one of the men a drink. An argument is in progress.*]

JACK STRAUSS: To me, Shenandoah is a beautiful name, original
and strange. I will give fifty dollars to be this boy's godfather.
ELSIE FISH [*to her sister,* EDITH]: He is just trying to win favor
with the man he works for.
BERTHA LASKY [*to her husband*]: What's the matter with you?
Make an offer quickly: don't let him get ahead of you.
HARRY LASKY: I will give sixty dollars to be the boy's god-
father—
JACK STRAUSS: I will go higher and make it seventy-five—
WALTER FISH: Gentlemen, Gentlemen: you will make me think
I ought to have a few children a week.
SHENANDOAH:
Clearly these business men feel in the father
A man whose day will come: he will be rich,
They feel his power. They feel his strength. He is

A man whose friendship must be cultivated,
$$\text{sought and won}—$$

ELSIE FISH: Walter, you promised me. I want my brother Nathan to be the child's godfather.

WALTER FISH: I promised you and I will keep my promise. Nathan is a fine young man, studious and intelligent. What better godfather could a child be given than a promising young doctor? *Nothing is too good for my son.* Thank you, Jack and Harry, when the boy is old enough I will tell him how much money you were willing to spend to be the boy's godfather. No doubt, he will then feel kindly to you.

SHENANDOAH:
He has a brutal tongue, cannot resist
Speaking his brutal insights as if
No one else knew the human heart. Yet this
Proves that such motives are intense in him,
How would he know them, why would he mock them,
Smiling with keen pleasure when he sees them
At work in other hearts, except in great
Relief at finding colleagues, finding peers?

JACK STRAUSS: I bet the boy will make a million dollars—

HARRY LASKY: I bet that he will be a famous lawyer—

GRANDMOTHER HARRIS: I hope that he will be a famous doctor—

SHENANDOAH:
How utterly they miss the mark, how shocked,
How horrified if they but knew what I
Will one day be: if from their point of view
They saw me truly, saw my true colors,
$$\text{grasped}$$
And understood the rôle of my profession!
O, their emotions would approximate
Those of a man who has found out his wife
Has been unfaithful or was born Chinese—

[*Enter* NATHAN HARRIS, *a good-looking and tall young man who has recently become a doctor. It is obvious as he is greeted that he is well-liked and respected by all and as he shakes hands, his boundless self-assurance and sense of authority shows itself.*]

NATHAN HARRIS: Where is my wonderful nephew, Jacob or Jacky Fish?

ELSIE FISH: Nathan, we have decided to give him another name since my father-in-law has the same name. We are going to call him Shenandoah—

NATHAN HARRIS: Shenandoah! How in a hundred years did you think of such a foolish name?

WALTER FISH: I fail to see anything foolish about Shenandoah?

NATHAN HARRIS: It is foolish in every way. It does not sound right with Fish. The association of ideas is appalling. The boy will be handicapped as if he had a clubfoot. When he grows up, he will dislike his name and blame you for giving it to him.

SHENANDOAH:

How moved I am! how much he understands!

He is both right and wrong. He sees the danger,

But does not see the strange effect to come:

Yet what a friend he is to me, how close

I feel to him! He means well and he knows

How difficult Life is,

climbing on hands and knees—

JACK STRAUSS: You are exaggerating, Dr. Harris.

HARRY LASKY: This is not a matter of the human body, in which you are an expert, Dr. Harris.

NATHAN HARRIS: No, not the human body, but the human soul: nothing is more important than a name. He will be mocked by other boys when he goes to school because his name is so peculiar—

SHENANDOAH:

He is intelligent, that's obvious:

Perhaps his youth permits a better view

Of cultural conditions of the Age—

NATHAN HARRIS: Don't you see how pretentious the name is?

WALTER FISH: Nathan, there is nothing wrong with me. I am as good as the next one and maybe better. My son has a right to a pretentious name.

NATHAN HARRIS: Walter, to be pretentious means to show off foolishly.

[*The infant has begun to cry again and cries louder as they quarrel.*]

WALTER FISH: Thank you very much for explaining the English language to me. That's very pretentious of you—

NATHAN HARRIS: Excuse me, Walter: what I meant to say is that the two names of Shenandoah and Fish do not go well together—

WALTER FISH: I suppose you think something like Fresh Fish would be better? [*Laughter from the others.*]

NATHAN HARRIS: All right, go ahead and laugh. But if this helpless infant is going to be named Shenandoah, I don't want to be his godfather.

WALTER FISH: Don't do me any favors! Others are willing to pay for the privilege. I am glad that you don't want to be his godfather—

NATHAN HARRIS: I am glad that you are glad!

GRANDMOTHER HARRIS: Nathan, don't lose your temper. What a shame, to quarrel on a day like this: what will the minister think?

WALTER FISH: He has come here to insult me and to insult an eight-day old child. Who do you think you are, anyway? Just because you are a doctor does not mean you are better than us in every respect—

ELSIE FISH: Nathan, you ought to be ashamed of yourself: you should have heard the fine things Walter was just saying about you and how he wanted you to be the boy's godfather. I was the one who chose the name of Shenandoah—

NATHAN HARRIS: Then you ought to be ashamed of *yourself!*

I am not going to stay here another moment to see a helpless
child punished for the rest of his life because his parents have
an inadequate understanding of the English language—

[NATHAN *goes out as everyone follows him, trying to stop his departure. The child is given to* SHENANDOAH *again. Spotlight and
half-light once more, as* SHENANDOAH *comes to the footlights, trying to stop the child's tears.*]

SHENANDOAH:
    This is hardly the last time, little boy,
    That conflict will engage the consciousness
    Of those who might admire Nature, pray to God,
    Make love, make friends, make works of art,
                    make peace—
    O no! hardly the last time: in the end
    All men may seem essential boxers, hate
    May seem the energy which drives the stars,
    (*L'amor che move il sole e l'altre stelle!*)
    And war as human as the beating heart:
    So Hegel and Empedocles have taught.
    —It is impossible to tell you now
    How many world-wide causes work this room
    To bring about the person of your name:
    Europe! America! the fear of death!
    Belief and half-belief in Zion's word!
    The order of a community in which
    The lower middle class looks up and gapes
    And strives to imitate the sick élite
    In thought, in emptiness, in luxury;
    Also the foreigner whose foreign-ness
    Names his son native, speaking broken English—
    Enough! for this is obvious enough:
    Let us consider where the great men are
    Who will obsess this child when he can read:

Joyce is in Trieste in a Berlitz school,
Teaching himself the puns of *Finnegans Wake*—
Eliot works in a bank and there he learns
The profit and the loss, the death of cities—
Pound howls at him, finds what expatriates
Can find,
          culture in chaos all through time,
Like a Picasso show! Rilke endures
Of silence and of solitude the unheard music
In empty castles which great knights have left—
Yeats too, like Rilke, on old lords' estates,
Seeks for the permanent amid the loss,
Daily and desperate, of love, of friends,
Of every thought with which his age began—
Kafka in Prague works in an office, learns
How bureaucratic Life, how far-off God,
A white-collar class' theology—
Perse is in Asia as a diplomat,
—He sees the violent energy with which
Civilization creates itself and moves—
Yet, with these images, he cannot see
The moral apathy after The Munich Pact,
The'unnatural silence on The Maginot Line,
—Yet he cannot foresee The Fall of France—
Mann, too, in Davos-Platz finds in the sick
The triumph of the artist and the intellect—
All over Europe these exiles find in art
What exile is: art becomes exile too,
A secret and a code studied in secret,
Declaring the agony of modern life:
The child will learn of life from these great men,
He will participate in their solitude,
And maybe in the end, on such a night
As this, return to the starting-point, his name,
Showing himself as such among his friends—

[*The lighting changes as before, the whole cast comes back, and as the child is returned to the dining room by* SHENANDOAH, *it is obvious that the argument has continued with greater and greater heat. For a moment, as the argument waxes fast and furious, the infant is passed from person to person hurriedly and painfully, like something too hot to handle.* NATHAN *has been backed against the wall by his mother and several of the men, who are trying to keep him from making his departure.*]

NATHAN HARRIS: I say again that the name Shenandoah is inexcusable and intolerable, and I will not stay here unless the boy is given another name—

GRANDMOTHER HARRIS: What an unlucky thing for the baby, to have his godfather go away on this day: this day of all days—

WALTER FISH: Let him go, if he feels that way. He thinks he is too good for all of us—

ELSIE FISH: What name would you suggest for my child, Nathan? Just what is wrong with Shenandoah?

NATHAN HARRIS: I have explained again and again that Shenandoah is not a name, to begin with, and secondly, it does not go well with Fish.

MRS. GOLDMARK: He is just a snob—

JACOB FISH: I wish I had not started this whole business. But after all, a great tradition was at stake.

DOLLY FISH: You ought to be ashamed of yourself: you would like to live forever.

NATHAN HARRIS [*scanning the paper*]: Mrs. Goldmark, you are so resourceful, here, turn to the sport pages and read out the names of the entries at the race-tracks. [MRS. GOLDMARK *turns aside in anger.*]

SHENANDOAH:
My God in Heaven: what piercing irony,
To think of naming me after a horse—

NATHAN HARRIS: "Straw Flower, About Face, Cookie, Royal
Minuet, Sandy Boot, Rex Flag, Hand & Glove, Fencing, Key
Man, Little Tramp, Wise Man, Domkin—"
SHENANDOAH:
These names are fairly pleasant, after all:
But I am not the best judge, prejudiced—
WALTER FISH: This is too much: how long am I supposed
to stand here and be insulted without opening my mouth?
To name my son after a horse: who do you think you are,
anyway?
NATHAN HARRIS: Who do you think the child is, anyway?

[*The child howls and* SHENANDOAH *holds his hand to his head
and then to his heart with feeling.*]

SHENANDOAH: I often wonder who I am, in fact—
WALTER FISH: Please depart from this house at once—
SEVERAL RELATIVES: Nathan! Walter! Nathan! Walter!
NATHAN HARRIS: This is my sister's home. I refuse to go.
WALTER FISH: I am going to get a policeman—

[*Enter the rabbi,* DR. DAVID ADAMSON.]

DR. ADAMSON: Ah, this is the house blessed by the birth of a
child; what a wonderful thing it is to bring a human being into
the world—
SHENANDOAH:
Here is the man of God: what will he say?
How relevant are his imperatives?
Can he express himself in modern terms?
And bring this conflict to a peaceful end?
His insights, old as Pharaoh, sometimes work,
But there is always something wholly new,
Unique, unheard-of, unaccounted for,
Under the sun, despite Ecclesiastes—

Dr. Adamson: But why did I hear such shouting and angry voices? What must God think, seeing anger in the house of a newborn child? Men were not born to fight with one another—

Jacob Fish: Why not let Dr. Adamson decide who is right?

Walter Fish: This is my son: I am the one to decide his proper name—

Dr. Adamson: A child is not a piece of property, Mr. Fish—

Walter Fish: Are you here to insult me too?

Dr. Adamson: Now, now: my remark was ill-considered: but let us get to the bottom of this improper quarrel—

Elsie Fish: Let me explain quickly: we cannot name the child Jacob after my dear dead father because his other grandfather's name is Jacob and here he is—

Jacob Fish: Thank God for that!

Dr. Adamson: You are right, a child ought to not be named after a living man: that is the habit of the Gentiles.

Jacob Fish: Let us not imitate them—

Elsie Fish: We decided to name him Shenandoah because that sounds like such a fine name. But my brother Nathan seems to think it is disgraceful. What do you think, Dr. Adamson?

Nathan Harris: I wonder how much sense this anachronism has? He knows more than the father, however.

Dr. Adamson: It is a most unusual name. There are so many fine names which belong to our people: why go far afield?

Walter Fish: There has been enough discussion. I have made up my mind. The boy is going to be called Shenandoah.

Shenandoah:
This shows the livid power of my father:
For fifteen years he will behave like this—

Dr. Adamson: I do not want to add fuel to the flames of this regrettable dispute. I must admit that there is nothing seriously wrong with the name, although it is unusual—

NATHAN HARRIS: You see, he is not sure. He does not know. He would like to stop the quarrel, but he speaks without conviction—

SHENANDOAH:

"The best lack all conviction, while the worst
Are full of passionate intensity—"[2]

DR. ADAMSON: Young man, I am full of conviction.

WALTER FISH: Go on, Nathan, just go on like that: attack everyone in the house: did you ever see anyone so sure of himself?

ELSIE FISH: Walter, maybe Nathan is right, who knows? Why don't you call up Kelly and ask him?

SHENANDOAH:

What a suggestion! fearful and unsure,
She seeks the Gentile World, the Gentile voice!
The ancient wisdom is far from enough,
Far from enough her husband's cleverness—

WALTER FISH: *All right;* everyone always says that I am unwilling to take advice and listen to reason. I will show you I can and I do. I will call my lawyer Kelly and we will find out what he has to say about the name. Not that I think for one moment that you're right, Nathan—

NATHAN HARRIS: Go ahead, Walter, call up Kelly: I won't think for one moment that you think I am right—

JACOB FISH: Who is this Kelly?

HARRY LASKY: Kelly is Walter's lawyer, one of the best young lawyers in town, one of the *coming* men. And they say he knows the right people in Tammany through his wife's sister—

DR. ADAMSON: Mr. Fish, to one and all it is perfectly clear that you have no need of me, since you have your lawyer Kelly. I would like to suggest that he perform the ceremony of circumcision—

---

2. "… *passionate intensity—*": Schwartz's protagonist quotes from Yeats's poem, "The Second Coming."

[*He starts for the door. Walter stops him.*]

HARRY LASKY: Another one wants to go! Soon no one will be left!

WALTER FISH: Now, now, Dr. Adamson, no offense intended. With all due respect for you, you know it is always best to hear what everyone has to say. *After all, this child is going to live in a world of Kellys!* Just sit down for a moment while I call. I am going to make this worth your while.

DR. ADAMSON [*to himself*]: Forbearance and humility are best: what good will it do for me to become angry? The modern world is what it is.

[WALTER *goes out to call.* DR. ADAMSON *helps himself to a piece of fruit from the buffet.*]

SHENANDOAH:

His feelings have been hurt. The war between
Divine and secular authority,
Is old as man in Nature! Ah, he knows
He is a kind of chauffeur and no more,
Hence he adjusts himself with a piece of fruit—

[WALTER *can be seen in the hallway, holding up the telephone to his mouth.*]

WALTER FISH: Hello, Kelly: this is Fish. Fine and they're fine too. Nothing like being a father. And how are you? And the wife and children? That's good. Sorry to disturb you on a Sunday (hope you put in a good word for me with the Almighty! ha! ha!) I have a problem on my hands and I could use some of your advice (just put it on the bill, ha! ha!).

SHENANDOAH:

For this did Alexander Graham Bell
Rack his poor wits? For this? Was it for this

The matchless English language was evolved
To signify the inexhaustible world?

WALTER FISH: You know how today we are giving my boy a
name. The ceremony is just like a christening, except that it's
different—Yes, ha! ha!

NATHAN HARRIS [*to the rest, who are listening intently*]: What a
marvellous sense of humor—

WALTER FISH: I would like to have invited you, but you know
how it is. Now the thing is this: we thought of naming the boy
Shenandoah. Yes, Shenandoah: it seems to be some place
down South. But my brother-in-law is making a scene about
the whole thing. He says the name is no good—

NATHAN HARRIS: As if it were merely a matter of opinion!

SHENANDOAH:
Ah, what a friend! How close I feel to him!
Almost as close as to that sobbing child—

WALTER FISH: I don't agree with him. It sounds fine to me, very
impressive. But this is not the kind of thing you like to take
a chance about. After all, a name is one of those permanent
things. People will be calling him that every day in his life. O,
now you're joking: sure, Francis is a fine name, but not for us.
It would not go well with Fish—

NATHAN HARRIS: Inch by inch, against enormous odds, a certain amount of progress is, with luck, made now and then—

GRANDMOTHER HARRIS: Nathan, be quiet: no more fighting—

WALTER FISH: Now what do you think of Shenandoah, Kelly?

SHENANDOAH:
Mark the dominion of the Gentile world:
This Irish Catholic will not quote Aquinas
Who wrote a treatise on the names of God—

WALTER FISH: Are your sure? All right, then Shenandoah it will
be! Many thanks, and give my best to Mary: good-bye—

[WALTER *returns to the dining room with a look of triumph.*]

WALTER FISH: He says it is a fine name, an elegant name. *He guarantees that it is a good name!* What have you to say now, Nathan? I suppose you think you know more than Kelly?

NATHAN HARRIS: I give up. No one can say I did not do my best—

WALTER FISH: Let's shake hands, Nathan, let's eliminate all hard feelings. I am sorry that I lost my temper. Some day the two of us will tell the boy about today and the three of us will have a good laugh about the whole thing from beginning to end—

NATHAN HARRIS: He may not share your sense of humor—

DR. ADAMSON: Yes! let kindness, forgiveness, good will, and rejoicing triumph in every heart on a day like this, the day which belongs to the first-born child.

NATHAN HARRIS: Here is my hand, Walter, but my left hand is for little Shenandoah!

[*He stretches out his left hand at an angle toward the bassinet.* SHENANDOAH *stretches out his hand to* NATHAN. *But* NATHAN'S *back is turned.*]

SHENANDOAH:
Nathan! here is my hand, across the years—

[SHENANDOAH *regards his unacknowledged hand with great sadness.*]

I am divorced from those I love, my peers!

DR. ADAMSON: This is the way that all conflicts should end. They should end with a sacred rite. Nothing is so beautiful, nothing is so good for the heart and the soul, and the mind as a ceremony well-performed. Let us go into the next room and begin the ritual of circumcision. The sacred nature of the rite will uplift our hearts—

JACOB FISH: This ceremony of circumcision gives me more pleasure, the older I get, although I hardly know why. And after

that, the food and drink: no matter how old one is, that makes
Life worth living, if one has a good stomach—
SHENANDOAH:
    Prime Mover of this day, you are a card!
    How many lives the Pleasure-Principle
    Rules like an insane king,
                  even in dreams—

*[The men begin to go to into the living room. The women remain
behind, for they are barred from the ceremony.* SHENANDOAH
takes the infant in haste, and stands before the curtain.]

    They are about to give this child a name
    And circumcise his foreskin. How profound
    Are all these ancient rites: for with a wound
    —What better sign exists—the child is made
    A Jew forever! quickly taught the life
    That he must lead, an heir to lasting pain:
    Do I exaggerate, do I with hindsight see
    The rise of Hitler?
                  O the whole of history
    Testifies to the chosen people's agony,
    —Chosen for wandering and alienation
    In every kind of life, in every nation—

VOICE FROM THE LIVING ROOM: May the All-Merciful bless the
    father and mother of the child; may they be worthy to rear him, to
    initiate him in the precepts of the Law, and to train him in wisdom—

*[There is the sound of moving about and arranging and preparing
in the living room.]*

    May the All-Merciful bless the godfather who has observed
    the covenant of Circumcision, and rejoiced exceedingly to per-
    form this deed of piety—

[Again there is the sound of moving about and murmuring, then a pause and silence, while the faces of the women are turned toward the other room, full of pained sympathy.]

For thy salvation have I waited, O Lord. I have hoped, O Lord, for thy salvation, and done thy commandments—

[There is an appalling screech, as of an infant in the greatest pain.]

And I passed by thee, and I saw thee weltering in thy blood, and I said unto thee, in thy blood, live. Yea, I said unto thee, in thy blood, live.

SHENANDOAH:

Silent, O child, for if a knife can make you cry,
What will you do when you know that you must die?
When the mind howls with the body, *I am I?*
When the horrors of modern life are your sole place?
When your people are driven from the planet's face?
When the dying West performs unspeakable disgrace
Against the honor of man, before God's utter gaze?
Though now and then, like the early morning light's pure greys,
Transient release is known, in the darkened theater's plays....

CURTAIN

Criticism

THE ISOLATION OF MODERN POETRY

The characteristic of modern poetry which is most discussed is of course its difficulty, its famous obscurity. Certain discussions, usually by contemporary poets, have done much to illuminate the new methods and forms of contemporary poetry. Certain other discussions have illustrated an essential weakness inherent in all readers, the fact that the love of one kind of writing must often interfere with the understanding of another kind. Wordsworth was undoubtedly thinking of this weakness when he wrote, in his justly well-known preface, that

> It is supposed that by the act of writing in verse an Author makes a formal engagement that he will gratify certain known habits of association; that he not only apprises the reader that certain classes of ideas and expression will be found in his book, but that others will be carefully excluded.

This seems to me to be a perfect statement of the first barrier which intervenes between the reader and any kind of writing with which he is not familiar. But it is far from being sufficient as a defense of modern poetry. Wordsworth was engaged in defending his poetry against the habitual expectations of the reader accustomed to Dryden, Pope, and Johnson. It is necessary now to defend the modern poet against the reader accustomed to Wordsworth. The specific difference between such a poet as Wordsworth and the typical modern poet requires a specific explanation.

There is another defense of the modern poet which seems utterly insufficient to me. It is said that the modern poet must be complex because modern life is complicated. This is the view of Mr. T. S. Eliot, among others. "It appears likely," he says, "that poets in our civilization, as it exists at present, must be *difficult*. Our civilization comprehends great variety and complexity, and this variety and complexity, playing upon a refined sensibility, must produce various and complex results." Mr. Eliot's explanation seems to me not so much wrong as superficial. I need hardly say that Mr. Eliot is seldom superficial in any regard; here, however, I think he is identifying the surface of our civilization with the surface of our poetry. But the complexity of modern life, the disorder of the traffic on a business street or the variety of reference in the daily newspaper is far from being the same thing as the difficulties of syntax, tone, diction, metaphor, and allusion which face the reader in the modern poem. If one is the product of the other, the causal sequence involves a number of factors on different levels, and to imply, as I think Mr. Eliot does, that there is a simple causal relationship between the disorder of modern life and the difficulty of modern poetry is merely to engender misunderstanding by oversimplification.

Now obscurity is merely one of the peculiar aspects of modern poetry. There are others which are just as important. Nothing could be more peculiar than the fact that modern poetry is lyric poetry. Almost without exception there is a failure or an absence of narrative or dramatic writing in verse. With the possible exception of Hardy and Robinson, it is impossible to think of any modern poet who will be remembered for his writing in any form other than that of the lyric.

It is obvious by contrast that the major portion of the poetry of the past, of poetry until we reach the latter half of the nineteenth century, is narrative and dramatic as well as lyrical in its most important moments; and it is equally evident that all of that poetry is never obscure in the modern sense.

I need not mention further characteristics of modern poetry which coexist with its obscurity and its limitation to the lyric form. The two characteristics seem to me to be closely related to each other and to spring from the essential condition of the modern poet. The way in which this condition, if that is the adequate word for what I mean, the way in which this essential circumstance affects the modern poet is a rather involved matter, but had better be stated bluntly and crudely at this point. The modern poet has been very much affected by the condition and the circumstance that he has been separated from the whole life of society. This separation has taken numerous forms and has increased continually. It is a separation which occurs with an uneven development in all the matters with which the modern poet must concern himself. Different poets have been differently affected, and their efforts to cope with this separation have been various. But there is a common denominator which points to a common cause.

The beginning of the process of separation, if one can rightly discern a beginning in such things, is the gradual destruction of the world picture which, despite many changes, had for a long time been taken for granted by the poet. Amid much change, development, and modification, the Bible had provided a view of the universe which circumscribed the area in which anyone ventured to think, or use his imagination. It would of course be a serious mistake to suppose that this view of the universe had not been disturbed in numerous ways long before the modern poet arrived upon the scene. But it is doubtful if the poet before the time of Blake felt a conflict between two pictures of the world, the picture provided by the Bible and the one provided by the physical sciences.

In Blake's rage against Newton and Voltaire, in his interest, as a poet, in the doctrine of Swedenborg, and in his attempt to construct his own view of the universe, we come upon the first full example of this difficulty of the poet. There is a break between intellect and sensibility; the intellect finds unreasonable what the sensibility and the imagination cannot help but accept because of centuries of imagining and feeling in terms of definite images of the world. Milton's use of a Ptolemaic cosmology, though he knew that the Copernican one was mathematically superior, is an example from a still earlier period; it shows with exactitude the extent to which the poet depended upon the traditional world picture of Western culture. After Blake, the Romantic poets are further instances; not only were they intensely interested in new conceptions of the world, new philosophies; but in turning to Nature as they did, they displayed their painful sense that the poet no longer belonged to the society into which he was born, and for which, presumably, he was writing his verse.

But these authors are not modern poets. And it was not until the middle of the nineteenth century that the progress of the physical sciences brought forth a body of knowledge which was in serious and open conflict with the picture of the world which had been in use for so long a time. This conflict had been going on, of course, for centuries, but it was not until we come to an occasion like the publication of the Darwinian theory that the conflict becomes so radical and so obvious that no poet of ambition can seriously avoid it. I am not referring to any conflict between religious doctrine and scientific knowledge, for this conflict, if it actually exists, is hardly the direct concern of the poet at any time. It is a question of the conflict between the sensibility of the poet, the very images which he viewed as the world, and the evolving and blank and empty universe of nineteenth century science.

The development of modern culture from Darwin and Huxley to Freud, Marx, and the author of *The Golden Bough*, has merely extended, hastened, and intensified this process of removing the picture of the world which the poet took for granted as the arena of his imagination, and putting in its place another world picture which he could not use. This is illustrated broadly in the career of such poets as Yeats. Hearing as a young man that man was descended from the ape, Yeats occupied himself for many years with theosophy, black magic, and the least respectable forms of psychical research, all in the effort to gain a view of the universe and of man which would restore dignity and importance to both man and the universe. We may invent an illustration at this point and suppose that when Yeats or any other modern poet of similar interests heard of how many million light years the known regions of the universe comprise, he felt a fundamental incongruity between his own sense of the importance of human lives and their physical smallness in the universe. This is merely a difficulty in imagining—one has an image of a very small being in an endless world; but that's just the point, the difficulty with images. The philosopher and the theologian know that size is not a particularly important aspect of anything; but the poet must see, and what he has had to see was this incongruity between the importance man attributes to himself and his smallness against the background of the physical world of nineteenth century science.

Now this is only one aspect of the poet's isolation; it is the aspect in which the sensibility of the poet has been separated from the theoretical knowledge of his time. The isolation of the modern poet has, however, taken an even more difficult form, that of being separated by poetry from the rest of society. Here one must guard against a simple view of what this separation has amounted to in any particular context. It is not a simple matter of the poet lacking an audience, for that is an effect, rather than a cause, of the character of modern poetry. And it is not, on the other hand, the simple matter of the poet being isolated from the usual habits and customs and amusements of his time and place; for if this were the trouble, then the poet could perhaps be justly accused of retiring to his celebrated ivory tower; and it would then be quite reasonable to advise the poet as some have done: to tell him that he ought to get "experience," see the world, join a political party, make sure that he participates in the habitual activities of his society.

The fundamental isolation of the modern poet began not with the poet and his way of life; but rather with the whole way of life of modern society. It was not so much the poet as it was poetry, culture, sensibility, imagination, that were isolated. On the one hand, there was no room in the increasing industrialization of society for such a monster as the cultivated man; a man's taste for literature had at best nothing to do with most of the activities which constituted daily life in an industrial society. On the other hand, culture, since it could not find a place in modern life, has fed upon itself increasingly and has created its own autonomous satisfactions, removing itself further all the time from any essential part in the organic life of society.

Stated thus, this account may seem abstract and even implausible. It would be best before going further to mention certain striking evidences of what has taken place. There is, for instance, the classic American joke about how bored father is at the opera or the concert; the poet too has been an essentially comic figure, from time to time. But this homely instance may seem merely the product of vulgarity and lack of taste. A related tendency which has been much observed by foreigners is the belief in America that women were supposed to be interested in literature, culture, and "such things," while men had no time for such trivial delights because they were busy with what is called *business*. But this instance may seem local in that it is American and inconclusive since it has to do with the poet's audience rather than with the poet himself. There is then a third example, one which seems almost dramatic to me, the phenomenon of American authors of superior gifts going to Europe and staying there. Henry James is the most convincing case; one can scarcely doubt that he lived in Europe because there the divorce between culture and the rest of life, although it had begun, had by no means reached the point which was unavoidable in America. George Santayana, Ezra Pound, and T. S. Eliot are cases which come later in time; we do not know exactly why these men went to Europe; the significant fact is that they do not come back to America. I do not merely wish to suggest a critical view of the role of culture in American life, for the same process was occurring in Europe, though at a slower rate and with local modifications. The important point is the intuitive recognition on the part of both the artist and the rest of the population that culture and sensibility—and thus the works by means of which they sustained their existence—did not belong, did not fit into the essential workings of society.

At this point, it might be objected that culture has never played a very important part in the life of any society; it has only engaged the attention and devotion of the elect, who are always few in number. This view seems utterly false to me, and for the sake of showing briefly how false it has been historically, I quote one of the greatest living classical scholars on the part that dramatic tragedy played in the life of Periclean Athens. Werner Jaeger writes that

> After the state organized the dramatic performances held at the festival of Dionysus, tragedy more and more evoked the interest and participation of the entire people.... Its power over them was so vast that they held it responsible for the spirit of the whole state ... it is no exaggeration to say that the tragic festival was the climax of the city's life. (*Paideia*, pp. 245–246.)

No contrast could be more extreme than this one between the function of the Greek dramatist and that of the modern poet in their respective societies.

One significant effect of this divorce has been the poet's avowal of the doctrine of Art for Art's Sake, a doctrine which is meaningful only when viewed in the context in which it is always announced, that is, to repeat, a society which had no use and no need for Art, other than as a superfluous amusement or decoration. And another significant and related effect is the sentiment of the poet, and at times his convinced belief, that he has no connection with or allegiances to anything else. Nowhere is this belief stated with more clarity than in the following prose poem by Baudelaire, who in so many ways is either the first or the typical modern poet:

> "Whom do you love most of all, enigmatic man, tell me? Your father, your mother, your brother, or your sister?"
> "I have neither father, mother, brother, nor sister."
> "Do you love your friends then?"
> "You have just used a word whose meaning remains unknown to me to this very day."
> "Do you love your country, then?"
> "I ignore the latitude in which it is situated."
> "Then do you love Beauty?"
> "I love her with my whole will; she is a goddess and immortal."
> "Do you love gold?"
> "I hate it as you hate God."
> "Well then: extraordinary stranger, what *do* you love?"
> "I love the clouds ... the clouds which pass ... far away ... far away ... the marvelous clouds!"

It would be possible to take this stranger who is the modern poet with less seriousness, if he were merely affecting a pose, attempting to dramatize himself or be clever. The shocking passages in modern poetry have sometimes been understood in this way as Bohemiánism, and the conventional picture or caricature of the poet has been derived from this Bohemianism, considered as a surface. But the sentiments which Baudelaire attributes to his stranger are the deepest feelings of the modern poet. He does feel that he is a stranger, an alien, an outsider; he finds himself without a father or mother, or he is separated from them by the opposition between his values as an artist and their values as respectable members of modern society. This opposition cannot be avoided because not a government subsidy, nor yearly prizes, nor a national academy can disguise the fact that there is no genuine place for the poet in modern life. He has no country, no community, insofar as he is a poet, and his greatest enemy is money, since poetry does not yield him a livelihood. It is natural then that he should emphasize his allegiance, his devotion to Beauty, that is to say, to the practice of Art and the works of art which already exist. And thus it is that Baudelaire's stranger announces that what he loves most of all is to look at the clouds, that is, to exercise his own sensibility. The modern poet has had nothing to do, no serious activity other than the cultivation of his own sensibility. There is a very famous passage in Walter Pater advising just this course.

From this standpoint, the two aspects of modern poetry which I marked at the start can be seen as natural and almost inevitable developments. In cultivating his own sensibility, the modern poet participated in a life which was removed from the lives of other men, who, insofar as they could be considered important characters, were engaged in cultivating money or building an industrial society. Thus it became increasingly impossible for the poet to write about the lives of other men; for not only was he removed from their lives, but, above all, the culture and the sensibility which made him a poet could not be employed when the proposed subject was the lives of human beings in whom culture and sensibility had no organic function. There have been unsuccessful efforts on the part of able poets to write about bankers and about railroad trains, and in such examples the poet has been confronted by what seems on the surface a technical problem, the extraordinary difficulty of employing poetic diction, meter, language, and metaphor in the contexts of modern life. It is not that contemporary people do not speak or think poetically; human beings at any time in general do not speak or think in ways which are immediately poetic, and if they did there would be no need for poetry. The trouble has been that the idiom of poetic style and the normal thought and speech of the community have been moving in opposite directions and have had little or no relationship to each other. The normal state of affairs occurs when poetry is continually digesting the prose of its time, and folk art and speech are providing sustenance for major literary efforts.

Since the only life available to the poet as a man of culture has been the cultivation of his own sensibility, that is the only subject available to him, if we may assume that a poet can only write about subjects of which he has an absorbing experience in every sense.[1] Thus we find that in much modern poetry, the poet is writing about other poetry, just as in modern painting the art works and styles of the past have so often become the painter's subject. For writing about other poetry and in general about works of art is the most direct way of grasping one's sensibility as a subject. But more than that, since one can only write about one's sensibility, one can only write lyric poetry. Dramatic and narrative poetry require a grasp of the lives of other men, and it is precisely these lives, to repeat, that are outside the orbit of poetic style and poetic sensibility. An analogous thing has, of necessity, happened in the history of the novel; the development of the autobiographical novel has resulted in part from the inability of the novelist to write about any one but himself or other people in relation to himself.

From this isolation of poetic sensibility the obscurity of modern poetry also arises. The poet is engaged in following the minutest movements, tones, and distinctions of his own being as a poetic man. Because this private life of his sensibility is the chief

---

1. The connection between the way in which an author lives and his writing is of course a complicated one. But how close the connection is and how effective can be seen if we ask ourselves: would Eliot have written *The Waste Land* as we know it, if he had lived in London? would Pound have written the later Cantos, if he had not lived on the Italian Riviera? would either have written, using culture as they have, if they were not expatriate Americans? Certainly Joyce might not have written *Finnegans Wake* if he had not taught in a Berlitz school and Perse could not have written *Anabase* if he had not been sent to Asia as a diplomat, and Yeats might not have written his later poetry, if he had lived on Lady Gregory's estate.

subject available to him, it becomes increasingly necessary to have recourse to new and special uses of language. The more the poet has cultivated his own sensibility, the more unique and special has his subject, and thus his method, become. The common language of daily life, its syntax, habitual sequences, and processes of association, are precisely the opposite of what he needs, if he is to make poetry from what absorbs him as a poet, his own sensibility.

Sometimes, indeed, the poet has taken this conflict between sensibility and modern life as his subject. The early fiction of Thomas Mann concerns itself repeatedly with the opposition between the artist and the bourgeoisie, and in such a story as "Tonio Kröger" we see the problem most explicitly; the artist feels at home nowhere and he suffers from an intense longing to be normal and bourgeois himself. Again, there is the famous device of modern poetry which was invented by Laforgue and used most successfully by T. S. Eliot, the ironic contrast between a past in which culture was an important part of life and the present in which the cultural monument sits next to vulgarity and insensitivity. This has been misunderstood very often as a yearning to go back to a past idyllically conceived. It is nothing of the kind; it is the poet's conscious experience of the isolation of culture from the rest of society.

I would like to cite one more instance of this condition. Four years ago one of the very best modern poets lectured and read his own poetry at Harvard. As a normal citizen, this man is an executive of an important corporation. It may reasonably be presumed that most of his writing is done on holidays and vacations. At the conclusion of his reading of his own poetry, this poet and businessman remarked to one of the instructors who had welcomed him: "I wonder what the boys at the office would think of this."

But I have spoken throughout as if this isolation was in every sense a misfortune. It is certainly a misfortune so far as the life of the whole community is concerned; this is evident in the character of popular taste, in the kind of fiction, play, and movie which is successful, as compared with the popular authors of the nineteenth century, who were very often the best authors also. But on the other hand, it seems to me that the period of modern poetry, the age which begins with Baudelaire, is undoubtedly one in which the art of poetry has gained not only in the number of fine poets, but in technical resources of all kinds. If the enforced isolation of the poet has made dramatic and narrative poetry almost impossible, it has, on the other hand, increased the uses and powers of languages in the most amazing and the most valuable directions.

I have also spoken as if this isolation of the poet had already reached its conclusion. Whether it has or not, and whether it would be entirely desirable that it should, may be left as unanswered and perhaps unanswerable questions. It is true, at any rate, that during the past ten years a new school of poets has attempted to free itself from the isolation of poetry by taking society itself as the dominant subject.[2] The attempt has been a brilliant and exciting one in many ways; the measure of its success is not yet clear, particularly since it has been inspired by the present crisis of society; and its relative popularity may also be limited to contemporary and transient interests. But the very nature of the effort testifies in its own way to the isolation which haunts modern poetry, and from which these poets have been trying to escape.

---

2. These are the poets who, significantly enough, have invented the recurrent figure of "the island," as a symbol of isolation. From the point of view of this essay, the leading themes of the Agrarian-Regionalist poets, such as Tate and Ransom, would represent another, very different effort to get back to the center of the community and away from the poet's isolation.

THE VOCATION OF THE POET IN THE MODERN WORLD

To have a vocation is to have a calling, to be called. One may be called by the powers of evil as well as the powers of good, but it is clear that one must respond with the whole of one's being. In this sense it is also clear that to have a vocation is very much like being in love. Being in love and being called to write poetry are often linked, and many people feel the need to write poetry when they are in love. As there are many errors in love, so there are many errors in the writing of poetry. And as there is puppy love, there is adolescent poetry.

Since there are errors and since a calling is a very important matter, since one is called during the formative and decisive years of existence, there is much doubt and hesitation about the fact of having a calling, and a period of trial is prescribed in some vocations, while one of the reasons for going to school, after a certain point, is to determine if one has a true vocation, if one has truly been called; and it is in some kind of school that we prepare ourselves to be adequate to our vocation.

In poetry, it is particularly true that many are called and few are chosen. And to be a poet in the modern world means a certain important renunciation which does not hold of all vocations: it means that there is little hope or none of being able to earn a living directly by the writing of poetry; and this has been true in the past, although in other ways, as well as in the modern life; for example, Dryden speaks of "not having the vocation of poverty to scribble." In the modern world, it is hard to think of any poet who has had from the start any real economic support for the writing of poetry. There are prizes, grants, patrons, and poetry is honored by much generosity and much prestige. Unfortunately, these are provided after the poet has established himself—and not always then—but during the first and perhaps most difficult years of being a poet, the best a poet can do is to get some other job to support his effort to be a poet. In recent years, the job of teaching English has provided a good many positions which help the poet during his first years, but it is not entirely clear that this is a good thing. For to have a vocation means that one must respond with the whole of one's being; but teaching should be a vocation too, and not a job, and when the poet takes teaching as a job, he may injure or weaken himself as a poet, or he may not be adequate to all that the task of teaching requires. All the temptations of the world, the flesh, and the devil combine to lure the poet to success as a teacher and to the rewards of successful academic ambition. At the same time that the poet resists these temptations, he must resign himself to the likelihood that a genuine poetic reputation can be achieved only among others who are poets—for it is mostly poets who read any poetry except what is to be found in anthologies—and the kind of fame (that last infirmity of noble mind, as Milton said) which he would like will come to him, if it comes at all, only in middle age.

What I have just said should distinguish roughly the difference between being a poet in the modern world from what it may have been in other historical periods. If we turn again to the wisdom, tried and inherited for so many years, to be found in the origins of words, we remember that to be a poet is to be a maker, to be the maker of something new, to make something new by putting things and words together. The distinguishing mark of the poet, that aptitude which more than any other skill of the mind makes him a poet, is metaphor, according to Aristotle. Now metaphor is literally a bearing-across, or a bringing-together of things by means of words. And composition, which is what the poet accomplishes by all the elements of his poem when they are brought together in a unity, structural, formal, intuitive, and musical—composition means putting things together, bringing them together into a unity which is original, interesting and fruitful. Thus the poet at any time may be said to be engaged in bringing things together, in making new things, in uniting the old and the new, all by the inexhaustible means which words provide for him. In this way, the poet as creator, and metaphor-maker, and presiding bringer of unity is a kind of priest. He unites things, meanings, attitudes, feelings, through the power, prowess and benediction of words, and in this way he is a priest who performs a ceremony of marriage each time he composes a poem. Unfortunately, not all marriages are happy.

In the modern world, the poet who has been truly called cannot respond as poets did in idyllic and primitive periods when merely the naming of things, as Adam named the animals, was enough to bring poems into existence. On the contrary, he must resist the innumerable ways in which words are spoiled, misused, commercialized, deformed, mispronounced, and in general degraded. We can see clearly how much this resistance is part of the vocation of the poet if we consider the recurrent references to language itself in the poems of that truly modern poet, T. S. Eliot. These references occur in his poems from the very start, continue in each volume he has published, and culminate in a passage in his most recent book of poems, *Four Quartets*:

> So here I am, in the middle way, having had twenty
>   years—
> Twenty years largely wasted, the years of *l'entre deux
>   guerres*—

237

Trying to learn to use words, and every attempt
Is a wholly new start, and a different kind of failure
Because one has only learnt to get the better of words
For the thing one no longer has to say, or the way in
    which
One is no longer disposed to say it.

Elsewhere in his work there is a sensitivity to colloquial speech—
and a kind of horror or anguish about it—which arises from the
fact that for a modern poet, as for any poet, words are the keys to
what he wants.

Eliot's play in verse, "Sweeney Agonistes," is the best example of this aspect of his feeling about language, which is used to
express a profound anguish about human beings and human existence. When language is degraded in speech, then the basis in
community life for the art of poetry is diseased; and it is appropriate and perhaps inevitable that the great modern poet who should
have felt this fact with as much acuteness as any other poet should
at the same time be an author who acquired an English accent
after arriving at the age of reason. Nevertheless, just as certain
kinds of disease make for a greater sensitivity to experience or a
more precise observation of reality (the blind know more about
how things sound and how they feel to the touch than those who
have normal vision), so, too, the disease which degrades language
in the modern world may help to bring about the remarkable and
often multilingual sensitivity of the modern poet to the language
which is the matrix from which he draws his poems.

Degradation and disease are strong words of condemnation,
and a great claim is also made when one says that the degradation
and disease to which poetry is subjected in the modern world are
also one of the fruitful and necessary conditions of genuine poetry and of a genuine vocation for the art of poetry. For the sake
of justifying these claims, let us examine small and convenient examples. The word, *intrigue,* is a noun which has four legitimate
meanings. It means something which is intricate; it means "a plot,

or a plotting intended to affect some purpose by secret artifice"; thirdly, it is "the plot of a play or romance"; fourthly, it is "a secret and illicit love affair; an amour; a liason" (this fourth meaning probably derives from the third). And the synonyms of intrigue are *plot, scheme, machination,* and *conspiracy.* Notice that there is no sense in which the word means something overwhelmingly attractive and fascinating, unless one thinks of secret and illicit love affairs as overpowering in their fascination. However, at present, the use of the word as a noun has fallen into decay. Although there are still references to schemers who engage in conspiracies and intrigues, the noun has become a verb in popular usage: anyone who is said to be *intriguing* is said to be very attractive, in fact, fascinating like a Hollywood star, or like the spy Mata Hari. An intrigue was something unpleasant, dishonorable, underhand, and immoral. But now to be intriguing is to be wonderfully desirable or interesting and has no unfavorable or dishonorable association. The sense of the same word has thus been turned upside down; it has changed, in popular usage, from signifying something unscrupulous to representing in a vague but unmistakeable way something which is extremely interesting, desirable, or beautiful, and has no immediate connotations of moral disrepute.

What has happened to one word has happened to many words and can happen to many more. And the causes are not, as is sometimes supposed, limited to a poor teaching of English, or a disregard of the dictionary. In this instance, the shift is probably involved in the radical trial which conventional morality has undergone in the last twenty-five years, and certainly there is also involved the influence of newspapers, the stage, the films, and the *literary* zest with which most people read of the sins of others.

This example does not make clear how a degradation in the meaning of a word can be fruitful as well as foolish. There is a shift of meaning and a new richness of meaning, of course, but some of the exactness has already been lost and more is going to be lost. Let me point out two more examples in which the complicated and mixed benefits and losses of the change may appear more fully. For a number of years I taught English composition. I taught because I was unable to support myself by writing poetry (for the most part, however, I like to teach very much). When I began to teach, I was confounded by simple misuses of languages of which *intrigue* is a fairly representative example. One student wrote that "swimming is my chief *abstraction*," and another student said that "a certain part of my native city is *slightly ugly*." A third student who was attempting to describe the salutary effects of higher education upon all members of the fairer and weaker sex said that it was good for a girl to go to college because "it makes a girl *broader*." When I corrected the last word in accordance with my instructions as to the proper usage of English—and with a physical sense of one of the meanings of broader—the student protested that I had a peculiar mind; otherwise I would not object to the way in which she used *broader* instead of *broadens*.

These errors—errors at least from the point of view of conventional and prescribed usage—made me reflect upon the character I played as a teacher of composition. The students thought I was pedantic when they did not think I was idiosyncratic. The difficulty was that so many of them made the same errors that, in a way, they were no longer errors. Moreover, the longer I thought about some of the errors, the more they seemed to be possible enlargements of meaning and association which might be creative. There was a real sense in which swimming, for an urban human being, was an abstraction as well as a distraction. So too, to say that something was slightly ugly was to suggest that a word or words denoting degrees of ugliness from homeliness and plainness to what was utterly ugly were lacking in English. And finally, it was true enough that education might make a girl broader as well as broaden a girl's outlook, although I doubt that this would have occurred to me if it had not been for this fruitful error.

The experience of teaching English literature and English poetry directly confronts the poet who teaches English with what can only be described as the most educated part of the population. Before the poet has taught English, he may well have been under the impression that no one except poets read modern poetry (with a few and misleading exceptions). When he teaches poetry in the classroom, he finds out something which may be a great hope or a great delusion. It may be a delusion now and a hope for the future. At any rate, he does discover that he can persuade any student to understand any kind of poetry, no matter how difficult. They understand it as long as they are in the classroom, and they remain interested in it until they depart from school. Since so many poets have more and more undertaken the teaching of English and of poetry, it does seem possible that this may be the beginning of a new audience trained in reading and aware of how marvelous and exalted the rewards of poetry can be. But this is a matter which must be realized in the future. In the present, it is true that as soon as the student leaves school, all the seductions of mass culture and middle-brow culture, and in addition the whole way of life of our society, combine to make the reading of poetry a dangerous and quickly rejected luxury. The poet who teaches has immediate experiences in the classroom which give him some reason to hope for a real literary and poetic renaissance. As soon as he departs from the pleasant confines of the university, he discovers that it is more and more true that less and less people read serious poetry. And the last straw may be the recognition that even poets do not read very much poetry: Edwin Arlington Robinson confessed that during the latter half of his life, he read hardly any poems except his own which he read again and again, and which may explain the paralysis of self-imitation which overcomes many good poets in mid-career. Here then is another trait which distinguishes the vocation of the modern poet from poets of the past: he not only knows how language is inexactly and exactly used, he also knows that for the most part only other poets will read his poems.

One reason that language is misused, whether fruitfully or not, is that in modern life experience has become international. In America itself the fact of many peoples and the fact that so large a part of the population has some immigrant background and cherishes the fragments of another language creates a multilingual situation in which words are misused and yet the language is also enriched by new words and new meanings. To make fun of errors in the use of language and to make the most comedy possible of foreign accents—or for that matter, an English accent—is an important and vital part of American humor, which is itself a very important part of American life. Moreover, the pilgrimage to Europe has for long been an important episode in the national experience. The American tourist in Europe, Baedeker in hand, has for generations spelled out the names of places, and works of art, and delicious foods. And most crucial of all, the experience of two world wars has made Americans conscious of the extent to which the very quality of their lives depends upon the entire international situation. Whether the danger is from Germany or from Russia, whether a banking scandal occurs in Paris, or Spain becomes Fascist, or the Vatican intervenes in American politics and American morality and American education, no one at this late date can fail to be aware of the extent to which the fate of the individual is inseparable from what is happening in the whole world.

These facts are, of course, in one sense platitudes; and yet it may not be clear how they affect the modern poet in his vocation as such. I want to resort to examples again before trying to define the way in which the international scene and an involvement with it affect the poet as a poet and have to do with his calling.

To quote once more from that truly modern poet, T. S. Eliot, here is a passage from one of his best poems, "Gerontion." Christ, the protagonist says is:

> To be eaten, to be divided, to be drunk
> Among whispers; by Mr. Silvero
> With caressing hands, at Limoges
> Who walked all night in the next room;
>
> By Hakagawa, bowing among the Titians;
> By Madame de Tornquist, in the dark room

Shifting the candles; Fraülein von Kulp
Who turned in the hall, one hand on the door.

Let us think a little merely of the names of the people he remembers, Mr. Silvero, Hakagawa, Madame de Tornquist, Fraülein
von Kulp. Is it not evident that the experience which provides the
subject-matter of the poet or inspires him to write his poem is not
only European, but international, since Hakagawa is presumably
Japanese; and involves all history, all culture, since the reference
here to Titian is matched elsewhere by allusions to ancient Egypt,
Buddhist sermons, and the religion of classical Greece? Another
aspect of the same involvement and of how it has a direct impact
on the writing of the poetry is illustrated in "Sweeney Agonistes"
where "two American gentlemen here on business" arrive in London and rehearse the clichés of colloquial American speech: London, one of them explains with great politeness to his English
friends, is "a slick place, London's a swell place,/London's a fine
place to come on a visit—," and the other adds with equal politeness: "Specially when you got a real live Britisher/A guy like Sam
to show you around/Sam of course is at *home* in London,/And
he's promised to show us around." In the same work, at a moment
of great anguish, another character reiterates the poet's extreme
sensitivity to and concern for language when he says: "I gotta use
words when I talk to you."

If Eliot as a transplanted American in Europe seems to be a
special case (a great poet, however, is always a special case, if one
chooses to regard him in that light), the example of James Joyce
should help to reinforce the somewhat complicated (because
ubiquitous) thesis I am trying to elucidate. Joyce was an impov-
erished Irishman. As Eliot had to toil for some time in a bank
while he tried to write poems, Joyce supported himself during
the composition of *Ulysses* by teaching in a Berlitz school in Trieste during the first World War. The publication of *Ulysses*—an
event which was described by a French critic as marking Ireland's
spectacular reentry into European literature—was sufficiently a

success to make a rich Englishman provide Joyce with financial security almost until the end of his life. Two years before, Joyce had completed his last and probably his best work, the stupendous *Finnegans Wake*, a book which would in itself provide sufficient evidence and illustration of the vocation of the modern poet in modern life.[1] All that has been observed in Eliot's work is all the more true of *Finnegans Wake:*—the attention to colloquial speech, the awareness of the variety of ways in which languages can be degraded and how that degradation can be the base for a new originality and exactitude, the sense of an involvement with the international scene and with all history. But more than that, the radio and even television play a part in this wonderful book, as indeed they played a part in the writing of it. Joyce had a short-wave radio with which he was able to hear London, Moscow, Dublin—and New York! In *Finnegans Wake,* I was perplexed for a time by echoes of American radio comedy and Yiddish humor until I learned about Joyce's radio and about his daily reading of the Paris edition of the New York *Herald-Tribune.* The most important point of all, however, is that *Finnegans Wake* exhibits in the smallest detail and in the entire scope of the work the internationality of the modern poet, his involvement in all history, and his consciousness of the impingement of any foreign language from Hebrew to Esperanto upon the poet's use of the English language.

It is foolish to speculate about the future of anything as precarious as the vocation of poetry—an eminent critic said some years ago that the technique of verse was a dying one, but Joyce may have

---

1. Joyce's two best works, *Ulysses* and his last book, are not poems in the ordinary sense of the word; and he wrote several volumes of poetry, most of which consist of verses far inferior to anything in his major books. But any view of poetry which excludes *Finnegans Wake* as a poem and Joyce as a poet merely suggests the likelihood that Joyce transformed and extended the limits of poetry by the writing of his last book. If we freeze our categories and our definitions, (and this is especially true in literature) the result is that we disable and blind our minds.

persuaded him to change his mind—but to think of the future is as inevitable as it is dubious. Joyce's last book suggests certain tentative formulations about the future of the writing of poetry. It suggests that there can be no turning back, unless civilization itself declines as it did when the Roman Empire fell. Yet it is also clear that poets cannot go forward in a straight line from the point at which *Finnegans Wake* concluded. What they can do is not evident in the least, apart from the fact that a literal imitation or extension of Joyce would be as mechanical as it is undesirable: too much in the very nature of his work depends upon personal and idiosyncratic traits of the author, his training as a Jesuit, his love of operatic music, the personal pride which was involved in his departure from Ireland and the infatuation with everything Irish which obsessed him in this as in his other books. There are other important elements in Joyce's work and in his life which do lead, I think, to some tentative generalization about the future of poetry and the vocation of the poet. One of them was pointed out to me by Meyer Schapiro (who has influenced me in much of what I have said throughout): the question has been raised as to why Joyce, both in *Ulysses* and in *Finnegans Wake,* identified himself with Jews, with Leopold Bloom, an Irish Jew, and with the character of Shem in his last book (Shem is, among other of his very many kinships, a son of Noah, and he is compared with Jesus Christ, to the ironic denigration of both beings). The answer to the question of Joyce's identification with Jews, Schapiro said, is that the Jew is at once alienated and indestructible, he is an exile from his own country and an exile even from himself, yet he survives the annihilating fury of history. In the unpredictable and fearful future that awaits civilization, the poet must be prepared to be alienated and indestructible. He must dedicate himself to poetry, although no one else seems likely to read what he writes; and he must be indestructible as a poet until he is destroyed as a human being. In the modern world, poetry is alienated; it will remain indestructible as long as the faith and love of each poet in his vocation survives.

from T. S. ELIOT: A CRITICAL STUDY

Editor's note

In the early 1940s, Delmore Schwartz signed a contract with James Laughlin—accompanied by the largest advance New Directions had yet paid—for a volume in Laughlin's Masters of Modern Literature series of critical books devoted each to a single author. Schwartz chose T. S. Eliot as his subject. This was a busy and difficult time in Schwartz's life, following the publication and resulting fame of his first book, when he was filled with ambition and energy, but he was also desperate for money, teaching uncertainly at Harvard, advising Laughlin on manuscripts for ND, and struggling with his marriage to Gertrude Buckman. Gertrude was working in an administrative capacity for New Directions, and the press's offices were partially housed for a time in Schwartz's Boston apartment.

In the correspondence between Schwartz and Laughlin, the Eliot book is mostly discussed in terms of money and the fulfillment of contractual obligations as Schwartz tried to goad Laughlin into freeing him to publish a novel with a bigger, more lucrative publisher—the abiding affection between the two men was often challenged by these kinds of exchanges, though they always, until near the end of Schwartz's life, found a way back to friendship. The book became a low priority for Laughlin, and Schwartz's energy and concentration eventually drifted elsewhere, mostly toward his sprawling and failed epic, *Genesis*.

But Schwartz idolized Eliot above almost all other authors, finding in him a model of the poet/critic/dramatist/editor and literature-altering figure he hoped to be. This necessarily resulted in ambivalence surrounding Eliot's work and person—Schwartz felt mastered by Eliot, and also hoped to master him to become a great man himself.

Schwartz's ambivalence, his frantic personality, and money difficulties made the Eliot book a near-impossible task. It was never finished, though Schwartz made many attempts, and it now survives in four disorganized folders in the Schwartz archive at Yale.

These folders contain several drafts of an introduction to the book, along with an aborted attempt at an entertaining anecdotal justification for writing the book and for Schwartz's literary activities in general. This is the first time these pages have appeared in print. Also in the folders are many drafts of chapters on Eliot's individual works—"Ash Wednesday," "The Four Quartets"—as well as aspects of his style and innovations, with titles such as "Separation as A Subject" and "Manners and Morals as A Subject," plus essays on Eliot's dramatic works, criticism, and influence. There is even a complex attempt at understanding and almost forgiving Eliot's anti-semitism.

Schwartz wanted to portray Eliot as the exemplary modern poet, the writer who actually brought on a new sense of the industrial world. Alas, he could not make it cohere. Nor could he even decide on a final form for the book, as various drafts indicate more or less formal and personal attempts at an overall scheme. A scholar might piece together a serviceable book from these folders, but it would probably offer little that other critics haven't since said better.

What is most useful to readers now is the chance this writing offers to better understand Schwartz the thinker and critic and literary fan. In the pages that follow, we see a young poet grappling with the overpowering influence of his chosen master, layering his personal philosophy and sensibility into his reading of Eliot, who offered, Schwartz insisted, a new "sense of the actual." Schwartz was increasingly tormented by his own shifting sense of actuality; what follows is one of his attempts at describing what seemed most true to him: literature.

THE REASON FOR WRITING THIS BOOK

In 1937, I lived in a rooming house near Washington Square. Because I read late at night and because it was difficult for me to fall asleep, I slept every morning until noon. I wrote all afternoon and then in the evening I went to the pictures, often walking the two miles to Times Square in order to do so, and going through the dark garment district of that part of the city until I came to the crowds moving about under the garish brilliance of Broadway. After the picture was over and I had left the theatre with my customary sense of guilt at the waste of an evening, I returned to the room where I lived with my brother and for the first time during the whole day enjoyed a genuine human relationship. All that I had done in that respect during the earlier part of the day was to tell the waitress behind the counter what I wanted for lunch and communicate in like terms with the waiter in a restaurant when I had my dinner. But when I came back from the movie, my brother was usually there and in bed, reading a tabloid. He had read my mail, which usually concerned literary matters, and we discussed these letters briefly. Then he began each night to tell me what had happened during the day at the office where he worked, a business concern which marketed artificial flowers and made a good deal of money, but not enough, it seemed, to keep the four brothers and their brother-in-law who owned the business on good terms with each other. [I would try with all the will in me to listen to my brother's stories, but they scarcely ever interested me very much, and so I would soon find myself turning the pages of my brother's tabloid while he continued to talk, wholly unaware of my lack of interest. Then he went to sleep usually, unless he had found some novel among my new books which interested him, and I sighed to think how far apart we were, although we had been in the same house and slept in the same bedroom almost always from the day he had been born.][1] These thoughts preoccupied me for a few moments, and then I would begin to read, placing four or five books beside my bed because I never could bring myself to believe that any one book would interest me sufficiently.

I came home one Saturday night in mid-winter and was surprised to find my brother there with his best friend.[2] I was surprised because Saturday night was their big night, the one on which they were determined to have a good time, or at any rate to stay out late. If they stayed out late they would not feel they weren't making the best use of the one night of the week when they did not need to go to sleep and get up the next morning and to go to work.[3]

Neither of the boys had been paying any attention to the other. My brother Stanley was reading the evening edition of the next day's Sunday paper and his friend Howard was studying the colored comics with profound attention, grunting now and then with amusement.[4]

Howard said to me: "We have just been talking about you and trying to decide why you spend your time the way you do, writing poems, stories, and reviews. What is it going to get you? No one or hardly anyone is interested in these things and you don't make much money, do you?"

---

1. Schwartz seems to have wanted to cut this bracketed portion, having handwritten the brackets and crossed it out on the typescript.
2. In the manuscript there is an illegible handwritten correction above "his best friend."
3. There is more illegible handwriting around "would not feel."
4. Schwartz's brother's name was actually Kenneth.

"No, I don't, and you're right, only about ten thousand people in the whole United States are truly interested; perhaps not even that many."[5]

"Then why do you do it? How do you know that anything you write is any good? Here you are writing articles of criticism in which you say whether a book is good or not. Now what I want to know is, How do you know what is good?"

"Would you really like to know how I try to decide? Because I'll tell you if you're willing to listen to me."

"Well, as a matter of fact," he answered, "we were just getting ready to go out."

Both boys arose, knowing they had left me in a lurch, in the middle of a sentence, so to speak. My brother, a person of infinite tact, said that he would like to hear about it tomorrow.[6] But Howard could not suppress one parting shot—

"Just remember", he said aggressively, "that a hundred and forty million human beings feel differently than you do and like the books you dislike and dislike the books you like, that is, if they waste any time paying attention to them. *I* don't like the books you read, and I can't even understand your poems or stories.[7]

The same kind of question arose in different forms upon other occasions and among other people. Once a relative of mine returned from a performance of "Mourning Becomes Electra" to ask why human beings, unhappy themselves, should be expected to enjoy and pay for a view of unhappiness for hours on end. On another occasion, another person looked at a story of mine and then at a poem; and then inquired why I never attempted to *beautify* anything.

------

5. In the manuscript, "two thousand" is changed to "ten thousand."
6. In the manuscript, "much more delicacy" is changed to "infinite tact."
7. This couplet is inserted here in the manuscript with no explanation: "One of the low on whom assurance sits / Like a silk hat on a Bradford millionaire."

T. S. Eliot is a great poet and the best literary critic in the English language.

I begin with this extreme statement so that the purpose of this book will be clear. Sainte-Beuve, a great critic, said that the purpose of the literary critic was to show the reader how to read more and more. This plain statement assumes that there are many ways in which to read the same book. By examining his own experience, the reader will remember how interesting and how illuminating the reading of other readers has often been. It is the best means of checking and extending and correcting our own experiences of the book. Do we not look at the introduction, converse about the book, and look for book reviews, always or chiefly with the purpose of seeing how our reading is the same or different from the experience of other readers? how we missed what other readers saw? how we projected into the book what was in our own existence, not in the book itself?

Implicit in this is the social nature of experience and of literature. Each one must read for himself, but he must be taught how to read by the society in which he exists and has come to belong. And each one's understanding of the words which he reads is determined by the way in which words are used by society.

We must remember our own society as well as the poet and the reader when we come to the first metaphor in T. S. Eliot's first book. This metaphor may very well be the beginning of modern American and English poetry, for it is likely that the reader will begin with this poem and this metaphor, when he begins to read the poetry of this age.

> .... When the evening is stretched out against the sky,
> Like a patient etherized upon a table

With this metaphor, J. Alfred Prufrock, the protagonist of the poem, begins to express—which means to press out what is within—his inner anguish of being.

To compare an evening sky to a patient upon an operating table is perhaps a forced comparison, considered in itself. For the visual image of the patient must be inverted; we must look down at the patient, but we must look up at the evening sky. What is important about the metaphor, considered as poetry, is the way in which two very different things have been joined. Considered in the most general way, within the context of how poetry is written in English, the important thing about this metaphor is the width of its sensibility or sensitivity. Although Keats studied to be a doctor, he could not have written such a metaphor; and neither Tennyson, Arnold, Swinburne, Rossetti, nor the poets of Yeats' generation were capable of a consistent apprehension of experience in such a way. A conception of poetry and of the nature of the poetic prevailed, which prevented these poets from thinking in terms of such a metaphor. This very conception of the nature of poetry was itself installed by Wordsworth and Coleridge, who in turn introduced a sensibility or sensitivity different from the eighteenth-century conception of poetic style and diction.

Wordsworth, by means of a new poetic style, a new use of words, rhythms, and images, made possible a new consciousness of nature. Eliot and other modern poets have made possible a new consciousness of modern life.

Yet to speak in this way of a new consciousness of modern life is to risk a misunderstanding which has deceived many poets, critics, and readers. A poet does not achieve a new apprehension of experience merely because he writes about new experience, and many poets have made the error of supposing that they were holding a mirror up to nature because they wrote poems about the automobile or the railroad train. In the same way, some poets have been misunderstood and condemned because they did not write about automobiles, trains, and the industrial character of modern life. But to expect this of the poet is to expect him to be a camera, an automatic register of experience.

The new experience of modern life made possible by Eliot's poetry is a new sense of the actual, new in that it joins for us things which in ordinary experience exist far apart from each other. Our sensitivity to experience has been widened not because two objects have been newly joined, but because the relevance of *any* two such objects to each other and to human thought and emotion has been shown.

It is thus essential to consider the actual, and the sense of the actual in Eliot's poetry. The sense of the actual and the supreme power to grasp it has been one of the great virtues of Eliot's poetry from the very start.

The actual is that which exists. It is not that which we would like to exist, nor what we hope will exist, nor what we are taught should exist. The failure to distinguish between what is actual and what is not is the cause of much weakness and blindness. The power to grasp the actual is also very important in any effort at understanding what is possible and what is ideal.

The actual is like a moist handshake, damp with nervousness or the body's heat. This should suggest degrees of actuality and the difference between such a handshake and the gloved hand of an ambassador. The latter is also actual, but one has encountered less of the reality of the person.

"Rocks, moss, stone-crop, iron, merds," as Eliot writes in one poem, are instances of actual things. But it would be wrong to suppose that things are more actual than feelings or motives. "I don't like eggs; I never liked eggs" is an instance of how colloquial speech brings us an actual person, or a definite time and place. "Disordered papers in a dusty room" are an instance of the decay and disorder of the actual.

Yet the sense of the actual is narrow and deceptive when the actual is identified or limited to the sordid, the squalid, and the dirty. On the other hand, it is the refusal to admit or pay attention to this aspect of the actual which makes many human beings shut their eyes, draw the window shades, or seek out the many other devices for escaping from reality. Thus it is significant that in some of Eliot's early poems there is an effort to satirize the genteel in speech and in manners. But if "carious teeth" are actual, the "inexplicable splendor of Ionian white and gold" is just as actual. And order is as actual as disorder. We are wrong only when we take the aspiration or the wish for order for actual order.

Hence Eliot as a critic speaks of the peculiar honesty of the great poet. This honesty is the moral quality of mind which insists upon knowing what is actual, no matter how unpleasant the judgement may be.

The actual eludes formulation because it is the foundation for all formulation and for all statements about what is true and what is not true. One must attempt definition merely by pointing. In the end, one must point to the color, blue, in order to identify it, and this pointing is useless, too, to the blind.

The sense of the actual must be refreshed repeatedly, and in the course of this book, the reader ought to try what is said and what is cited by invoking his own sense of what is actual. As the reader continues to examine Eliot's work and this effort to describe his work, the actual and the sense of the actual will turn out repeatedly to be the very heart, the inner warmth and source of movement, of the subject.

The progress of poetry—the process by which one method and style of writing is succeeded by a new one—is inspired by the way a given convention of style that once made possible the experience of the actual has been made habitual and stock, to the point at which, instead of helping the poet to arrive at the actual, it is a block or barrier between him and his subject. It is also a barrier between a new kind of poetry and a reader who is devoted to the style of a previous period. The style and idiom of Victorian and Pre-Raphaelite poetry was the barrier which Eliot had to break through when he began to write poetry, and it was precisely the familiarity with this kind of poetry which made his new work seem wrong and unpoetic to habitual readers of poetry. Such a scorn is natural because it is natural for the reigning taste to take for granted and proclaim its universality.

Letters

To Ezra Pound

73 Washington Place
New York City
April 9, 1938

Dear Mr. Pound,

It was a very great pleasure to receive your letter. I am idolatrous or perhaps the word is "superstitious," and one of my superstitions is the great poet, especially the three or four who are not yet dead. Your corrections of my piece in *Poetry* are thus very welcome, and I hope that you will be moved to correct me in the future.[1] But you will not mind, I am sure, if I try to explain more exactly the notions to which you are objecting.

First, however, to answer your question about George Dillon and *Poetry*. Dillon is a very weak poet and not in the least intelligent. He was Harriet Monroe's pet child, he won the Pulitzer Prize once, and he translated with Edna St. Vincent Millay all of Baudelaire very poorly (using an alexandrine in English because Baudelaire used it in French). It is no exaggeration to say that he knows nothing. This obviously puts him in the same class as

---

1. "Ezra Pound's Very Useful Labors," *Poetry*, March 1938, a favorable review of Pound's *Fifth Decade of Cantos*.

Harriet Monroe, and he seems to have like her one saving virtue, only one, the willingness to give all parties a chance to speak their pieces, and I should guess that he will be more or less as amenable to your desires as Harriet Monroe was. I for one have never been able to understand how you could tolerate so foolish a woman for so many years even with an ocean between the two of you. As for whether I was writing against the editor or with his consent, this question perplexes me. At any rate, I asked him to let me review your new book, expecting only two or three pages and he told me to write a long article, probably because he had read my long piece in the *Southern Review* in which I put Yvor Winters in his place. When the piece was finished, he said it was very good, and this probably means that I was writing with his consent. As for what I as contributor intend to do about the sabotage of your labors, let me know what you would like me to do and I will probably do it. But I actually cannot see why you should be concerned at all about *Poetry*. It has had its day and that day is long past, was over in 1920, so far as exercising a genuine influence goes, and the future for that sort of thing belongs or is going to belong to J. Laughlin IV. He has the interests, the energy, the ability and the intelligence which are needed where Harriet Monroe seems to me to have had nothing but a vague desire to be helpful, and it is obvious to me that you can go on with your useful labors with much more ease and satisfaction now than ever before.

Now for your objections. "suppose you Read some of these writers before telling grandpa he ain't been fotografted in his dress suit." This is only a shot in the dark and a pretty poor one at that. I have read with much care and attention Dante, Homer and Shakespeare, and also, though not as fully, Ovid. One reason, in fact, that I studied Greek was your own translation from the *Odyssey*—if Homer was like that, I wanted to read all of him. I found out that he was not really like that and as a matter of fact even better. All literary judgement seems to me to be comparative and on this basis it still seems clear to me that the best "frame" for a long poem is narrative. I may be very naive and literal about it, but when you say that "The *Divina Commedia* has practically no narration and no plot/it presents a scheme of values/merely a walk upstairs to a balloon landing," I can only keep in mind the literal fact that the poem in question is about a man who was lost in a dark wood where he met various animals and then a great poet's ghost and learned that in order to escape from the wood and the animals, he would have to travel thru Hell, Purgatory, and Heaven. And thus the enormous exaltation of the cantos toward the end of Purgatorio derives from the character of the story, the narrative that Dante is going to meet the lady with whom he was very much in love for a long time and who has been dead for ten years. I do not expect you to take over broken-down values from fat Aquinas nor in fact do I suppose that the absence of narrative in your poem *as a whole* is a simple thing, a pure matter of choice. It seems to me that narrative began to go out of poetry when Coleridge had to write marginal summaries for *The Ancient Mariner* and by the time we get to *Sordello* it has become even harder to tell a story and again there are marginal summaries (at least in some editions) and all this is, I think, a part of a whole complex of both history and literature, partly the increasing quest of certain poetic effects which must of necessity eliminate or at least halt the story narrative—could Mallarmé, for example, conceivably have told a story using his style; and partly the development of the novel as a way of getting everything about a character into a medium; and partly the very breakdown of those values which focus interest upon the life and death of the individual soul—thus even the novel now tells almost no story and the leading beliefs on all sides are, as in Marxism, beliefs about classes, not individuals, about history as a whole.

I do not know how clear this is, and perhaps it is superfluous, but what I mean to say is that the very virtues of your writing *necessitate* the absence of narrative—at least some of those virtues, such as the wonderful excitement one gets as *The Cantos* move about the centuries. But given these virtues and with full awareness of your situation, I mean situation in a definite time, the contrast still exists as an objective fact, the contrast between what one gets in Dante and Shakespeare and Homer, and what one gets in *The Cantos*. It works both ways, of course, and there are, I need hardly tell you, effects in *The Cantos* which have never before been heard of. I said this in my piece. It also seemed worth saying that there is the correlative lack.

"NEXT/as to the seereeyus and solemp and perlite/'A tailor might scratch her where ere she did itch,' *'cul far tombetta.'*" It is right after this that you tell me to read some of these writers, so that it is only in fairness to the quotations that I point out that you seem to have misquoted both, if you are referring to *"ed egli avea cul fatto trombetta"* (Inf. XXI, 139) and that song from *The Tempest*. But really, you are mistaking me. By serious I do not mean solemn and polite. T. E. Hulme—there was a serious man, and that is what I mean by being serious, and I was trying to say that no matter what you, Ezra Pound, believe, the fact is that very estimable persons have all kinds of beliefs about life and death and uncontrollable mysteries which you as a poet sometimes (sometimes, I say, not always and who knows what the next 49 cantos will bring except yourself) sometimes neglect or pass over because you are more interested for the time being in some uproarious story (they are really uproarious). The marvellous comedy which takes place at the end of *Iliad* I, and the comedy in Shakespeare are proportionately less important in the structure of their writing than in yours. But notice this—perhaps I am repeating myself again—this kind of judgement and comparison is made only with the assumption that your poem is good enough to bear such a contrast.

At any rate, you can see that I have not been speaking without also thinking about what I was saying—not that that ever saves a stupid one from his own stupidity. There is a good deal more which I would like to say to you, but this letter is already too long.

Sincerely yours,
Delmore Schwartz

To Ezra Pound

8 West 105 St.
New York City
March 5, 1939

Dear Mr. Pound:

I have been reading your last book, *Culture*.[1] Here I find numerous remarks about the Semite or Jewish race, all of them damning, although in the course of the book, you say:

> Race prejudice is red herring. The tool of man defeated intellectually, and of the cheap politician.

which is a simple logical contradiction of your remarks about the Jewish people, and also a curious omen of a state of mind—one which can support both views, race prejudice and such a judgment of race prejudice, at the same time, or in the same book.

A race cannot commit a moral act. Only an individual can be moral or immoral. No generalization from a sum of particulars is possible, which will render a moral judgment. In a court of law, the criminal is always one individual, and when he is condemned, his whole family is not, qua family, condemned. This is not to deny, however, that there are such entities as races. Furthermore, this view of individual responsibility is implicit in the poetry for which you are justly famous.

But I do not doubt that this is a question which you have no desire to discuss with anyone who does not agree with you, and even less with one who will be suspected of an interested view. Without ceasing to distinguish between past activity and present irrationality, I should like you to consider this letter as a resignation: I want to resign as one of your most studious and faithful admirers.

Sincerely yours,
Delmore Schwartz

---

1. *Guide to Kulchur* (1938).

To James Laughlin

Friday, December 16, 1941

Dear Jay:

I am sending you the first two hundred pages of *Genesis* today in a copy which is a mixture of carbons, revisions, and older versions, but as close as I could get to the final version without parting with what I need here. These 200 pages are substantially the basis on which I was given a Guggenheim renewal.

I want you to publish it separately. It can be called *Genesis* or *Genesis Part I* or *Made in America* or *Made in New York* or *An Atlantic Boy* or *A New York Childhood*. Many other titles might be considered to take care of the fact that it is just the first part—*The Beginning,* or *Book One*.

This publication of the first two-fifths of the poem seems by far the wisest policy to me for a number of reasons, intrinsic and extrinsic. The intrinsic reasons are bound up with the difficulty of getting a proper conclusion right now. If I try to force one, I may wake up in six months and be sorry. But these 200 pages I am certain of, I have tried them out on myself in the worst despondency and lack of energy and I am sure they mean what I want them to mean and what they ought to mean. And if they don't, there will still be time to make changes whenever the whole poem is published. Long poems have been published in parts from *The Divine Comedy* to *The Cantos,* and no comparison in quality is needed here: The form is the same, the long narrative poem can be published in its natural divisions. But more than that, it is too much of a risk right now, with everyone thinking of war, to print 500 pages and expect it to get attention between one crisis in the Far East and another in Iceland and a third in Libya and a fourth in Southern Russia.

The fact that the Philistines of the Guggenheim committee were pleased with this two-fifths should serve as a good external gauge. Some of the internal gauges worth mentioning are as follows: It may seem for a while that the alternation of Biblical prose and blank verse is too predictable, but it will, I think, be felt as an acceptable *formal* device, like the refrain in a ballad or like rhyme or like a tragic chorus. If the dead as a chorus seem bizarre, remember that Dante wrote the best poem ever written by *using the dead as voices*. If the fusion of narrative and commentary seems strange, remember that, as I intend to point out in a short preface, this story-succeeded-by-commentary is one of the profoundest most deeply-rooted and most accepted experiences in modern life: The newspaper story-editorial, the play-and-review-of-the-play, the travel film with voice as commentator and newsreel with commentator are all primordial examples of what is going to be an inevitable literary form (inevitable because the life we live forces it upon us). In any case, as I just said, the chorus is one of the best and most popular devices invented in any time. Louise Bogan made a fool of herself again by denying this in reviewing *Shenandoah* (she says that the poet always disappears from the scene when Dante walks half the way through Hell and Purgatory with a poet next to him and stops to discuss versification with other poets on the way).

If you don't want to get in back of this separate publication in the way that you would back up the whole poem, that suits me perfectly. I feel that this is more than good enough to make its way to the point where, when the reviews are in, you will feel no further need for caution about my staying powers as a poet. You can regard it as a trial balloon, which will cost you no more than the new Miller book.[1]

The Christmas vacation comes in two weeks and by the end of the month, at the latest, I will be able to type final copy of the two hundred pages I want you to print, with a bridge passage at the end intended to make the reader look forward to more. Then I can *wait* (as all good poets should and as fruit-trees wait for

---

1. *the new Miller book: The Wisdom of the Heart*, a collection of essays and stories, was published by ND in 1941.

the proper season) until the right conclusion comes; I can wait through the summer when I do not have to mark eighty abuses of the English language a week. Perhaps I can write a first version of a first novel, or at least enough of one to make you think I am worth my leisure time.

I have a good deal more to say about this 200-page section in itself (especially about the roadhouse scene as the proper end to this separate publication), but it is pointless to do so until you have the mss. [*sic*] at hand and have read some of it.

I also want to answer your letter in detail as soon as I have time. One point worth mentioning in advance is that the question of matching another publisher's advance is beside the point. Whether I am worth what I am told by some publishers I am worth I may never know; they say they would spend from five to ten thousand dollars advertising a novel of mine. Not only would you not do this, but the organization of ND gets worse all the time and you have just put it all in the hands of one who, though a fine person in many ways, has just been running it into the ground because of ignorance, hysteria, and neuroses unequalled on the Eastern Seaboard. The only reason you put it in her hands is that you are busy with the ski hotel: What reason has anyone to believe that you will not always be busy with something else besides ND?[2] It strikes me that the whole thing would be much better moved completely to Hollywood, since you obviously intend to be in Utah most of the time. In fact, that seems to me the only possibly reasonable arrangement, moving everything including E. S. (who would do well enough with a superior nearby) near you. ND needs you as a bow needs an arrow. However, be this as it may, it is nothing I intend to do anything about until I give you a novel.

Another thing I ought to answer right now, since it may shine on the mss. I am sending is that, lucky or not (and I was not very

2. JL was running the ski lodge in Alta, Utah, in Big Cottonwood Canyon above Salt Lake City.

lucky with Rimbaud, for if I had not been at Yaddo because of poverty I would have shown it to someone at Columbia), and intrinsic merit apart, it should be clear to you by now that what I write attracts a great deal of attention (did you, for example, see the spread for *Shenandoah* in Sunday's *Times?*). Perhaps it is a streak of vulgarity or something else, but almost everything I have published has rung the gong for four years; the instance of the translation shows that it is not my beautiful eyes or winning personality or Aryan background which is responsible; it is the work itself, whether for the wrong reasons or not I do not know.

Please read the mss. as soon as possible and with the best attention. Printing this first part will solve many problems at one stroke. I will try to get a final version to you quickly; don't let rough spots here and there throw you off.

> Yours,
> Delmore

265

To James Laughlin

Thursday, 11 a.m.
Jan. 7, 1942

Dear Mr. Laughlin:

Henceforth I will communicate with you in the cold objective style. This may or may not prevent you from remarking from Norfolk to romantic Alta that I am a drunkard. Your new method of getting at me and insulting me appears to be imputation. First, I play the part of Judas and write the *Advocate* review; then I write when drunk. I drink only to get to sleep when I have been writing all day; to drink at any other time would be a waste because I would then have to drink so much more to sleep.

Send me back my two Monday letters, so that I can make out what it is, except an epistolary style modelled or rather inspired by yours, that made you think I was drinking. Also send me back my poem. I want both these things and I want them very much, so let us not argue about it.

Answer me about Kazin: Did you tell him I was going to review his book? I take it you are not interested in the story; this suits me, since I can get paid for it now. Also I demand a retraction again; what makes you think you can call me a traitor and schemer in that way without offense?

Why won't you be persuaded that jacket quotes are dangerous in this case? First, you may not even be able to get them because even those who much admire me think I have already been praised too much for a young man. Second, the reviewers will spend their time fighting the jacket quotes. Third, I can't postpone reviews and poems beyond March, and if I don't do them, the editors will be displeased with me. Fourth, the reviews I've already persuaded some of my friends to write on the ground of your putative campaign against me won't be written because of the delay and also because the jacket quotes will make it clear that there never was a campaign, only resentment, expressed loudly to you because it is thought that I have influence with you.

Never was there anyone so influenced by momentary fashions as you. Just because quotes work with Villa, you think it will do good in quite a different case, a long poem in which such a one as Louise Bogan will think this is her last chance of stopping me this side of immortality. If you visit the right editors, then we will get honest and sympathetic reviews, and this book can get along on its own speed.

The decision, perforce, is yours, but you'll be sorry if this book is not an immediate success because you won't want to meet the offers I've gotten and can get from other more well-to-do publishers when my novel is finished, as it probably will be by fall. I can get three thousand dollars instead of three hundred for a novel and in addition not be insulted as a drunkard, nor terrified by imaginary campaigns against me; nor would I have to fight to get the proper amount of advertising for a novel, namely, an amount which exceeds what you spend on all your books.

I have all the fame I want for the time being; now I want power to protect it or money and probably both. If this seems a drunken statement to you, come to Cambridge and I will make it in person after walking a straight line.

As for Arthur, I like him, but never admired him because he has nothing but his capacity to flatter. In that *Kenyon* review, he praised all who might do him good and damned those who could not harm him, such as poor Berryman.

For example, in sneering at those who praised Villa, he carefully omits to mention Van Doren, whose boots he has already licked earlier in the review. He kicks Berryman in the face, but is careful to put in a soothing word to me. Next time you see him, ask him how the shoe polish tastes which the Tates use. You can get a certain distance by bootlicking, *if* you have talent. Arthur has nothing but glibness; I suppose I ought to be sorry for him, because they scared him at Yale and it must be hard to be a

Mizener and Moore in a time of raging anti-semitism. But I am sorrier for Berryman who does have talent. Another instance of your fickleness: Last year, on reading his poems, you told me you thought he was really first-rate. Now Arthur says no, dishonestly, and you change your mind. Why are you so unsure of your own taste? Who scared you?

We must get another picture, or the old one may be used and I am sick of being kidded about that and also disappointing the Radcliffe girls. I am nervous and sensitive, and don't want to be kidded.

Furthermore, I am going to get a five-year contract from Harvard in May. One possibility which may interest you is that the Army may put all instructors into uniform and make them officers (since most of the students will be in uniform and it has been difficult to maintain discipline at training schools with civilian instructors). The classes will march into school in platoons and the first time this happens I will doubtless turn and run into the blackboard, thinking, Jay was right after all, there *was* an organized campaign against me, there are Patchen, Prokosch, and Barker coming to shoot me down.

As for Williams and his light o'love, this is an example of how your wish to have everything is impossible of realization. You say you want only good poems and an anthology with staying power. In the same paragraph, you say you want Patchen, Brown, and God knows what other bad poets included, all in 128 pages. How can this be? Will you explain? A good anthology full of bad poets? It might be done if we had four hundred pages. But 128 pages? It is you that must be drinking, James.

Which preface do you want me to write, the ghost book or the artist book? I would prefer the ghost one, since I already have thought about it a good deal, and have a lot to say.

Gertrude does not know which store ordered 50 copies. You have an exaggerated view of her interest in how many copies my books sell. She thinks, probably, San Francisco.

Now I have wasted all this energy on you, which would other-wise have gone into a new chapter. Enough of these insults and imputations. Please send me back poem and letters and please answer all the questions I've asked.

Yours truly,
Mr. Delmore Schwartz

P.S. If you must have quotes, why won't old quotes do? Maybe it is the extreme excitement of writing better than ever before that seems like drunkenness to you, when I relax into letter-writing?

To James Laughlin

[Date missing]

[First two pages missing]

... It is clear, is it not, that fame and fortune are mine, especially since, if I may improve upon a revolutionary hero of the past, I have just begun to write.

My chief weakness or Achilles' heel is an irrational devotion to you. However, I am even more devoted to my self, and to good behavior, and your conduct during the last year—Matthiessen, duress before publication, spite or insensitivity about publication matters, quarrels with one and all, and your complete lack of responsibility—has done much to teach me how costly it is to be devoted to you.

It is possible for us to continue on a new basis by means of several plans, all of which will have to be confirmed in front of witnesses: (The following need not be in conflict with my new publishing venture):

Plan A: You give me a half-interest in New Directions. This is the best plan of all, but I know that, smart as you are, you are not smart enough to see how profitable this would be for you. Since it does not seem likely that this plan will delight you or impress you with its infinite practicality, I pass on to Plan B;

Plan B: You mail me a check for two thousand dollars as a retainer for my services as editor and author during the coming year. This is not as an advance, just as payment for services to be rendered the publishing house. This plan must be put into effect within eight days or the check will have to be augmented by five hundred dollars. After two weeks have elapsed, there will be no more price rises because it will be too late. I will have gone to New York and transferred my services elsewhere.

This plan, too, does not strike me as being likely to win your approval. If it does not, I do not really care very much, I will prosper with more responsible characters who care less for skiing and insulting sensitive human beings.

Supposing then that you are not shrewd enough to seize upon either of these plans, there remains the question of previous agreements. Since I am an honest person, I am prepared to give you the two books promised you, the work of fiction and the sequel to *Genesis*, once you have kept some of your broken promises and made some new ones of an unfinancial nature.

Thus, *Plan C:* You must send me a complete accounting of my royalties, give me a contract for an introduction to Flaubert's *Three Tales* to requite me for the Matthiessen business, write me a letter apologizing for your reference in various quarters to Gertrude and Emily as "those lice in Cambridge," sign a statement saying that any such unfavorable remarks will void any contractual agreements entered into in the future, and pay me the fifty-seven cents a copy for each copy of my first book above the cost of publication, an item stated in our initial contract which, I am told, you have broken in a dozen ways, many of them stated in your succinct prose which Robert Fitzgerald once compared to Mozart.

I trust that whatever your emotions at the moment are, you will be reasonable enough to consider the fact that your criminal behavior is a matter which can be proven by other human beings and by your own letters. Meanwhile, I really don't demand an adherence to any of these plans. You can just disregard them. Each of them is a request for what is my just due, but I am perfectly content to forget about them. But since you have broken our contract in various ways, I will then have to consider it broken. There is no publisher in the country who would not be delighted to publish what I write, and there are several who are prepared to prove in court that you have broken your contract, if you are foolish enough to start a costly legal struggle in which your method of behavior comes out into the open.

I have not yet signed a contract for *America, America!,* and I do not intend to, unless equity is restored and I have a real guarantee that you will not in the future behave in such a fashion as to make life difficult for me: Such as abusing literary editors, applying duress on the eve of publication by threatening not to publish an already-printed book, losing mss. for months at a time, endangering my relationships with friends such as Matthiessen, insulting my wife (whose inefficiency was less than her predecessor's and who in any case did nothing to warrant your touching tribute), disturbing me with reports of conspiracies, and not promoting a book properly (as in the instance of *Genesis*) because of spite or timorousness or penuriousness or skiing.

All of this is merely a postscript, you will recognize, to the period last March when you taught me a lesson once and for all by writing me of Plans A and B. And all I want by way of restitution is either peace to go my own way, or two, the guarantee that so far as I am concerned, you will recognize and act upon the profound truth that Honesty is the best policy. That is the reason that Plan A strikes me as the most brilliant of the lot.

Our six years' association, so fruitful to you, so fruitful and difficult for me, opened with a letter in which you called me a crook. It continued by your opening a letter to me from Harcourt, Brace, a violation of the laws about the mail. It reached great humiliation when Gertrude and I were unloaded at Baton Rouge so that you might have more room for baggage and a whore. It achieved a height of torment when my translation of Rimbaud appeared, and although you behaved with much kindness then, nevertheless this would not have occurred if I had been with a responsible publisher and if I had not been forced by poverty to live at Yaddo, far from anyone to consult about my translation. Told of this poverty in the early fall, you sent me a check for $150., a handsome reward to an author who had just helped very much to give the publishing house and publisher an immense success. There is no need to continue with these memoirs; my purpose is to see that such episodes do not occur again.

I don't think you have any idea of the amount of ill-will you have accumulated in important places. Thus, the fact that you did little or nothing with Trilling's book is going to keep other critics who might do as well from writing in that series. You can always get the third-rate, but that will do no good, especially since the first-rate authors will write for others. What chance, for example do you think I have for the kind of success my book on Eliot ought to have, if you are too intent on skiing to make provision for new editions? I say nothing of the difficulty of merely buying a book from New Directions, such is the character of your office.

Once again, I refer to the fact that if you had been willing to listen to me, you would have published Karl Shapiro and Eudora Welty. As a perhaps last piece of advice, I suggest that you act quickly in order not to lose a poet, critic, playwright, editor and teacher who has added much to the prestige, prosperity, and character of New Directions. If you look with care through the new list or catalogue, you will see that so far as success goes, half of the credit is just sheer luck, half is divided in equal parts: One, your money and energy and ambition; two, my ideas, or the direction you went in because of my interests as a critic, or my initial success. You ought also to regard the list from the point of view of the possibility of another author, old or young, being capable of my many activities, no matter how much you promoted him. Williams, Patchen, Fitts, even Miller's lucid pornography, or Harry Brown, Paul Goodman, Robert Hivnor, Tennessee Williams, and whatever candidate attracts you at the moment.

As a reward, I've received some fifteen hundred dollars, many psychological attacks, and the news that you speak of my former wife, to whom I remain devoted, as "one of those lice in Cambridge," a remark not made in a moment's emotion, but typed and mailed.

Now if you are really sensible, you will not resort to charm, or anger, or threats, or anything but the decent behavior I have outlined above; which will not cost you anything, if you wish to save money in that pathological manner which leads to many of your worst errors. Don't take the trouble to break away from the pleasures of Utah in order to converse and dicker with me, because within two weeks it will be too late and you will learn as never before that Honesty is the best policy, it pays to be good, and you have cast a pearl away.

I remain devoted to you, although I don't know why. If you want to take the alternative of just calling off all bets, then our friendship can continue and be renewed on an uncommercial and disinterested level, though Utah is quite distant. But the best beginning would be a check and an apology.

Yours affectionately,
Delmore

To Gertrude Buckman

Dear Gertrude,

You have not heard from me because I went to New York on Monday night and to Princeton on Tuesday, trying to get away from the boredom and emptiness here. I should have thought of your letters to your mother, but I did not, and after much thought I did not try to get you in New York because it seemed unlikely that you would want to see me so soon, as I see by your letter where you tell me not to call you. I came back last night, although I was going to stay longer, because I had to run away from New York and Princeton, everyone was too unhappy or dead to bear, and be with.

I suppose you must tell your father, but if you do, be sure that he promises to tell no one else. Philip lives on 10th St. and William on 9th, Fred is nearby, the Zolotows go back and forth, and on 8th Street you will certainly meet some of the boys all of the time. The only thing to say when you meet them is that you have just come to New York in order to visit your mother in New Jersey several times a week. I told them you were at Morristown when they asked for you, and Nancy took the address because she wanted to write to you. It might be best for you to pay a state or official visit to the Macdonalds and Phillipses, to maintain the deception. Besides, you will be lonely and it is better to see them than to be at the mercy of the abysses of loneliness, as you know.

// Dwight liked your review very much, and Richard liked it very much, but felt that there was not enough of the lenience in you and you were a woman with a woman with Kay Boyle. But it

---

Gertrude Buckman was Schwartz's first wife, a writer. They divorced after six years.

reads very well, it reads as if you had written literary criticism for ten years. I will send the copies today.

I was told by Dwight no sooner had I crossed the doorstep that Paul Goodman was going to attack *Genesis*, and from William I heard that Frank Jones, which might as well be Clement Greenberg, would review it for *The Nation*, and that there had been a row at *Time* about reviewing it at all.[1] Matthiessen had not written his review, although Philip asked for it several times, and Richard had not written his, and spoke of putting it off, and when I looked dismayed, consoled me by a description of how Allen Tate had praised the book. Meanwhile Jay has written all over to say that he does not like the book, but thinks it deserves a serious review.

My last classes ended with surprising delightful prolonged applause, especially from the girls, and made me think I had perhaps not been as poor a teacher this year as I supposed. I boarded the train with Gogol's *Dead Souls*, determined hereafter to read a masterpiece on each trip, and when an RAF officer sat next to me after Providence, and seemed to want to hold a conversation, I was divided in half by Gogol delightful [*sic*] and the feeling that I ought as a matter of conscience to hear what this instance of a great historical reality had to say. But Gogol was too profoundly farcical and I let the great historical reality go.

Dwight was speechless with a sore throat and nothing if not annoying, which made me go to Princeton where Richard and Nela were in their own ways annoying, Richard with his class which I went to and with his detailed activities, Nela with her stories of Richard, Helen, and Nela. But I stayed for two days and came back with Nela who had to come to see Christine, and then went to the Wilsons, asked there because I had been answering Dwight's phone during his speechlessness, to find Lionel Abel, Dawn Powell, and Rolfe Humphries there, but also [Roberto] Matta [Echaurren] the painter, an effervescent soul

---

1. It was an enthusiastic review; Jones echoed Eliot's description of Pound's *Mauberley* by praising *Genesis* as "a positive document of sensibility."

who had brought Lionel, and Lionel's girl friend, and his own wife pregnant and from Ohio. Matta wanted all to take off their clothes. This would be truth and consequences, he declared. No one spoke to Lionel, because he had not been asked to come, and finally I spoke with him and heard him prove that Sidney Hook believed in God. Consequently the next day Lionel went about to tell everyone what a fine fellow I was. Wilson was very attentive to me for several hours and called me Mr. Schwartz when I came in, Schwartz after the second highball, Delmore after the fifth, and Mr. Schwartz once more when we arrived at the eighth refreshing. Now I will never know what would have happened at the tenth and twelfth, although I was tempted to stay just to find out. //

The next night there was a foolish party at William's, and Diana Trilling asked me if I thought I looked like her? to which I said after a stunned silence, it is very kind of you to ask me. Later William and I tried to decide what it could possibly have meant, and we went to see Meyer Schapiro and asked him, and he had several interpretations, but he was not sure. He looked worn out and old, and he said foolish things, and he told Philip Rahv that he did not know what he was harping about as they discussed the war. He had just written a piece for the magazine entitled "The Nerve of Sidney Hook," making Hook look like a fool and maintaining that if Hitler won the war, there would nevertheless be the possibility of a revolution in Europe.

But I see that this must sound as if it were a happy trip, but it was not. I felt immense depression to see everyone paralyzed, unable to go forward with their work, not different or better than in 1938, and having nothing to say or foolish things to say, most of all Schapiro who lost his temper with Philip as if he were Dwight, and reported himself unable to read *The Ambassadors* from beginning to end, and remarked that Joyce hated the English language, part of a typical theory that only an Irishman could have written *Finnegans Wake*.

Your little pictures make me remember how you were beautiful then as you are now.

Except for your letters, there was no mail that was interesting when I came back last night. //

I dreamed about your room last night, and I did not like the way it looked. But in your letter it sounds like a fine room, and the fireplace must please you.

I will write you more and more, but I went to get this off right now to end this silence and waiting, which I should have thought of, except that I did not think of your difficulty with your father. If my mother hears anything, she will come here again and refuse to go, and maintain that she wants to take care of me, and then there will really be a scene.

Very much,
Delmore

To William Carlos Williams

20 Ellery St.
Cambridge, Mass.
August 20, 1943

Dear Williams:

I like your little poem, "These Purists," very much, and we will use it soon, with Miller's "It's Not What You See, But How You See It." I'd like to take several more of Miller's pieces, but we're full of too many unused accepted verse right now. At some later date, I hope you will send us not just one poem, but a group, for I've noticed that readers tune in on what you write when they look at several poems, one after another.

I don't have your last letter here because I sent it to N.Y. to show the boys that there ought to be no more delays, about answering anyone (but they've been preoccupied with the business end of the review for the last two months). So, without your letter, I risk being told again that I did not read what you said. I risk it, anyway, letter or not.

However, the gist of the reply to your essay will be as follows, so far as I am in on it: Dr. Williams is an important poet and author of fiction. This essay is significant for that reason. In it, he maintains that the best kind of statesmen have been boobs, or at least none too bright. Intellectuals are too smart. They are smart to such an extent that they ought to be used very carefully, like any dangerous thing. They are by nature only "superficially colored by democracy." Jump. Maybe then they are fascists. They don't like to see a whitewashing of the totalitarianism of Soviet Russia (where two million peasants were deliberately starved in 1932) because such a whitewash has no military value whatever. Jump. Hence intellectuals, or at least [John] Dewey and Eastman, are aligning themselves with those who bombed Guernica. *Mission to Moscow* not only distorts the truth about Russia, but it also distorts the book on which it is based. Jump. This shows that intellectuals are too smart, and Russia may have its faults, but the fifth columnists (and, as you may know, the best living Russian poet, Pasternak) are behind barbed wire, unable to do any harm.

You can certainly reply to this in print if you like, after the other editors have added their remarks.

As I remember, you ended your letter by remarking that you and I were not intent on the same thing. So far as intent and intention go, this is not true; so far as performance goes, if I am half as good as you at fifty, I will be a lot more pleased with myself than I am now. But the intent is a common one: the exact description of what is loved and what is hated. If I may be even more personal about this, I might say that I guess my teaching at Harvard puts me under the general stigma of being academic. You have as much notion of what the academy is like now as I have of the care of infants. I teach the freshman how to use English, and when one boy writes that a neighborhood is slightly ugly or a person has an outstanding nose, I try to explain that they have misunderstood some words and might do better with other words. Or when a girl writes that "a liberal arts education makes a girl broader," I try to explain that words have idiomatic and metaphorical qualities which require careful handling. When the high school gets done with them and when the newspapers, films and radio get through with their minds, they arrive here to be repaired. Thus, obviously, I am a kind of dentist, as you are a doctor, and it is an honorable calling. The textbook the freshmen use, as you may know, contains not one, but two pieces by you, "The Use of Force" and "The Destruction of Tenochtitlan." The only other author with two pieces is your old chum, T. S. Eliot. It is in this way that you are treated by the academy. Meanwhile there are also the Navy boys to be taught, and it grows on me that the war will be over long before some of them learn how to spell, which I mention to explain the perhaps harassed tone of this letter.

The boys and the girls, by the way, seem to see no serious difficulty and inconsistency in reading both you and Eliot, nor do I, and your notion that Eliot keeps any good poetry from print is just as much fantasy as your idea that Macdonald likes Eliot. He resigned, saying among other things that he never wanted to run a review which printed such authors as Eliot. Another fantasy is that Lincoln was not an intellectual; how do you think he learned to practise law and to make the best speeches any politician is ever likely to make?

Well I've never won any argument with anyone and being in the middle of my twenty-ninth eternity, I don't have the energy of old to nourish often-defeated hopes, but I cannot resist adding that your view of the role of Eastman and Dewey is identical with the view expressed by Alfred Noyes that Proust was responsible for the Fall of France. By your jumping logic, this makes you the same kind of poet as Noyes, if Dewey is aligned with the Fascists who bombed Guernica.

Perhaps I ought not to argue with one of the few of my elders I admire very much, but it occurs to me that the difference in age between us is not likely to diminish, so that this is as good a time as any.

Yours sincerely,
Delmore Schwartz

To James Laughlin

20 Ellery
Cambridge 38, Mass.
Oct. 16, 1946

Dear Jay:

I've finally got a manuscript to the point where it seems satis-factory. It's a volume of two short novels and five stories entitled *The World Is a Wedding*. Will you let me know when you get this letter how soon it can be published? I can come down to New York with the manuscript as soon as you get back to America, and I think this would be the best procedure because there are extra-literary reasons for rushing as much as possible.[1] If you can get it out by early spring, both of us will profit by the speed.

How do you feel about my appearing with two books in one year? The book on Eliot is close enough to being ready, though there is no question of rushing about this.

Yours,
Delmore

---

1. The Laughlins were in France.

To James Laughlin

20 Ellery St.
Cambridge
Jan. 7, 1947

Dear Jay:

I am delighted more than I would have believed possible that you like the script.[1] Perhaps all the sad years since 1943 can be traced back to your contempt for my last work.[2] Can it be that your approval means so much to me? Be this as it may, I hope you will sustain your liking at least until the date of publication, and refrain from letters to editors telling them that you don't like the book. My uneasiness is occasioned by the fact that you liked *Shenandoah* very much until you started to lend an ear to rival authors: "Your effort is VERY GOOD," you wrote to me, "My congratulations on this evidence of the increasing tumescence of your esteemed literary powers."

"Tumescence," that's what the girls like.

I think it would be a good idea to include the story "In Dreams Begin Responsibilities," not as an appendix, but just like the other stories. I've been getting letters asking for the entire book. Is it out of print? And is *Shenandoah* out of print too?

Can you get the book out by June? The Dial Press, which is no great shakes, takes only three months with an anthology of 600 pages. If it appears in June, I will bet you Elinor Blanchard's address against two of my roundest, warmest and wettest students at Radcliffe that Orville Prescott will review the book in the *Times* and declare that I am almost as good as John Steinbeck.[3] Is it a bet? But only if the book appears by June, because it gets hot and Prescott goes

---

1. *the script:* Typescript of *The World Is a Wedding*.
2. *my last work: Genesis* (1943).
3. *Orville Prescott:* Principal book reviewer for the daily *New York Times*.

away because he does not like the heat and dear Alfred Kazin, who might review it on Sunday, will have departed to France.

How about giving me the introduction to Cocteau's *Selected Writings*? I will do as good a job as John L. Sweeney, but faster.[4] I also admire Svevo, Pasternak, and Valéry very much, but more than anything else I lust for The Almighty Dollar, just like you.

You can have the page of ads in *PR* for $40, if you will sign up for six times a year. $40 is $8 less than anyone else. Please advise.

I don't understand what "the Jewish problem" is, so far as my book goes.[5] No reader has ever accused me of providing anti-Semitic ammunition. In fact, I should think that this might well be the link with the gross public of New York, where most of the readers are, anyway.

The enclosures, which please return, are to show you that I always get good reviews. The gross public will love me, if it is given a chance. And now that I am an assistant professor, I am almost as authoritative as Harry Levin, n'est-ce pas?

Yours,
Delmore

---

4. *John L. Sweeney:* Sweeney edited the ND edition of *Selected Writings of Dylan Thomas* (1946).
5. *"the Jewish problem":* JL was having difficulty writing flap copy for *The World Is a Wedding*.

To James Laughlin

405 East 7th St.
Bloomington, Indiana
June 26, 1951

Dear Jay:

My brother was finally located in Seattle. The pursuit had narrowed down to some place between Los Angeles, San Francisco, and the Canadian border when at last Kenneth—a man of few words—wrote me that he had returned to the aircraft industry as a tool engineer, giving up household appliances because of credit restrictions. This illustrates once more a truth I have tried to force on the American reading public—the international character of our lives; I wonder why I seem to be the only one who finds it fascinating. However, many thanks for offering to put Marie Rexroth on the trail.[1]

Elizabeth and I want to buy a house which we saw last week in Flemington, New Jersey. It has six acres, three bedrooms, two sheds, a barn, a Bartlett's pear tree, two peach trees, a vegetable garden, a wonderful rooster, and among other valuable assets, a bathtub, for which I have yearned these last four years since leaving Cambridge. We have raised all but one thousand of the four thousand and five hundred dollars necessary to the purchase of it (the total cost is nine thousand, but half is a mortgage), and I wonder if you can lend us the one thousand we need, for a period of two years? You might lend the money to us either as a personal loan, or as an advance of five hundred to Elizabeth and five hundred to me, on books which ND published within the next two years. I will probably have a new book of short stories ready to show you by fall, and that with the addition of Elizabeth's second novel, ought to cover the advance. If it does not, then we will be able to repay you the loan at the end of two years, because both of us will have

---

1. *Marie Rexroth:* Kenneth Rexroth's first wife.

to take full-time jobs by the fall of 1952 unless we manage to make more money than we are making now. We figure that by getting the house and living in the country as much as possible, we will be able to get more work done during the coming year. I have the promise of a good teaching job for 1952–1953, and unless I succeed in writing for the slicks during the coming year (as I have been trying to do for the past month), I will have to teach anyway, the fall after this, since there will be no *P.R.* salaries after next December.

The house appears to be a good investment and the kind of a place we need very much, as you seemed to have noticed last winter when you suggested that we use your place in Norfolk during your absence and thus get rid of cabin fever. It is just an hour and a half from New York, neither too near nor too far, it is entirely rural, and it is just right for the young novelist and the ageing poet's declining years. I am sure that we can pay you back at the end of two years. However, if you are hard-up for cash or hard-pressed in one or another way, we will naturally understand, since we know how many other needs you have to handle. But do let us know as soon as you can.

We arrived here last Sunday and today I began to teach Yeats and Eliot at the School of Letters, which is the new name of the Kenyon School of English. It is very pleasant, but very hot. Arthur is here but he cannot play tennis with me because his doctor says that he is against it, so I am playing with Francis Fergusson who, as he confesses, is so eccentric a player that his eccentricity becomes a form of power. I never can tell—anymore than he can—what he will do next, while Arthur, while powerful, was entirely predictable. If Francis were but ten years younger, what matches we might have! Tate is here too; he has just become a Catholic and attacks Cardinal Spellman with a vigor he formerly reserved for Robert Hillyer.[2] All in all, it looks like a pretty hot six weeks,

---

2. *Robert Hillyer:* (1895–1961): Boylston Professor of Rhetoric at Harvard, led the campaign against the award of the Bollingen Prize to Ezra Pound in 1948.

and I wish you could come out and inspect the little boom in culture. Next week I lecture to the entire congregation on television and literature, and what chance there is that any sensible and sane portion of the reading public will ever open a book again once they get used to the television scream. As Shakesbeer said, "Some rise by vice, and some by virtue fall," and the main thing is just to keep swatting the ball.

We passed through Greenfield, Indiana, on our way out, and it turned out to be the former home of James Whitcomb Riley, which made me think of Marguerite Young, since the dear girl is writing a book about the great bard.[3] The heat and the strain of driving for three days was such that I was moved to compose the following masterpiece on the spur of the moment:

> Who's your Hoosier poet?
> Pure corn entirely?
> Marguerite would know it!
> James Whitcomb Riley!

As Tears Eliot remarked, and he ought to know, poetry is a mug's game—but if one is born a mug, one might as well accept the fact.

As ever,
Delmore

3. *James Whitcomb Riley:* (1849–1916), known as "The Hoosier Poet." *writing a book about the great bard:* Schwartz is mistaken or making another of his jokes. Young's *Angel in the Forest* dealt with Utopian aspiration in New Harmony, Indiana.

To Roy P. Basler

725 Greenwich St.
New York City 14, N.Y.
September 9, 1958

Dear Roy:

Enclosed is the corrected copy of my lecture. You have edited it very well indeed and it must have been a trying task. I also enclose a list of the names of people I would like copies to be sent to; if it is possible to send more than twenty-five copies I wish you would let me know: and if it is a question of the Library's budget I would be glad to pay for the additional copies. As you doubtless know, this is the practise of a good many literary reviews.

I am sorry to have to say that I will almost certainly have to make use of the letter you wrote me last September, about my being able to lecture in January. I would prefer of course to forget about everything that happened, including your letter, but it is impossible at present to do so. I am sure that you acted not only in all innocence and in natural concern about your program; nevertheless, the incident is important for a variety of reasons on which I will not dwell except to say what is relevant to your letter of inquiry concerning my health. It had not occurred to me when I last wrote you that it would have been possible to find out if I had lost my mental health in a good many ways other than that of writing a letter, the envelope of which was addressed to me— so that I would be certain to get it—but the body of which was addressed to my former wife. You will understand my feelings about the matter if I tell you, as I may [have], in part, before now, that I was the object of illegal arrest and detention in Bellevue for seven days, during which, as a result of improper treatment and false information, I had a heart attack on the fourth day and was put in a straitjacket and came close to dying. I did not know of this until last spring when I had a chance to examine the medical records. Your own letter was but one incident—there were a good many others—in which persons of great wealth, having involved themselves in a criminal conspiracy of the most serious kind—attempted to make it impossible for me to protect myself by preventing me from getting any financial help. Use was made of others as innocent of what was going on as you were and also of persons as unscrupulous as Conrad Aiken. During the past year I have repeatedly found that the defamation and the stigma consequent upon it have had serious consequences which I cannot do very much about personally, either through my work or by an explanation which sounds lurid and implausible to anyone who does not know the personas involved. I make this explanation to you with the same feeling that, although I owe it to you as someone who honored me by inviting me to lecture, it will nevertheless fail to be entirely convincing. This is one instance in which there is only one side of the story.

Sincerely,
[Unsigned carbon.]

To Dwight Macdonald

House of Mirth
The Crack of Dawn
December 14, 1958

Dear Dwight,

Events are in the saddle, as Emerson rather pallidly remarked 100 years ago. But before burdening you with what has occurred since Saturday at 3, I must tell you that I can't use your check until I hear from *Art News* and immediately add that this letter is *not* a new attempt of Laughing Boy to ask you for more financial aid. You've been more generous in all ways than anyone else, by far, and this sentence is, to be plethorically emphatic, sincere, candid, unequivocal, literal, etc.

However.

On Saturday night two hoodlums called on me at 2:30 A.M. and stayed until 5, trying to get me into a fight. When they left— partly because I had begun to ask them to stay—I went to the police station where the desk cop wrote my complaint into his intimate journals. He was rather impressed that one of my friends had taken a few dollars out of my pants pocket, and had been so dedicated to the task of throwing all my belongings on the floor (he was, he said, trying to find out whether I had what he called spunk) that he dropped his draft-board card amid the chaos of books and paper. The desk cop seemed to be delighted by this evidence that I had not been dreaming, but his delight was pure disinterested joy, for he has not sent a detective around, as he said that he would.

Last night my well-wishers and would-be friends, whoever they are, were tired or compassionate, for they restricted their courtesies to ringing the downstairs doorbell every hour from one to five.

Dwight Macdonald was an editor of *Partisan Review* from 1937 to 1943 and was a longtime friend and colleague of Schwartz.

The only reason I report this to you is the desire to do so. When I started the letter, I intended to describe a joint project called "Eggshells," but now that the dawn's mauve light has become a cotton pallor, I don't feel like writing about it. It is a serious project, however. But there is no hurry whatever.

Best,
Delmore

To Mrs. Odell

907 Harrison Street
Syracuse 10, N.Y.
August 20, 1964

Dear Mrs. Odell:

I intend to continue to pay one hundred and ten dollars a month rent and to stay in this apartment as long as it suits my convenience, or more precisely my immediate needs. If you believe that you are justified in raising the rent by ninety dollars a month—and thus one thousand and eighty dollars a year—I am sure that it would be wise to consult an attorney and go through the customary legal procedures of New York State when a landlord wishes to raise the rent or persuade a tenant to depart. As you may know, you will be wasting time and money; but if you do not know that this is true, it might be worth finding out for the sake of other such occasions.

The only reason you give for your incredible demands, "excessive damages," has no basis in fact whatever. There are no excessive damages whatever: there are no damages. One mattress, which was very old and torn when I moved here in August 1963, became entirely useless as mattresses invariably do. As I told you in June, I meant to buy a new one myself as soon as my teaching and writing permitted me the leisure. Even if the mattress's obsolescence had been hastened by me, to suppose that it justifies an increase of over one thousand dollars a year, or [is] a threat to the other facilities in any way at all, is so completely fantastic that it is difficult to believe that it is more than a pretext: only a severe lack of relation to reality could make anyone entertain the supposition seriously. The literal truth is that, since I never cook or entertain,

---

Mrs. Odell was Schwartz's landlady when he was teaching and living in Syracuse, New York.

I make almost no use of the facilities and furnishings outside of the bedroom and bathroom.

I must say again—though you may know this very well and imagine that I do not—there is an established legal procedure through which a landlord can seek to raise the rent or secure a tenant's departure, and this is not only a perfectly effective recourse based upon many landlord-tenant relationships, it is also the only way in which my plans at present can be altered. I would probably prefer to get another apartment and avoid this very unpleasant letter and to conclude by asking you not to write any more letters to me, but use a lawyer or friend for whatever communications may be necessary. I have already had twelve months of letters characterized by gratuitous and insulting advice, lengthy analyses of character and habits of an intimate nature which a close friend would hesitate to make, and in general an insensitivity, insolence, tactlessness and wholly unprovoked hostility.

In any case, I will not open any further communications from you, but if you do consult a lawyer, I will be glad to provide him, at his request, with copies of letters you have written me.

Yours sincerely,
Delmore Schwartz

P.S. There is a limit beyond which forbearance becomes encouragement—your obvious compulsion to bully, patronize and insult anyone you [becomes illegible and crossed-over].